PUBLISHED BY KOYAMA PRESS
KOYAMAPRESS.COM

FIRST EDITION: MAY 2017

ISBN: 978-1-927668-42-9

PRINTED IN CHINA

VOL- CANO TRASH

A DOUBLE+ ADVENTURE

PART 1

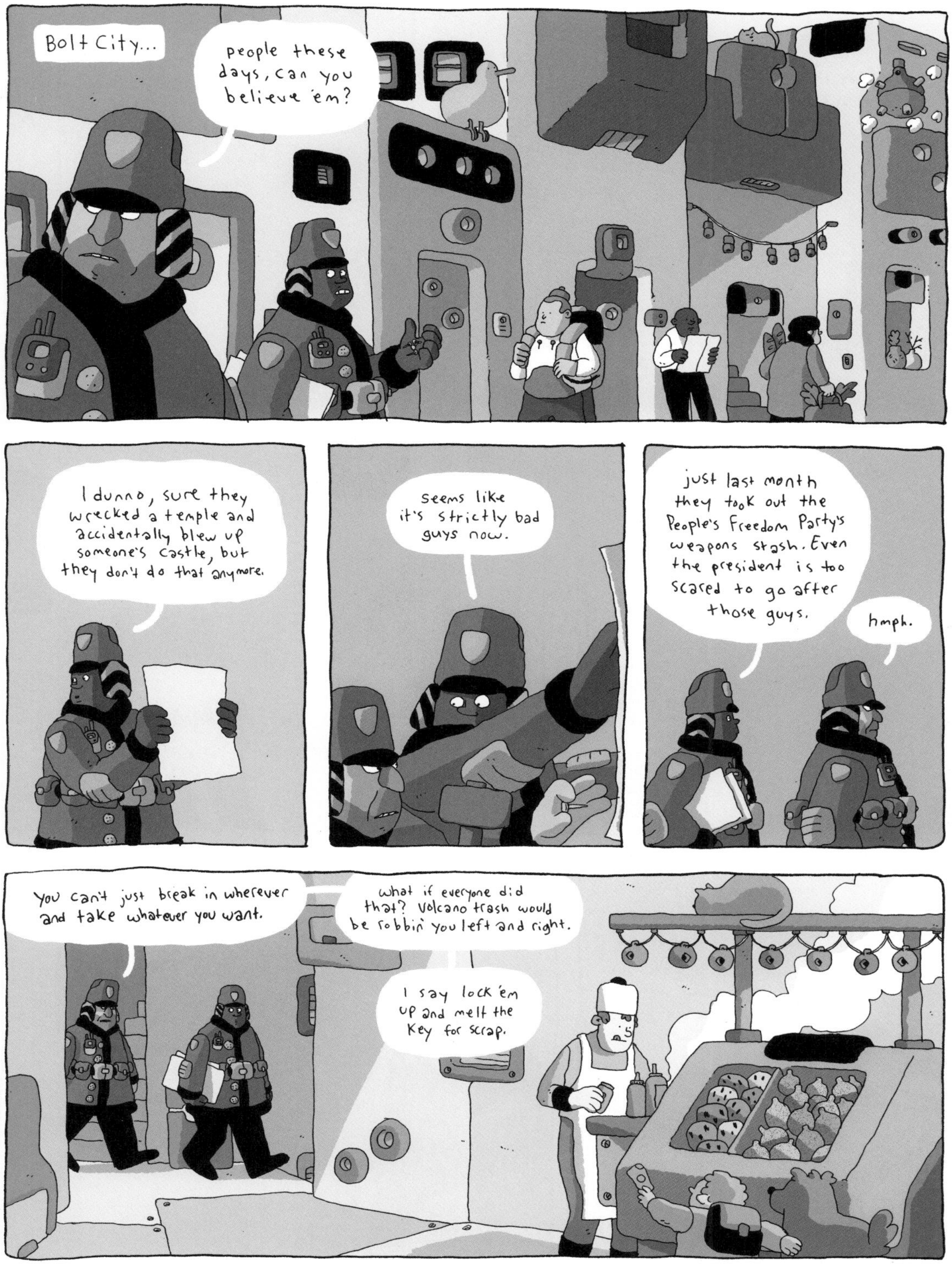
Bolt City...
people these days, can you believe 'em?
I dunno, sure they wrecked a temple and accidentally blew up someone's castle, but they don't do that anymore.
Seems like it's strictly bad guys now.
just last month they took out the People's Freedom Party's weapons stash. Even the president is too scared to go after those guys.
hmph.
You can't just break in wherever and take whatever you want.
What if everyone did that? Volcano trash would be robbin' you left and right.
I say lock 'em up and melt the key for scrap.

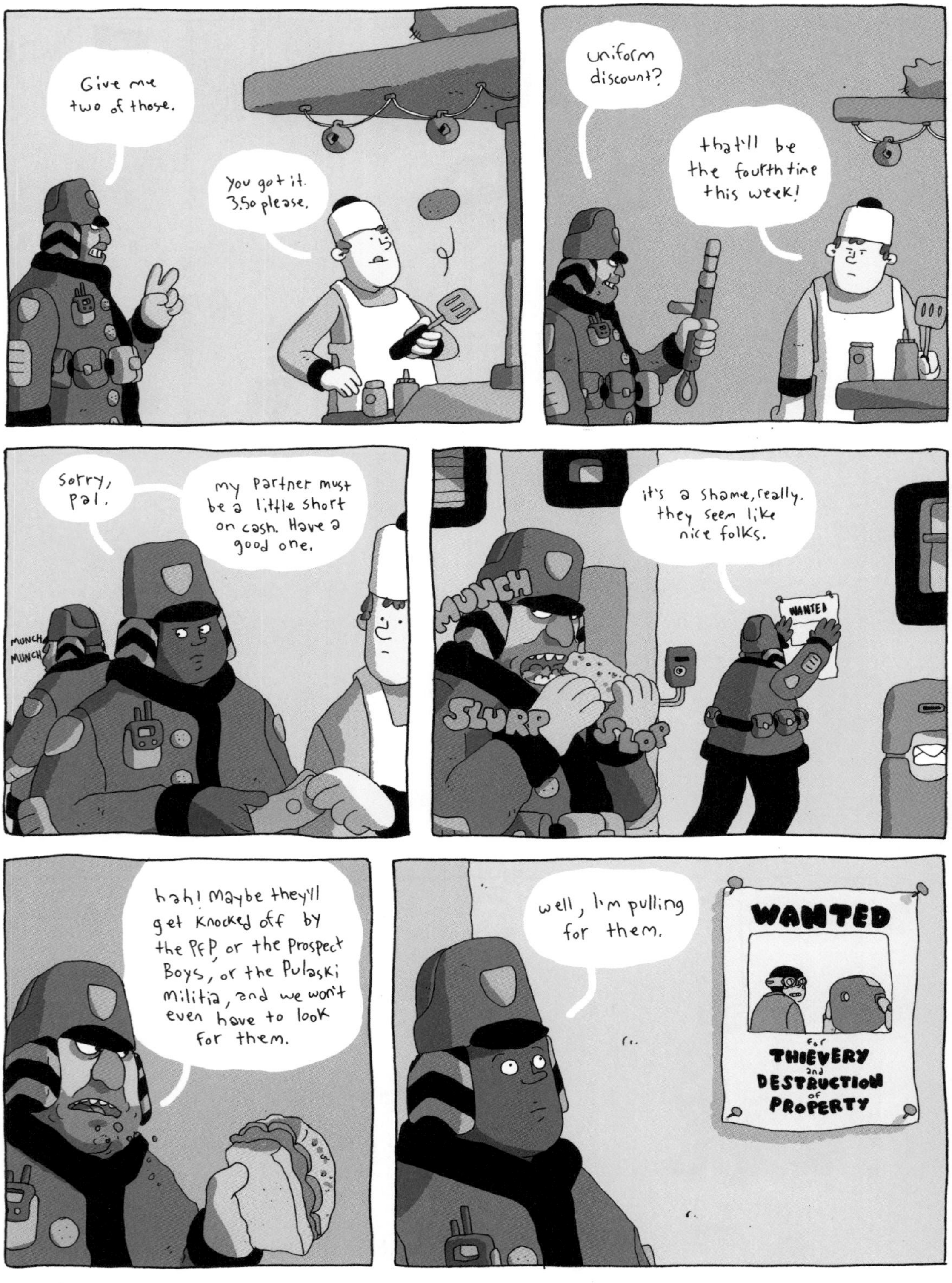
Give me two of those.
You got it. 3.50 please.
uniform discount?
that'll be the fourth time this week!
MUNCH
MUNCH
sorry, pal.
my partner must be a little short on cash. Have a good one.
MUNCH
it's a shame, really. they seem like nice folks.
WANTED
SLURP
SLOP
hah! Maybe they'll get knocked off by the PFP, or the Prospect Boys, or the Pulaski militia, and we won't even have to look for them.
well, I'm pulling for them.
WANTED
for
THIEVERY
and
DESTRUCTION
of
PROPERTY

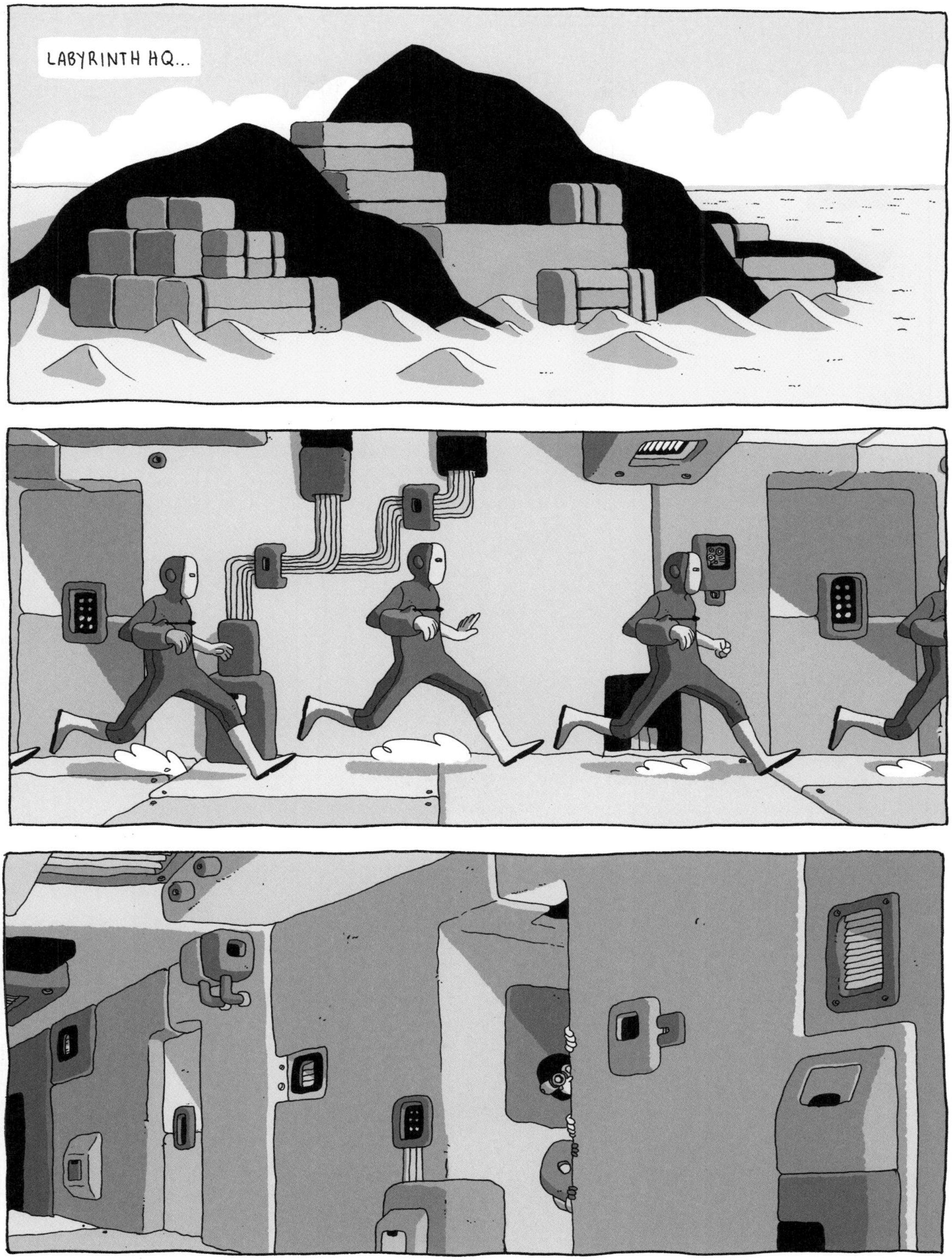
LABYRINTH HQ...

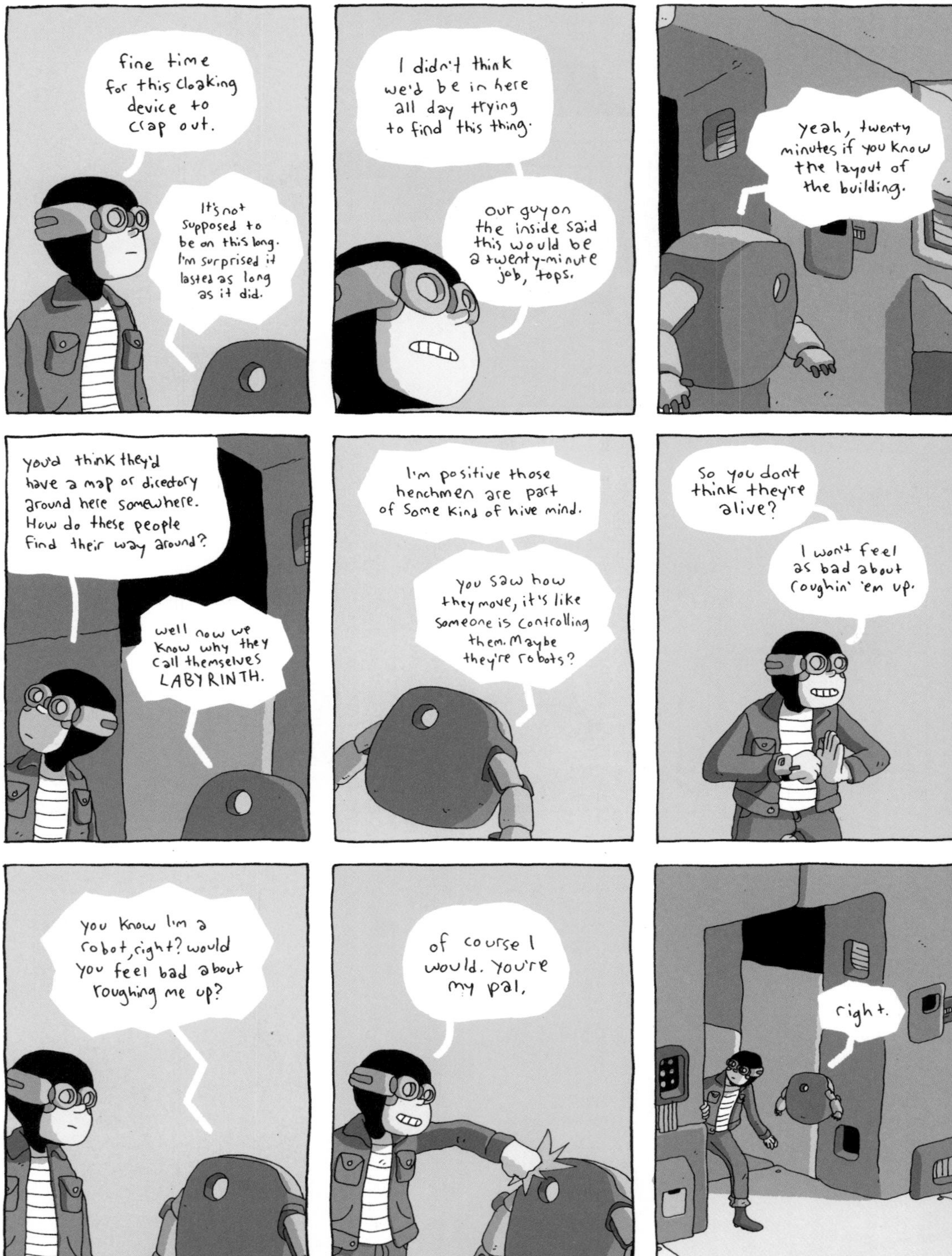
fine time for this cloaking device to crap out.
It's not supposed to be on this long. I'm surprised it lasted as long as it did.
I didn't think we'd be in here all day trying to find this thing.
our guy on the inside said this would be a twenty-minute job, tops.
yeah, twenty minutes if you know the layout of the building.
you'd think they'd have a map or directory around here somewhere. How do these people find their way around?
well now we know why they call themselves LABYRINTH.
I'm positive those henchmen are part of some kind of hive mind.
you saw how they move, it's like someone is controlling them. Maybe they're robots?
So you don't think they're alive?
I won't feel as bad about roughin' em up.
you know I'm a robot, right? would you feel bad about roughing me up?
of course I would. You're my pal.
right.

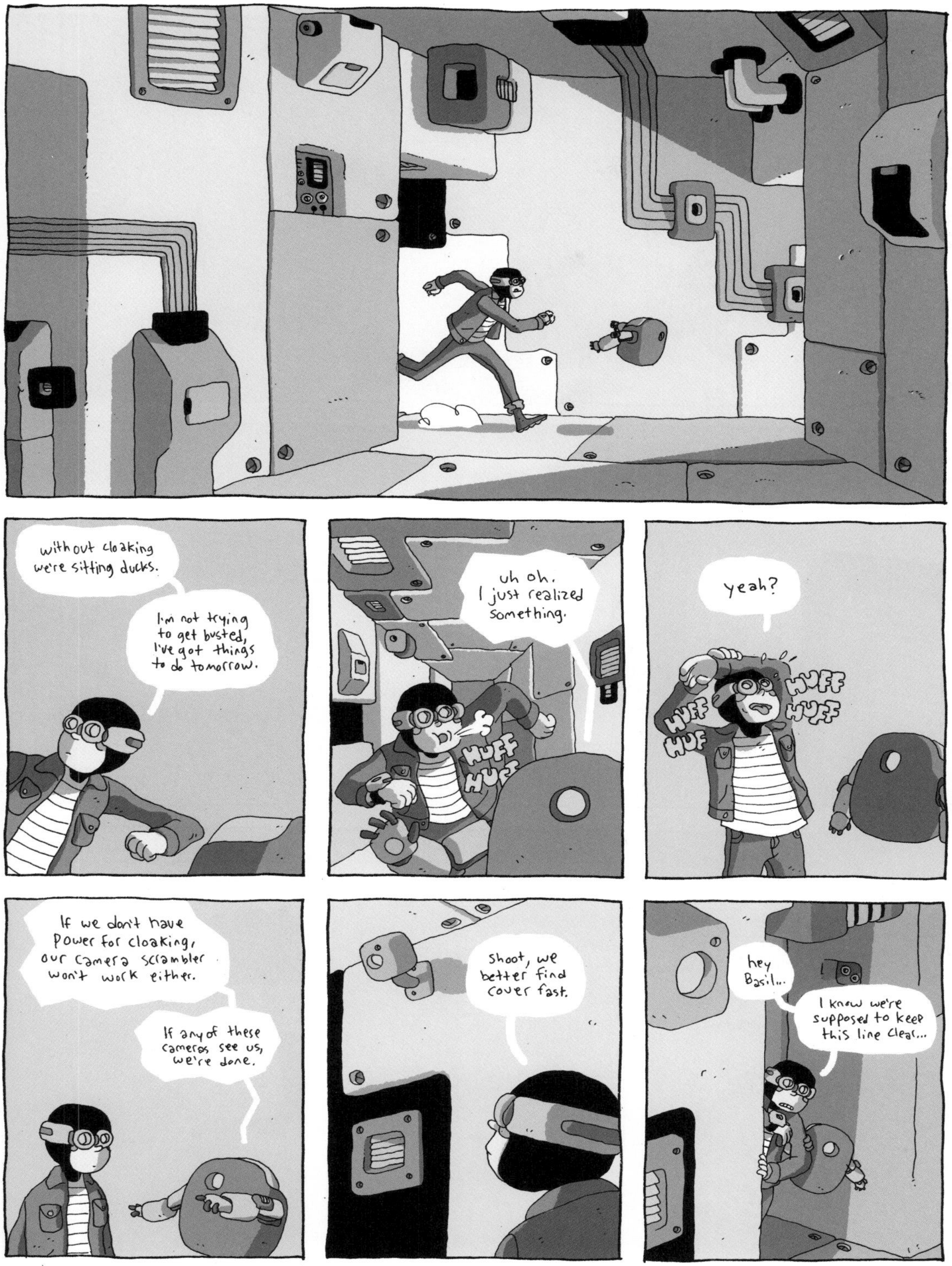
without cloaking we're sitting ducks.
I'm not trying to get busted, I've got things to do tomorrow.
uh oh. I just realized something.
HUFF HUFF
yeah?
HUFF HUFF HUFF HUFF
If we don't have power for cloaking, our camera scrambler won't work either.
If any of these cameras see us, we're done.
Shoot, we better find cover fast.
hey Basil...
I know we're supposed to keep this line clear...

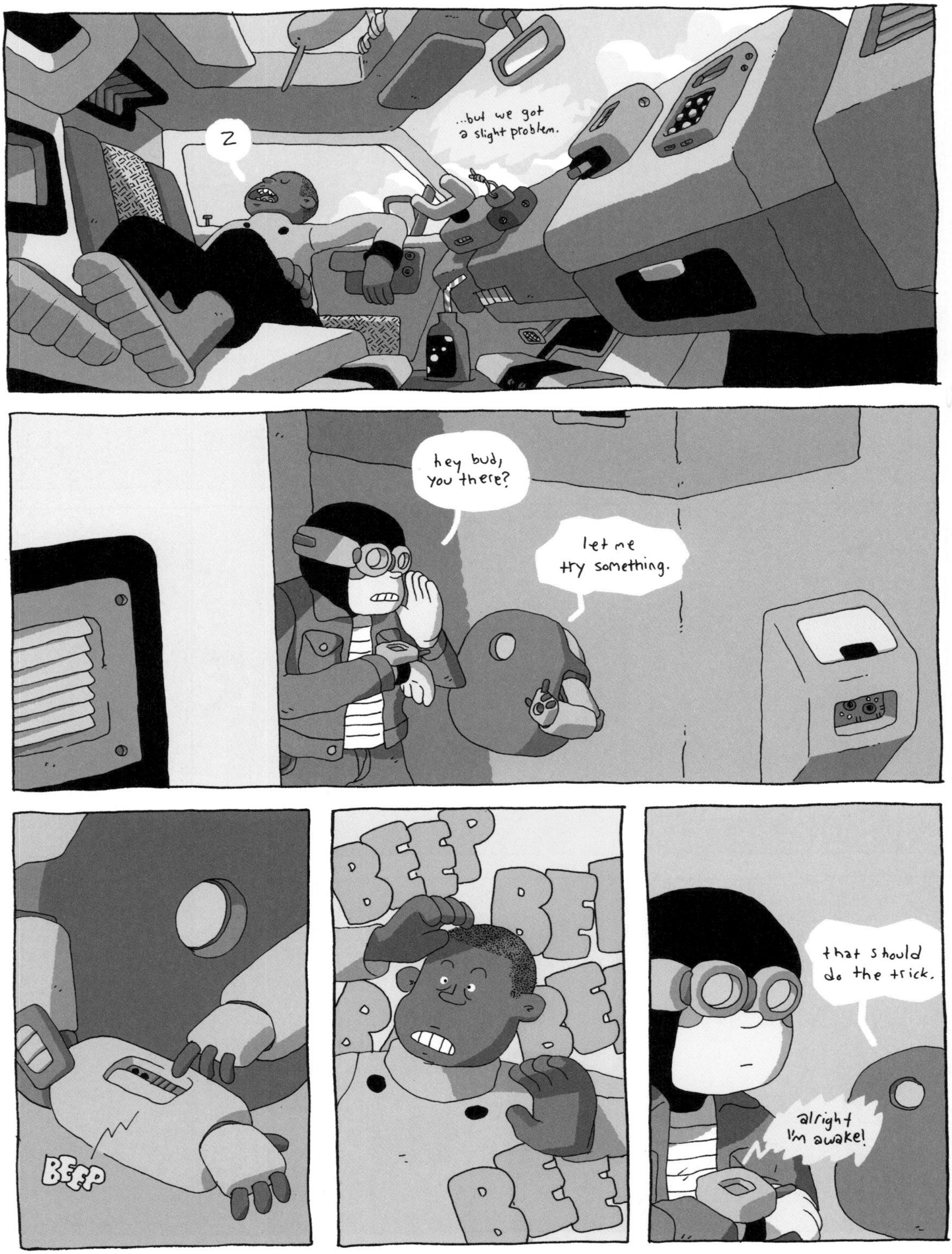
Z
...but we got a slight problem.
hey bud, you there?
let me try something.
BEEP
BEEP BEEP BEEP BEEP BEEP
that should do the trick.
alright I'm awake!

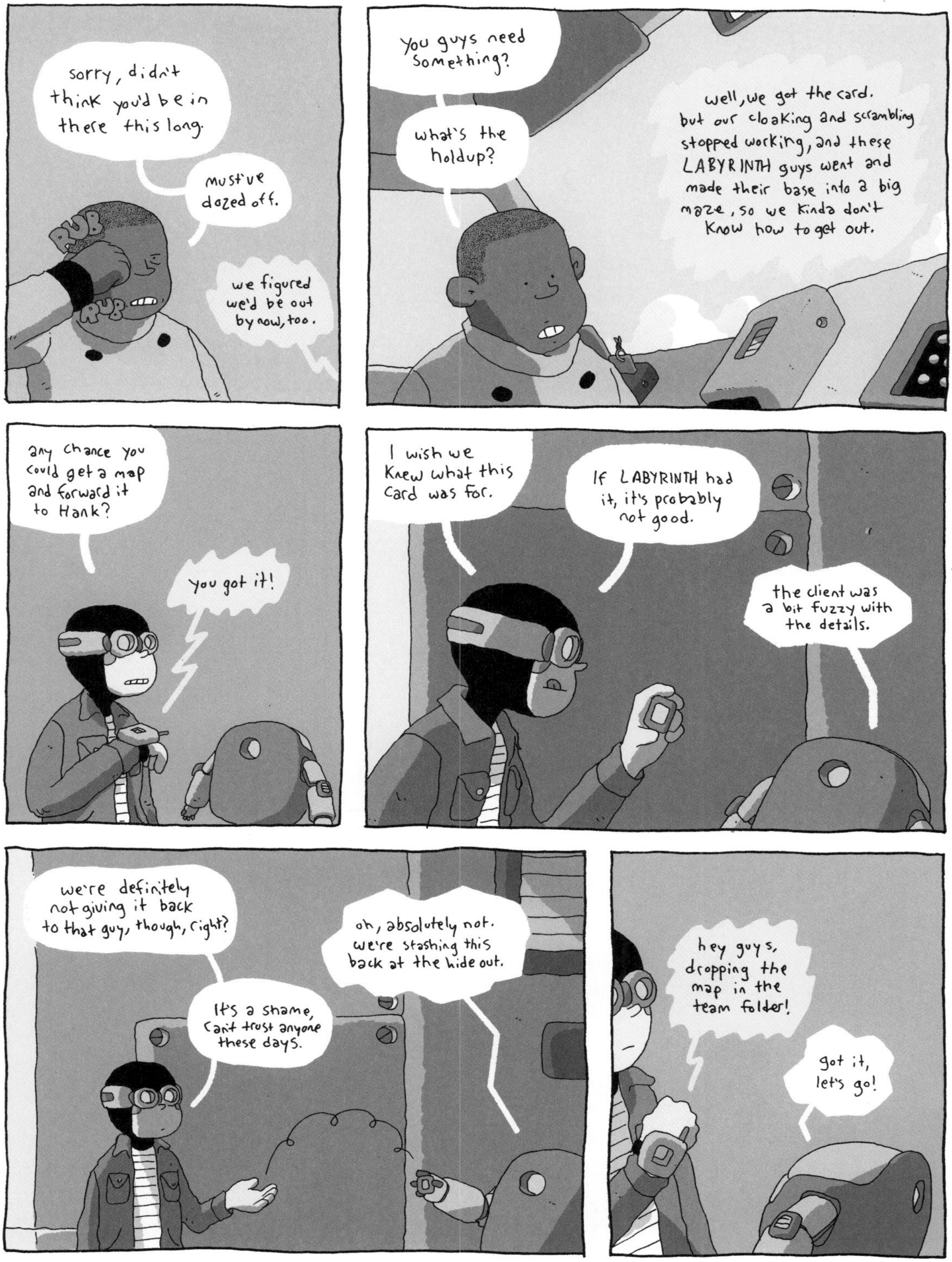
sorry, didn't think you'd be in there this long.
must've dozed off.
RUB
RUB
we figured we'd be out by now, too.
you guys need something?
what's the holdup?
well, we got the card. but our cloaking and scrambling stopped working, and these LABYRINTH guys went and made their base into a big maze, so we kinda don't know how to get out.
any chance you could get a map and forward it to Hank?
you got it!
I wish we knew what this card was for.
If LABYRINTH had it, it's probably not good.
the client was a bit fuzzy with the details.
we're definitely not giving it back to that guy, though, right?
It's a shame, can't trust anyone these days.
oh, absolutely not. we're stashing this back at the hide out.
hey guys, dropping the map in the team folder!
got it, let's go!

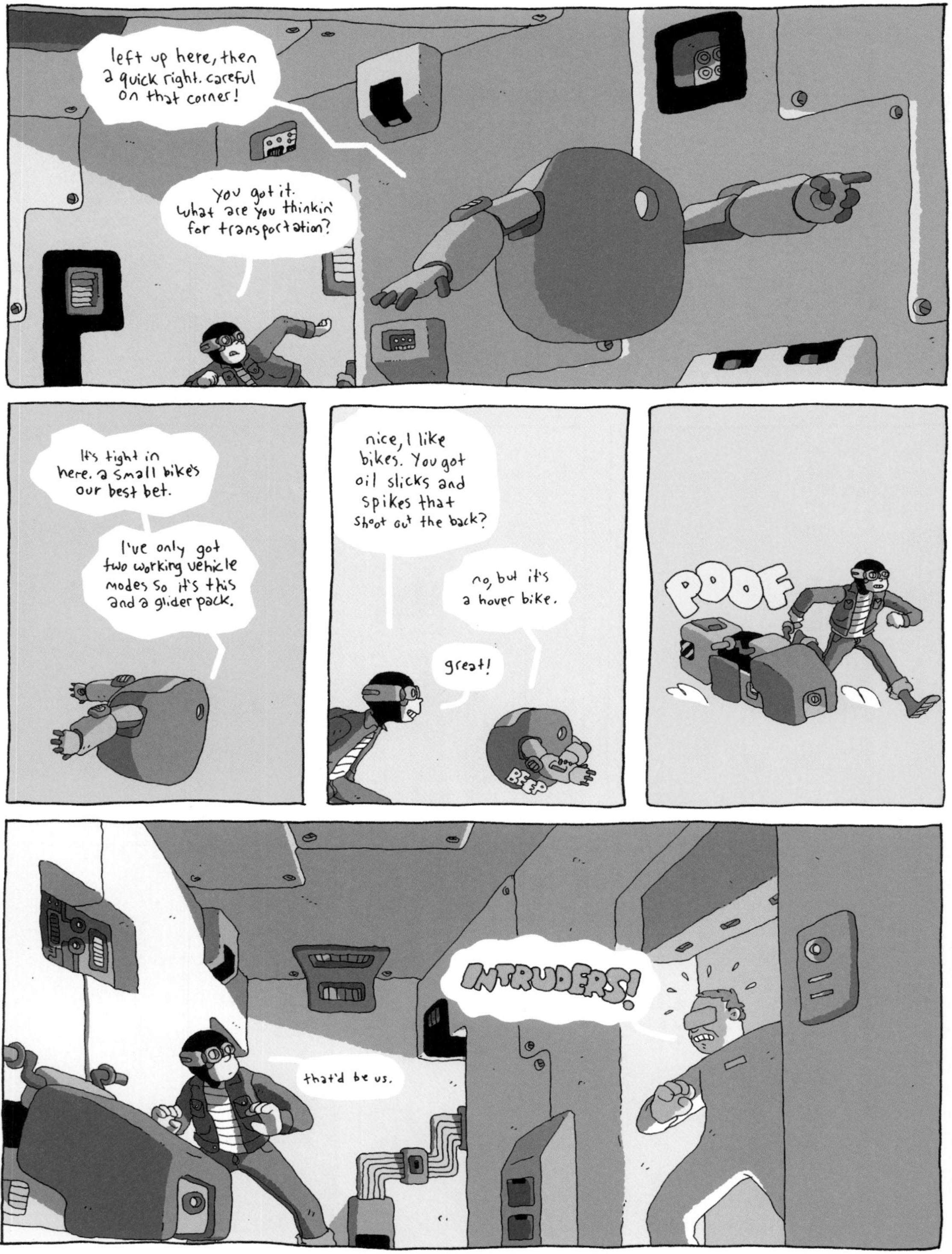
left up here, then a quick right. careful on that corner!
You got it. what are you thinkin' for transportation?
It's tight in here. a small bike's our best bet.
I've only got two working vehicle modes so it's this and a glider pack.
nice, I like bikes. You got oil slicks and spikes that shoot out the back?
no, but it's a hover bike.
great!
BEEP
POOF
INTRUDERS!
that'd be us.

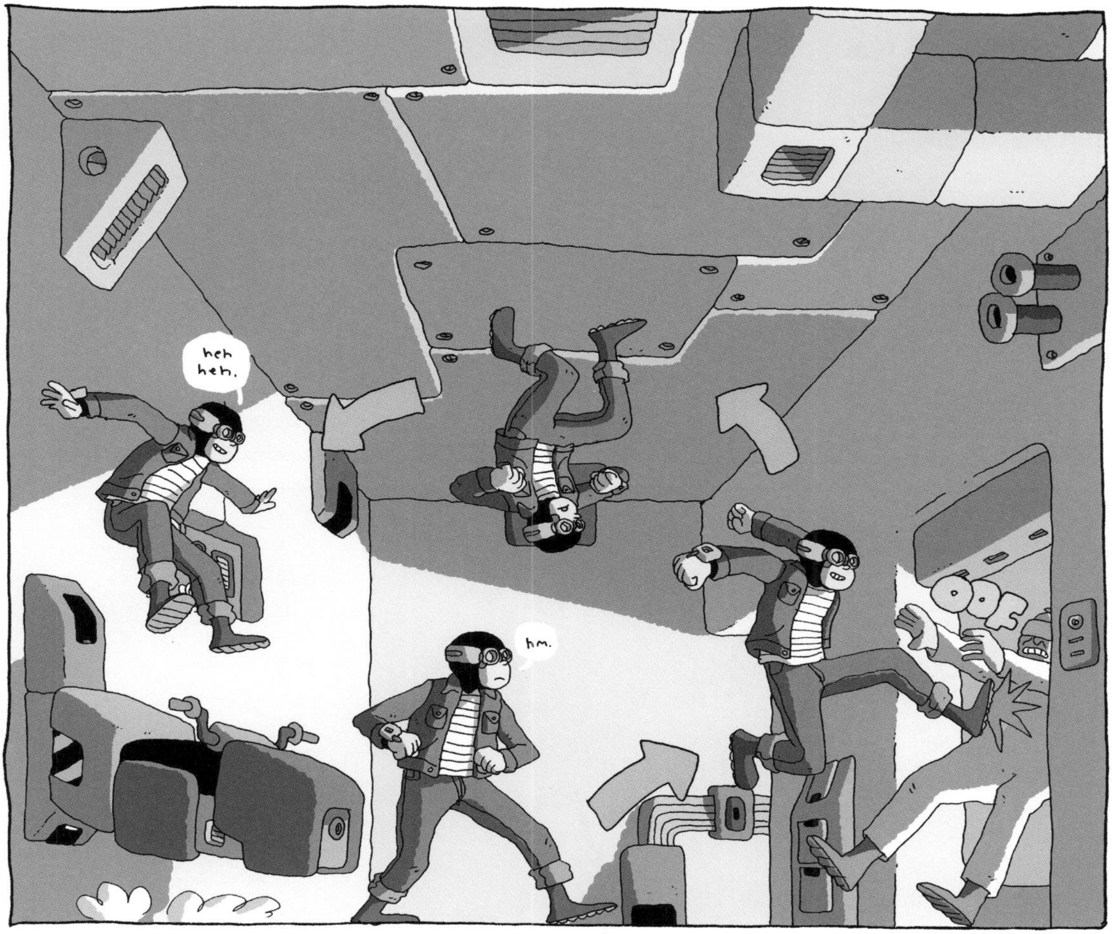
heh heh.
hm.
OOF

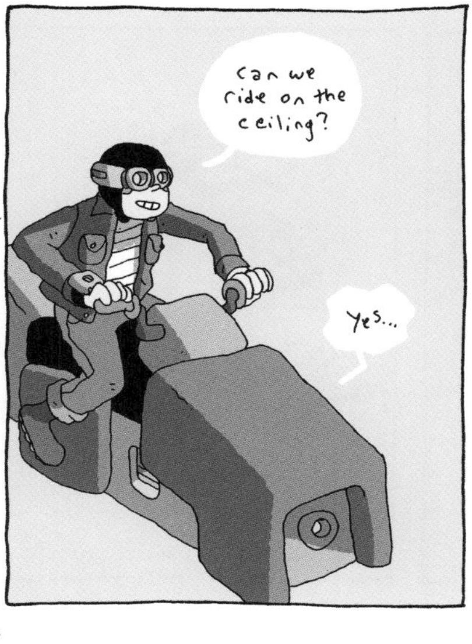
can we ride on the ceiling?
yes...

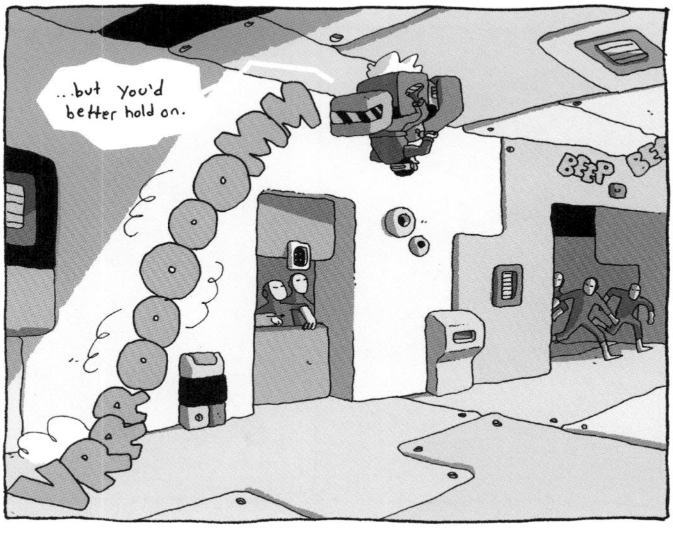
...but you'd better hold on.
VRRRROOOOOOMMM
BEEP BEE

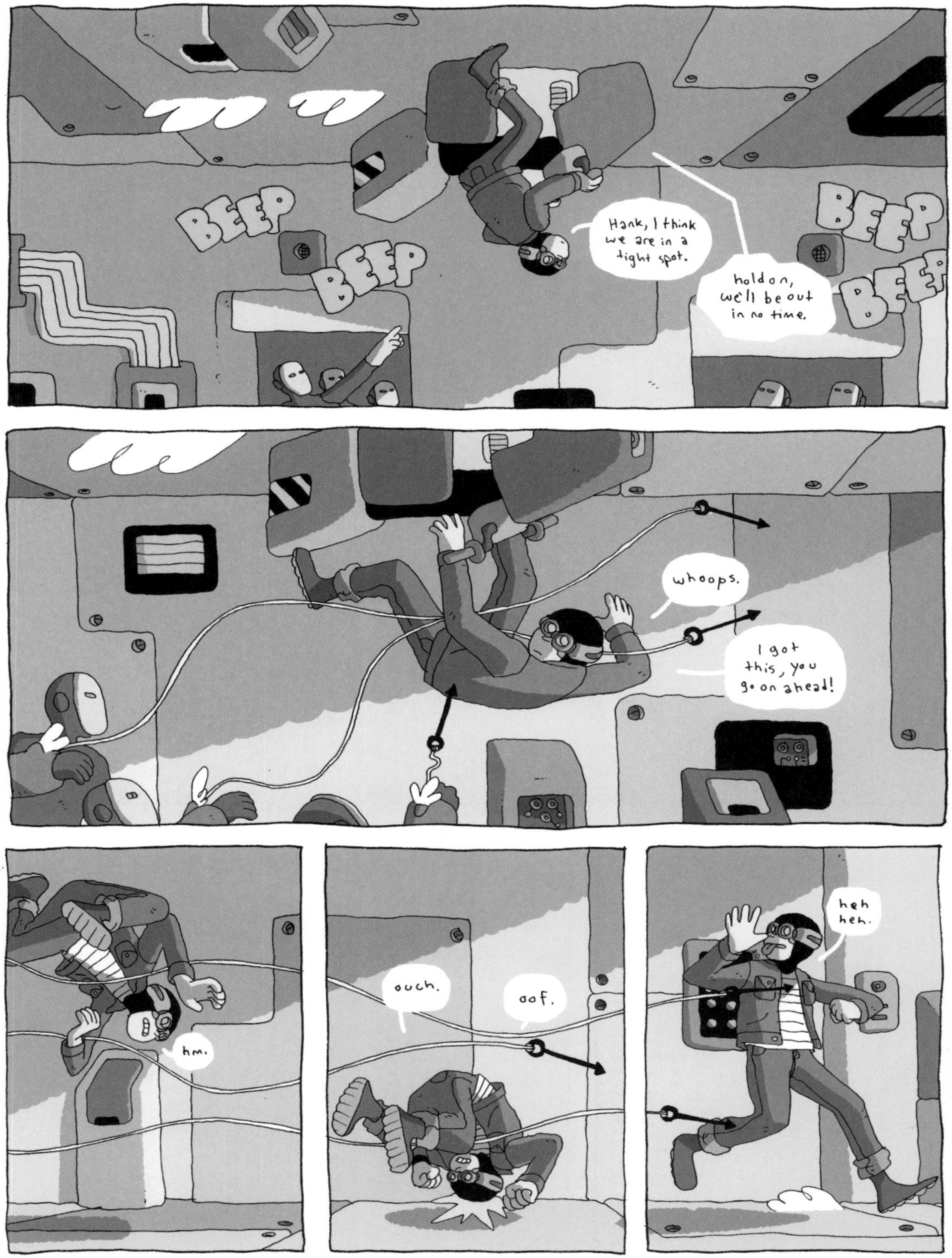
BEEP
BEEP
Hank, I think we are in a tight spot.
hold on, we'll be out in no time.
BEEP
BEEP
whoops.
I got this, you go on ahead!
hm.
ouch.
oof.
heh heh.

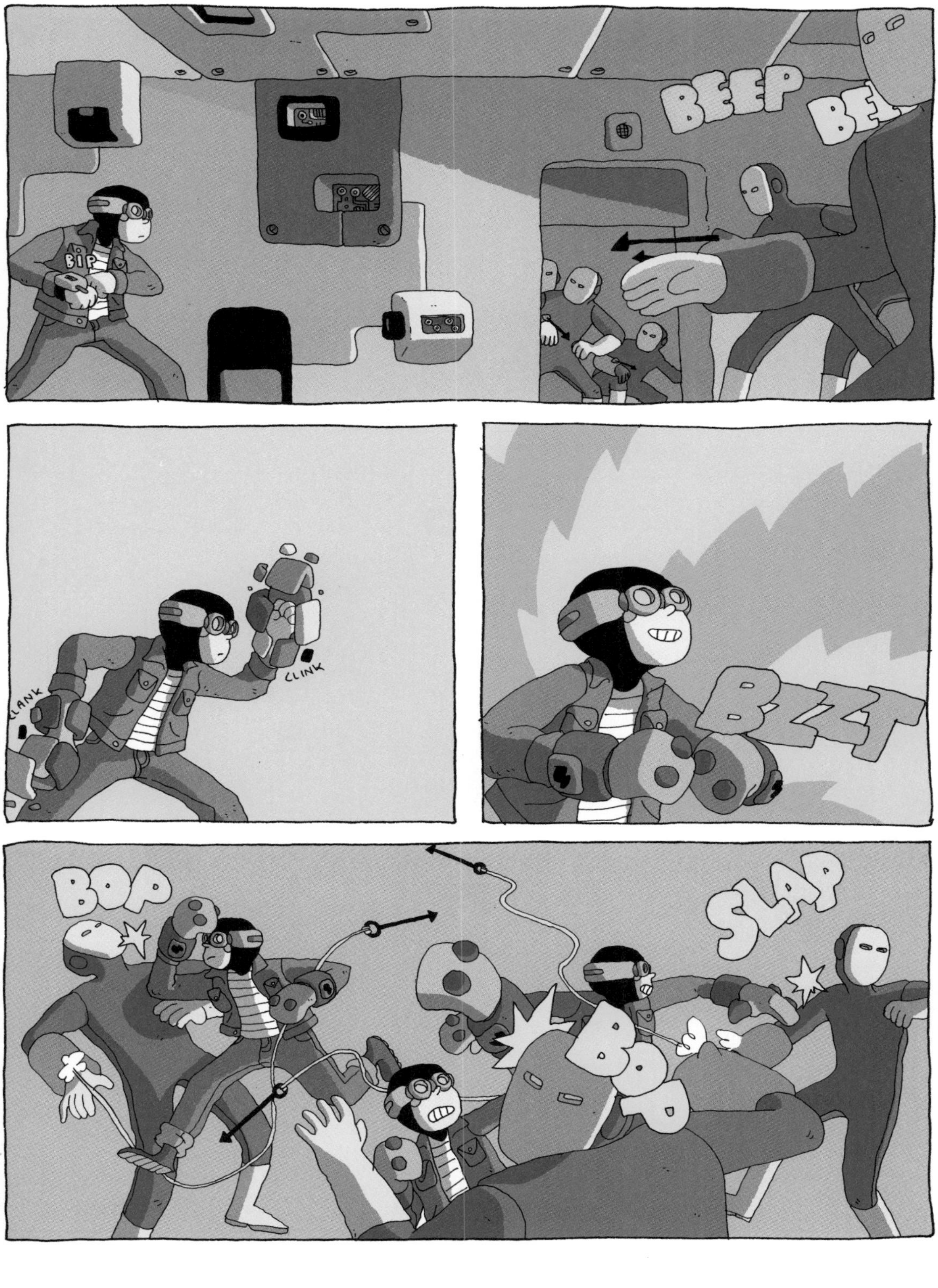
BIP
BEEP
BEE
CLANK
CLINK
BZZT
BOP
SLAP
BOP

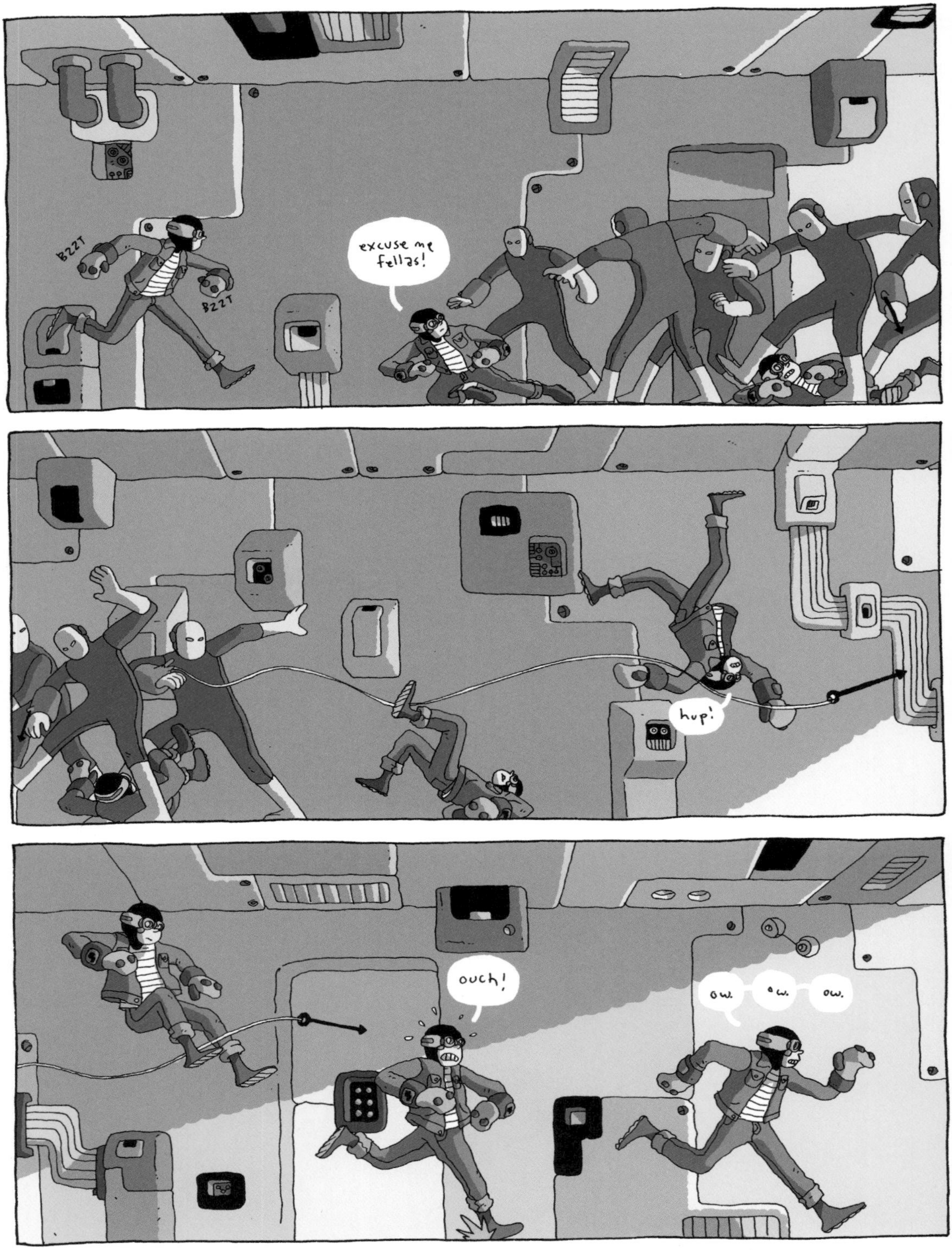
BZZT
BZZT
excuse me fellas!
hup!
ouch!
ow.
ow.
ow.

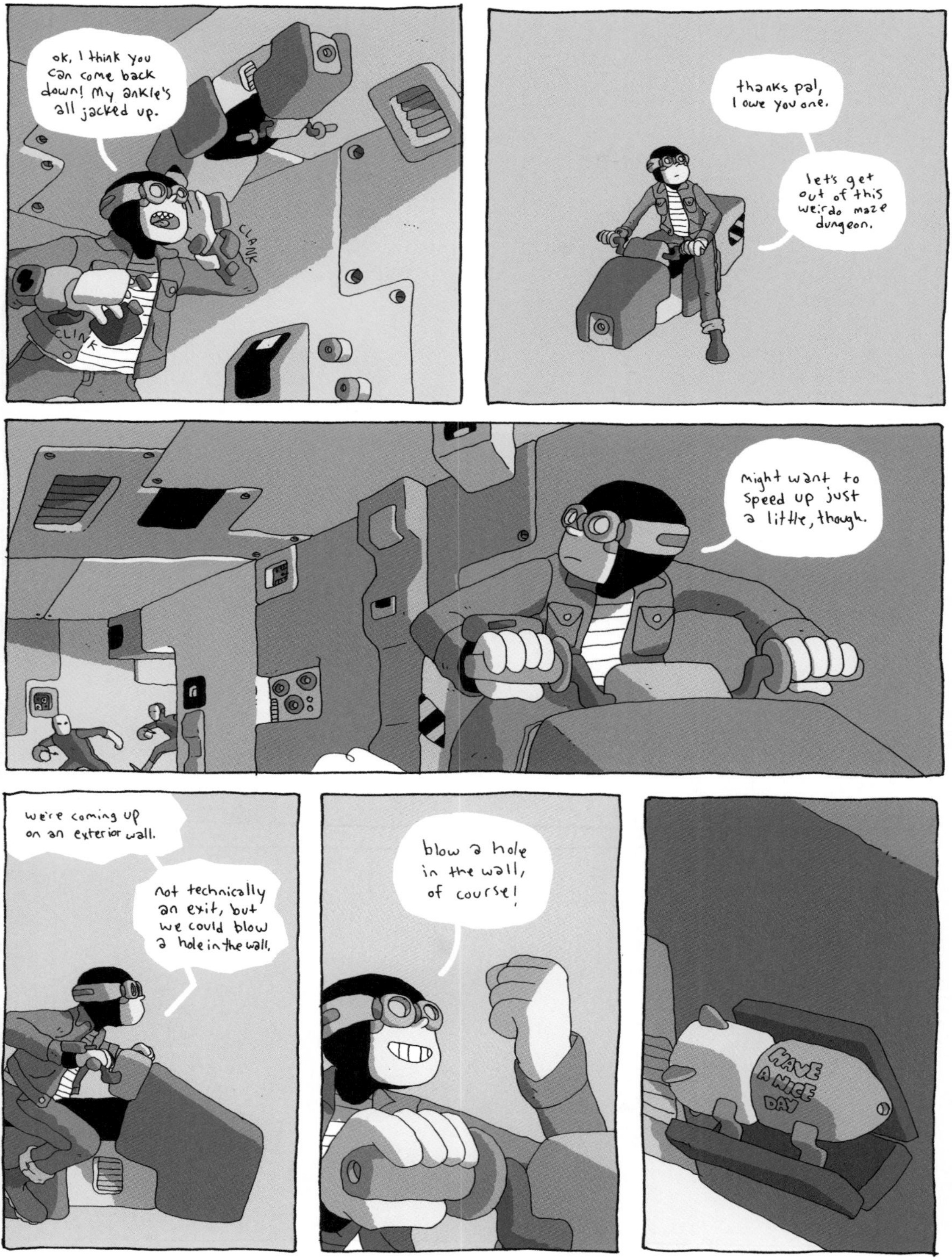
ok, I think you can come back down! My ankle's all jacked up.
CLANK
CLINK
thanks pal, I owe you one.
let's get out of this weirdo maze dungeon.
Might want to speed up just a little, though.
we're coming up on an exterior wall.
not technically an exit, but we could blow a hole in the wall.
blow a hole in the wall, of course!
HAVE A NICE DAY

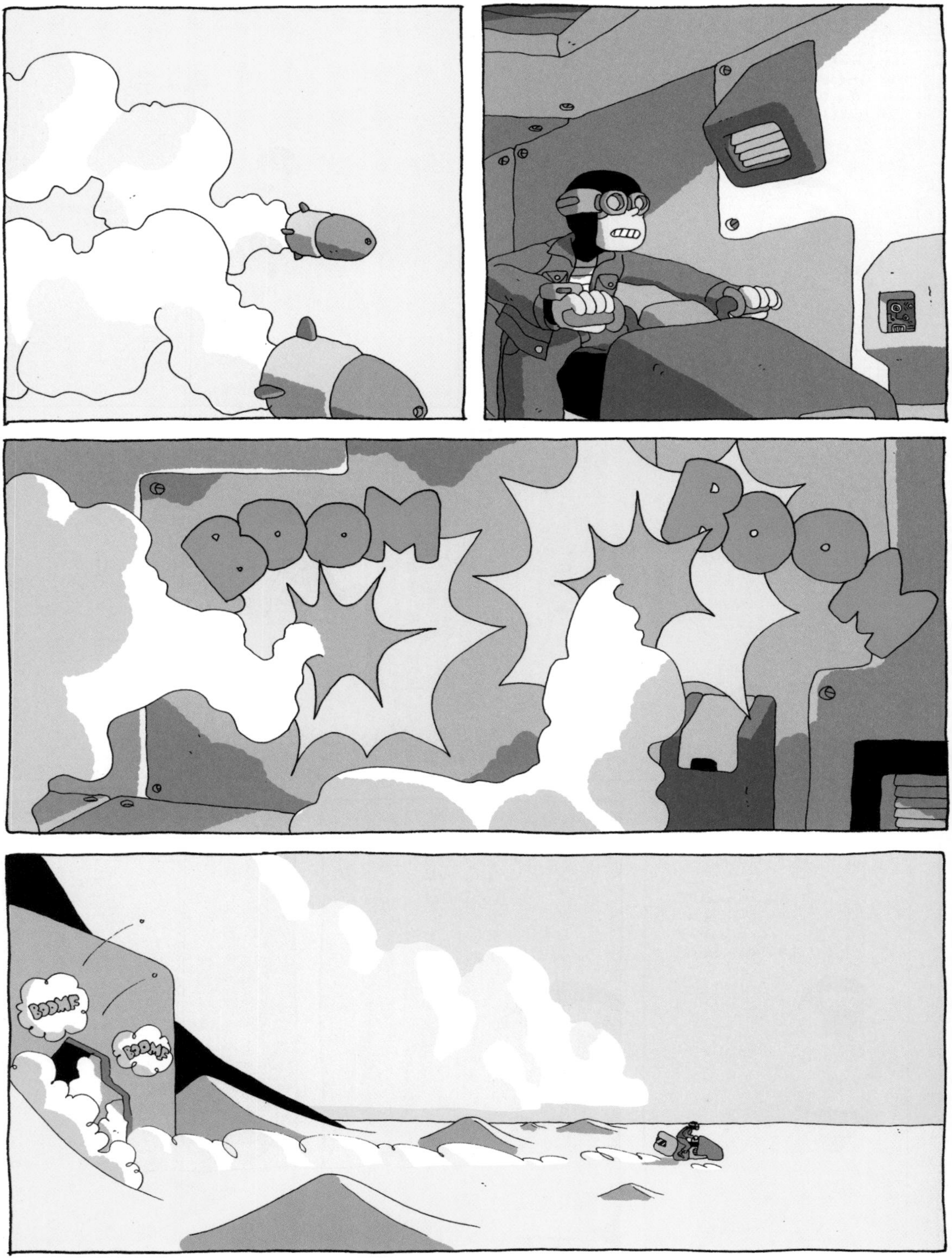
BOOM
BOOM
BOOMF
BOOMF

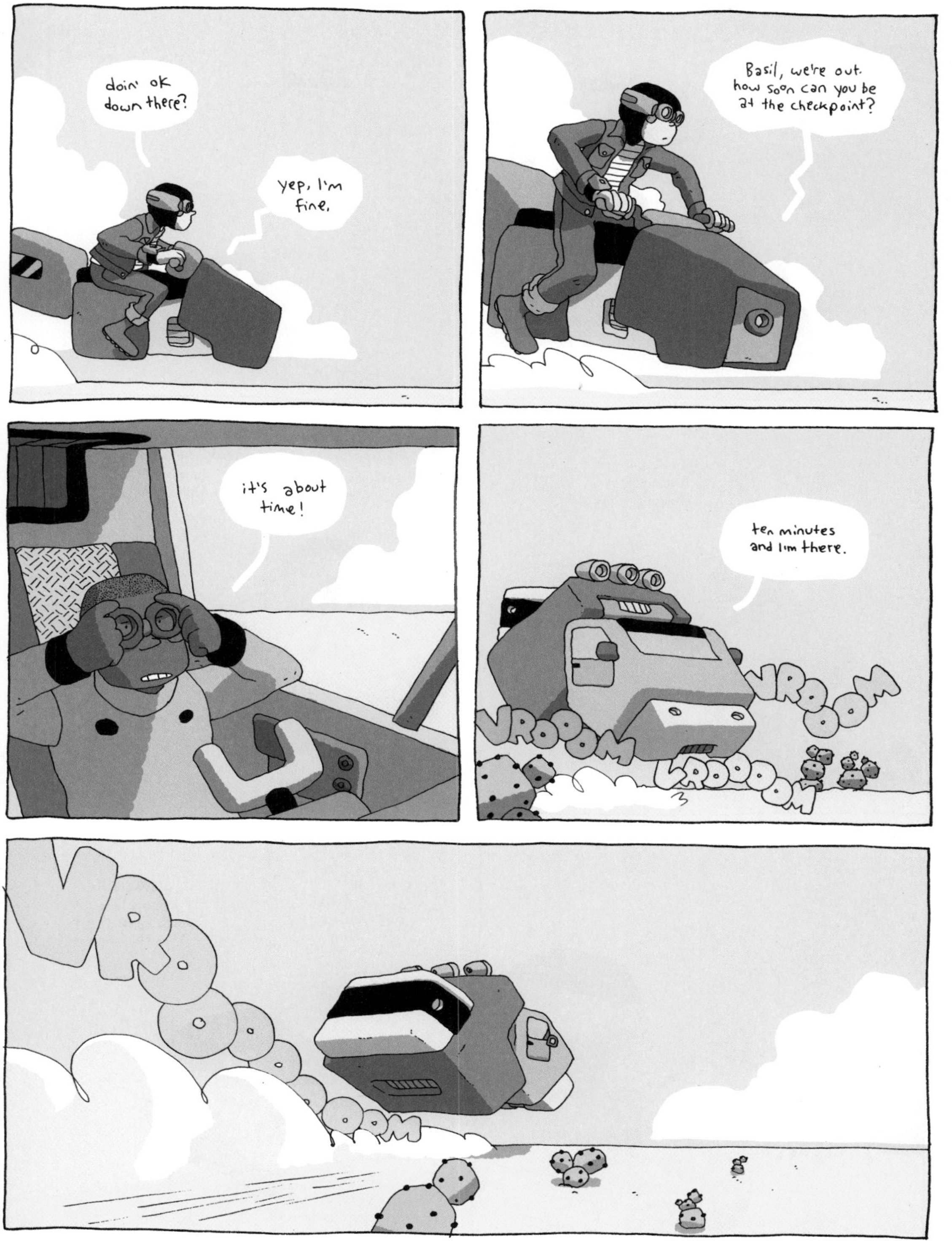
doin' ok down there?
yep, I'm fine.
Basil, we're out. how soon can you be at the checkpoint?
it's about time!
ten minutes and Im there.
VROOOM
VROOOM
VROOOOOM
VROOOOOOOM

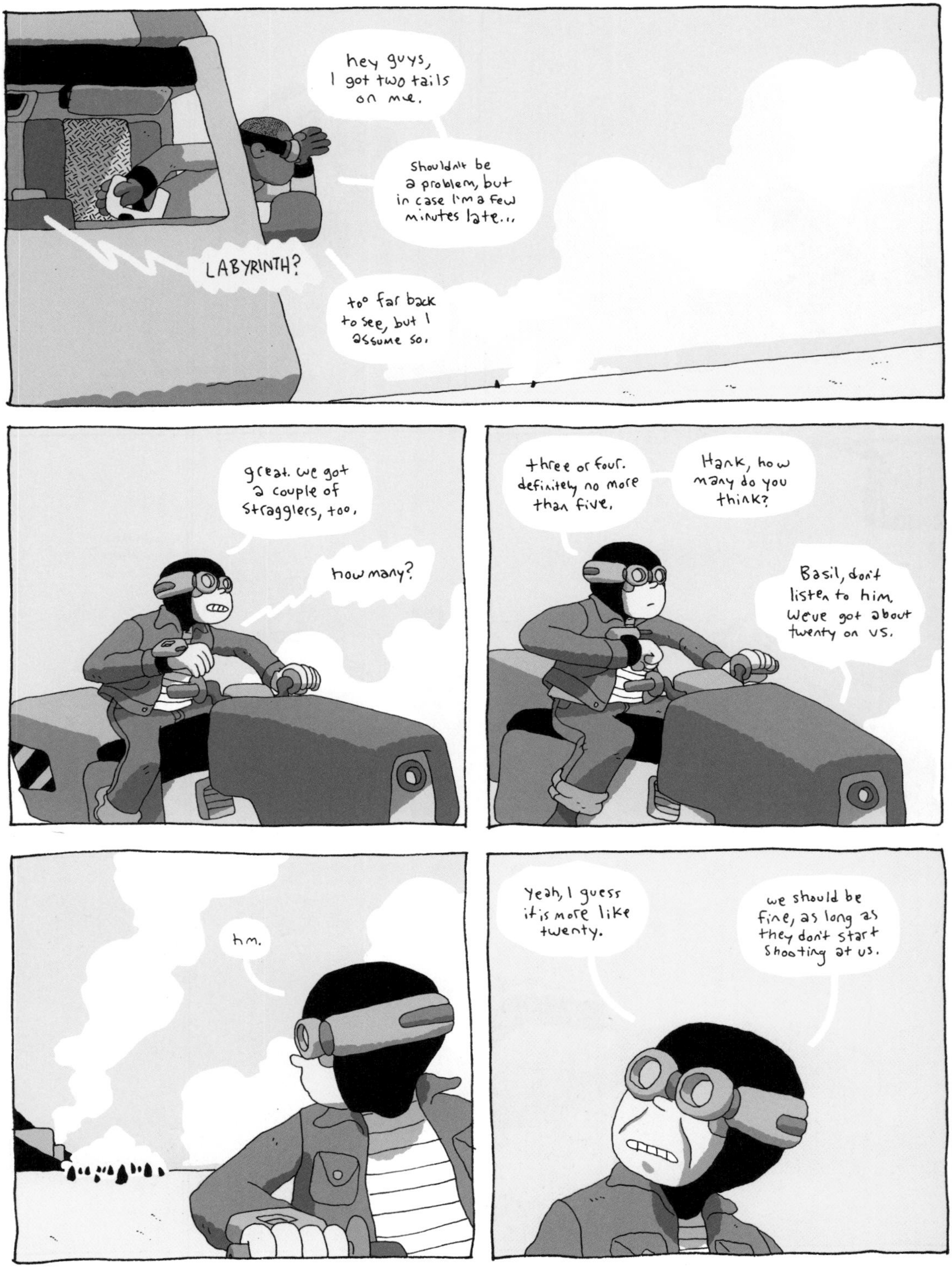
hey guys, I got two tails on me.
shouldn't be a problem, but in case I'm a few minutes late...
LABYRINTH?
too far back to see, but I assume so.
great. we got a couple of stragglers, too.
how many?
three or four. definitely no more than five.
Hank, how many do you think?
Basil, don't listen to him. We've got about twenty on us.
hm.
Yeah, I guess it is more like twenty.
we should be fine, as long as they don't start shooting at us.

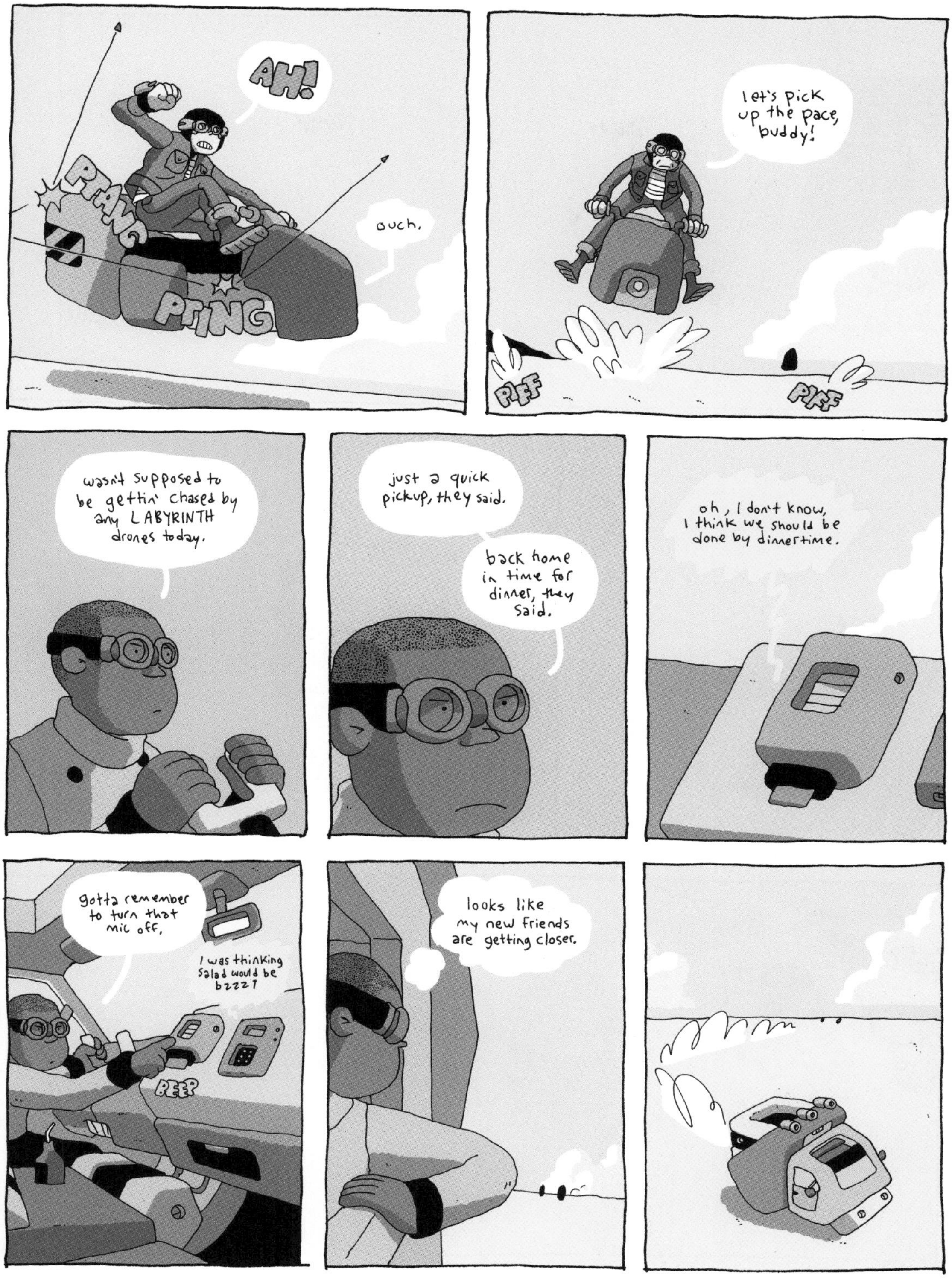
AH!
PTANG
PTING
ouch.
let's pick up the pace, buddy!
PIFF
PIFF
wasn't supposed to be gettin' chased by any LABYRINTH drones today.
just a quick pickup, they said.
back home in time for dinner, they said.
oh, I don't know, I think we should be done by dinnertime.
gotta remember to turn that mic off.
I was thinking salad would be bzzz?
BEEP
looks like my new friends are getting closer.

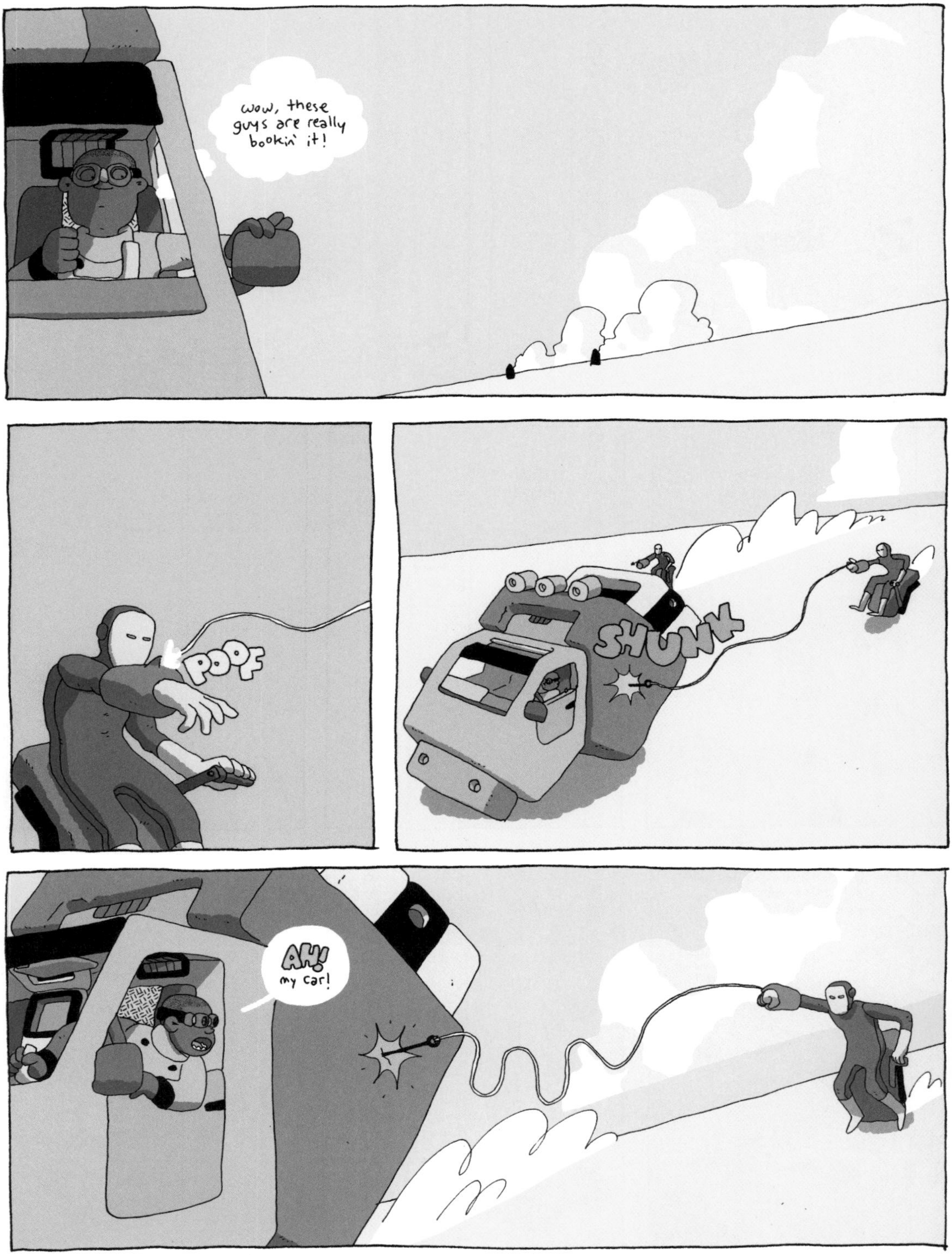
wow, these guys are really bookin' it!
POOF
SHUNK
AH! my car!

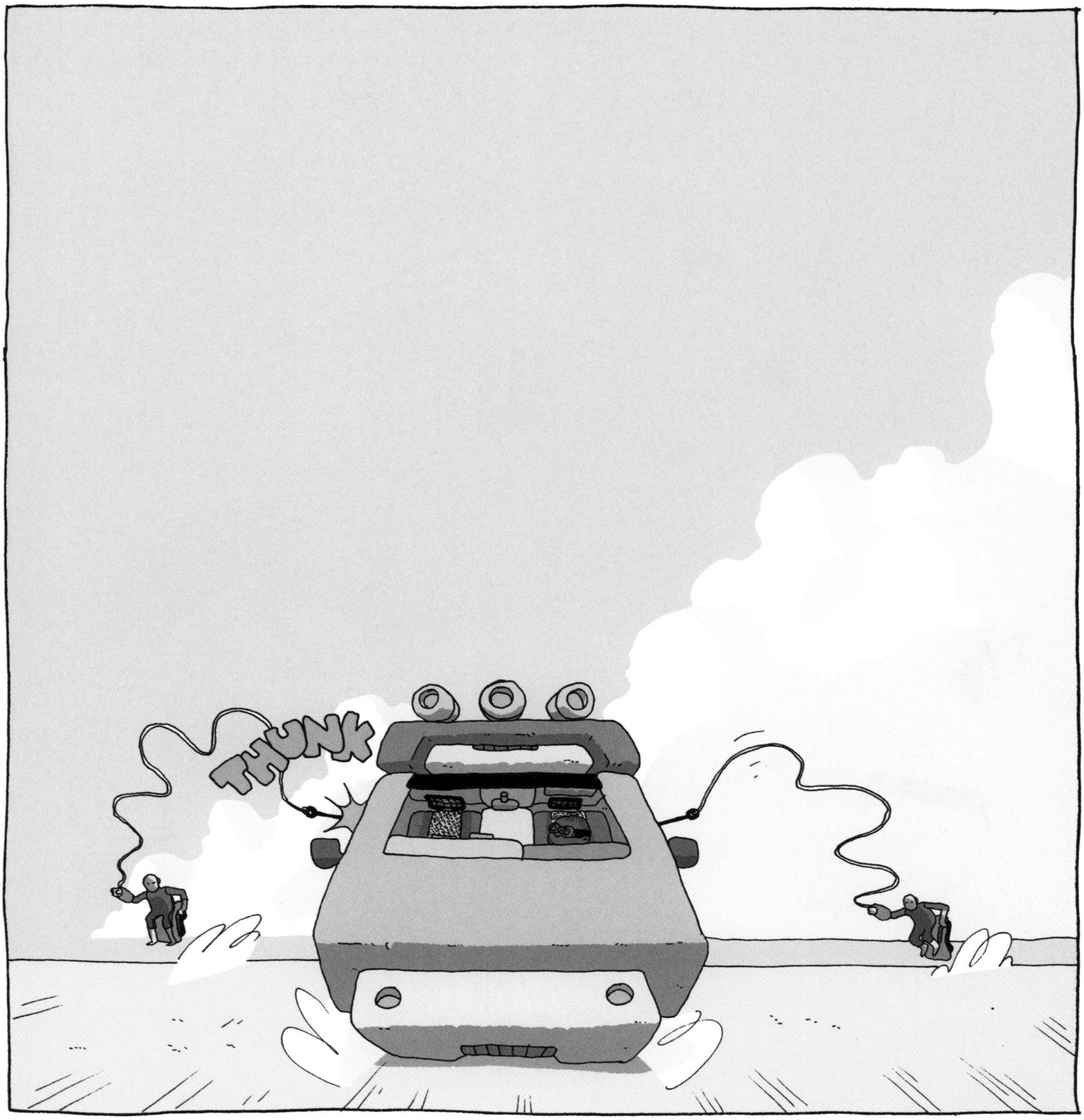
THUNK

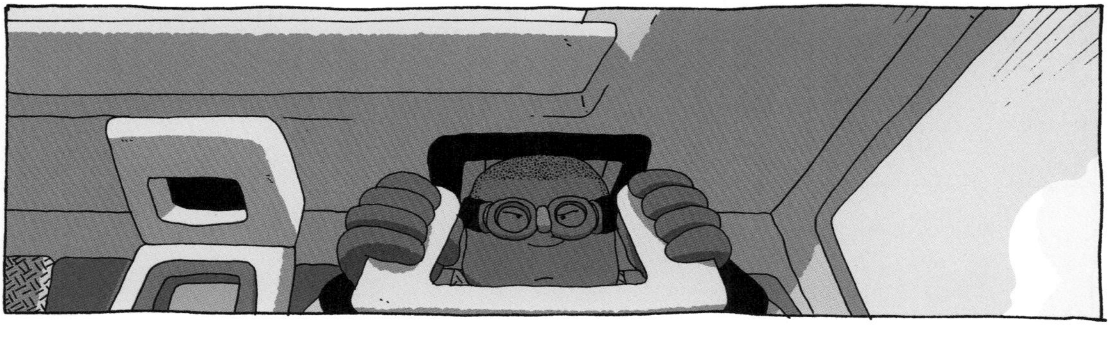

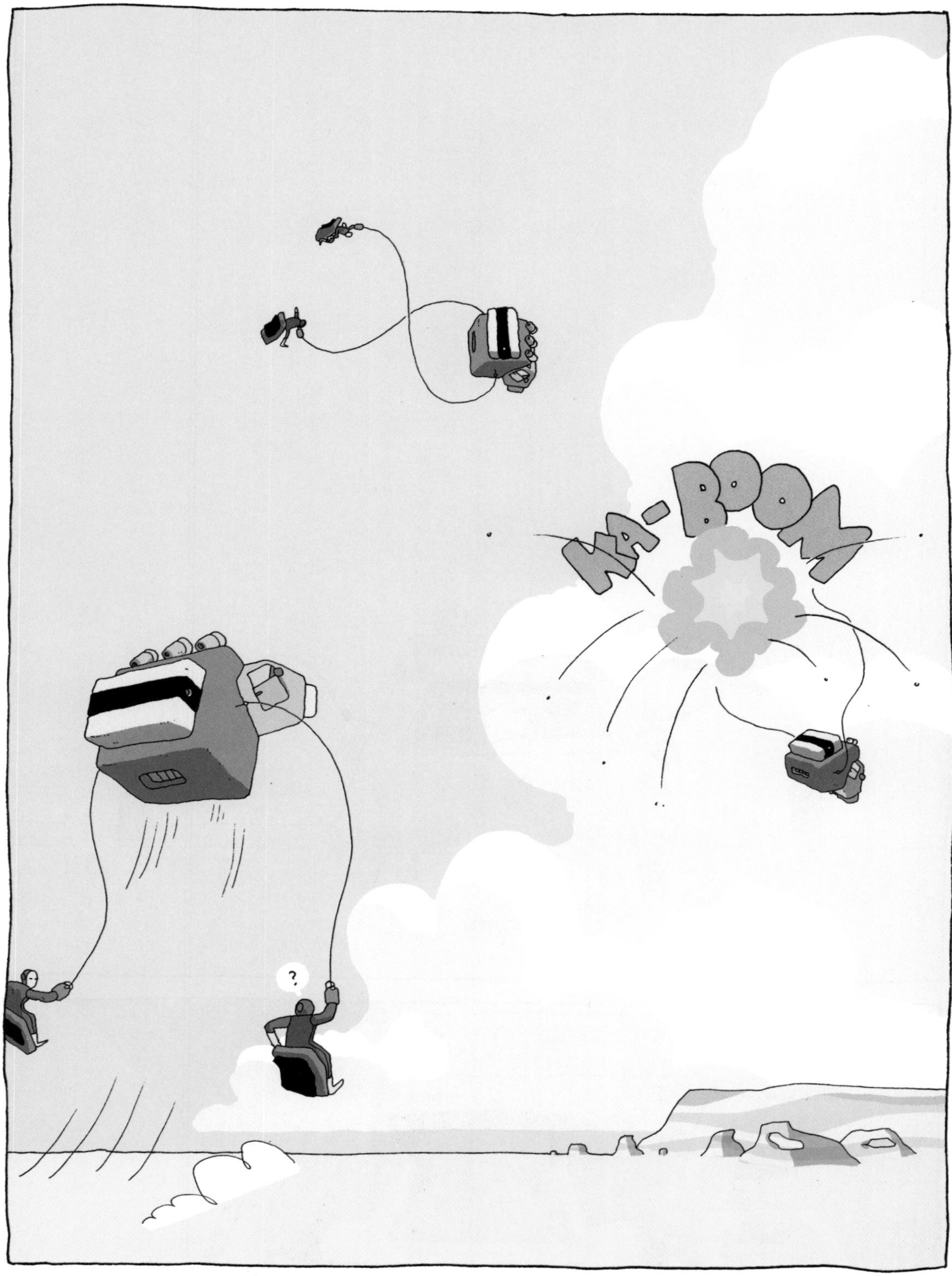
KA-BOOM
?

heh heh.

you did good back there.

PAT
PAT

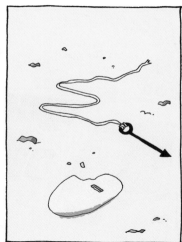

PUTT
PUTT
PUTT

hey, ace you guys almost here?

oh, hey Basil. we're just about there. small change of plans, though.

there should be a cliff pretty close to the checkpoint.

could you meet us there instead?

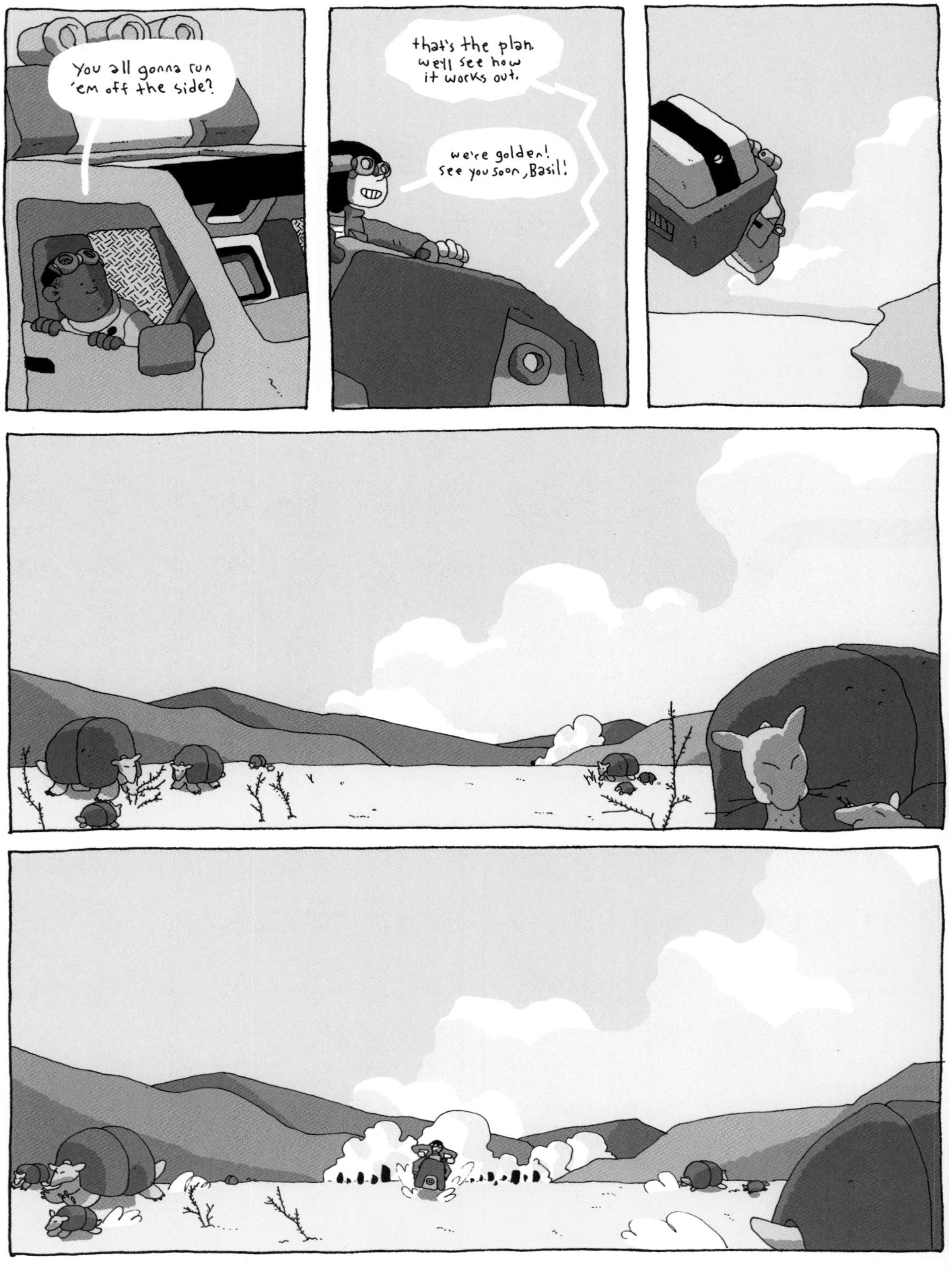
You all gonna run 'em off the side?
that's the plan. we'll see how it works out.
we're golden! see you soon, Basil!

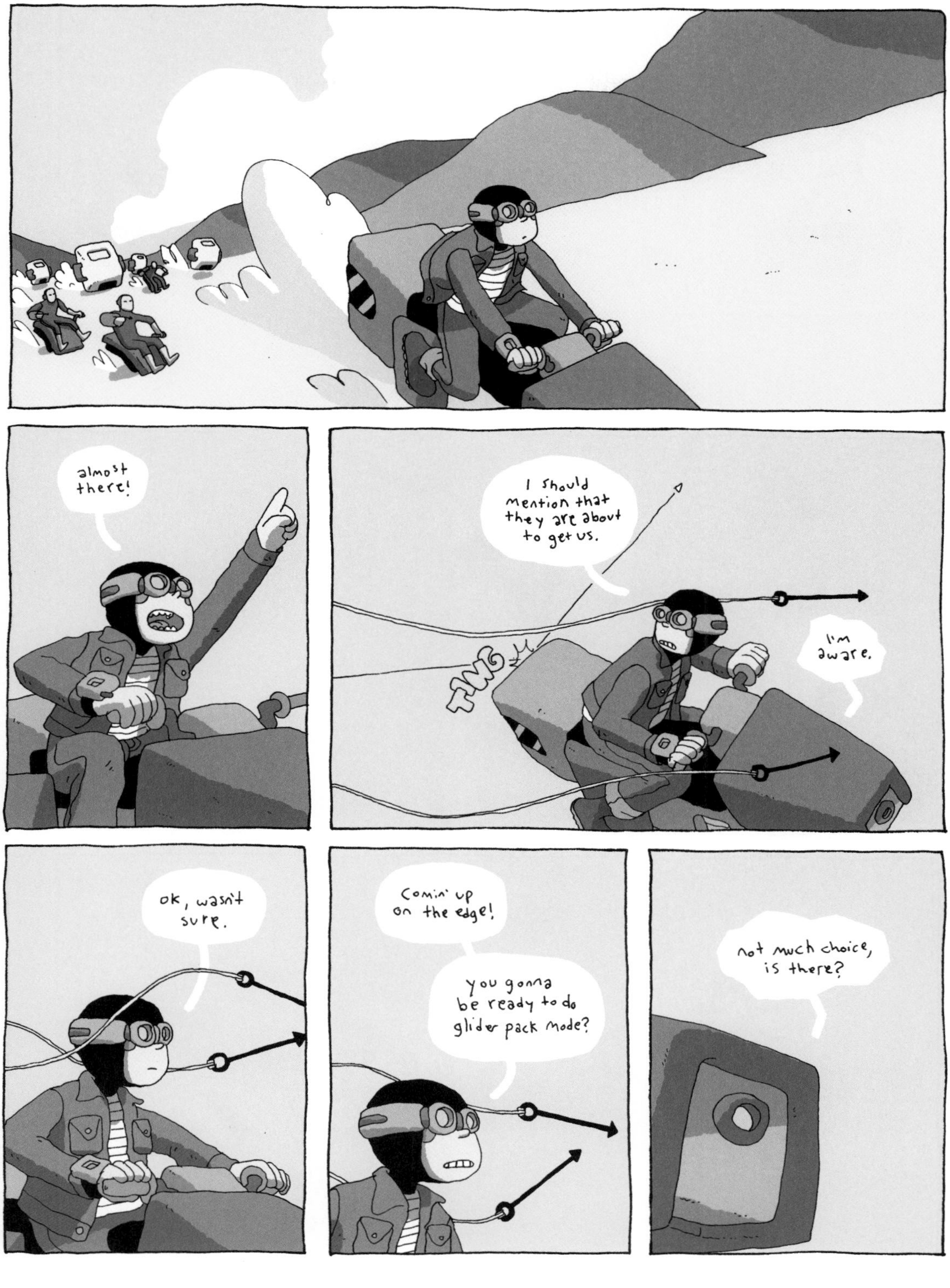
almost there!
I should mention that they are about to get us.
TWG
I'm aware.
ok, wasn't sure.
Comin' up on the edge!
you gonna be ready to do glider pack mode?
not much choice, is there?

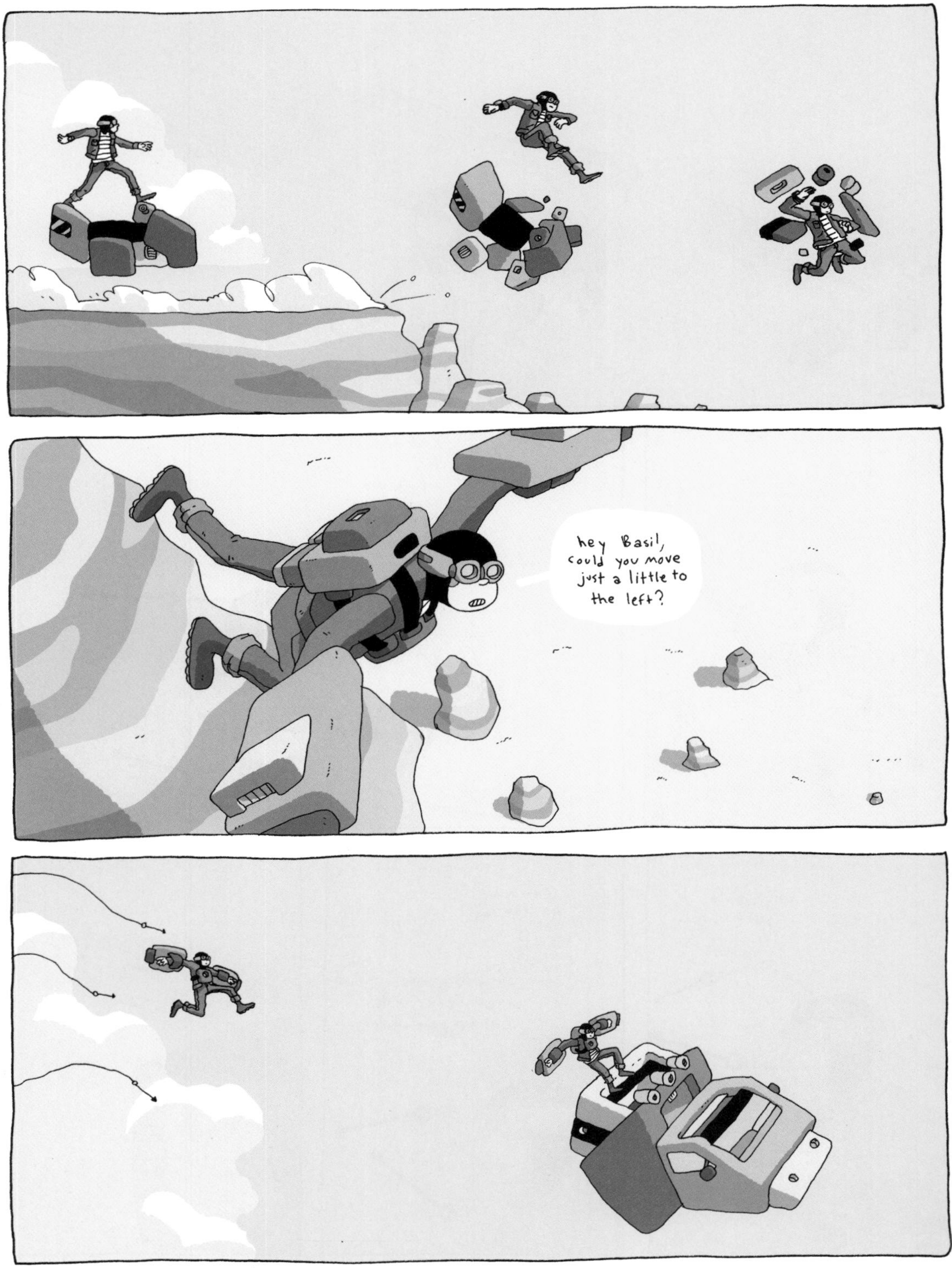
hey Basil, could you move just a little to the left?

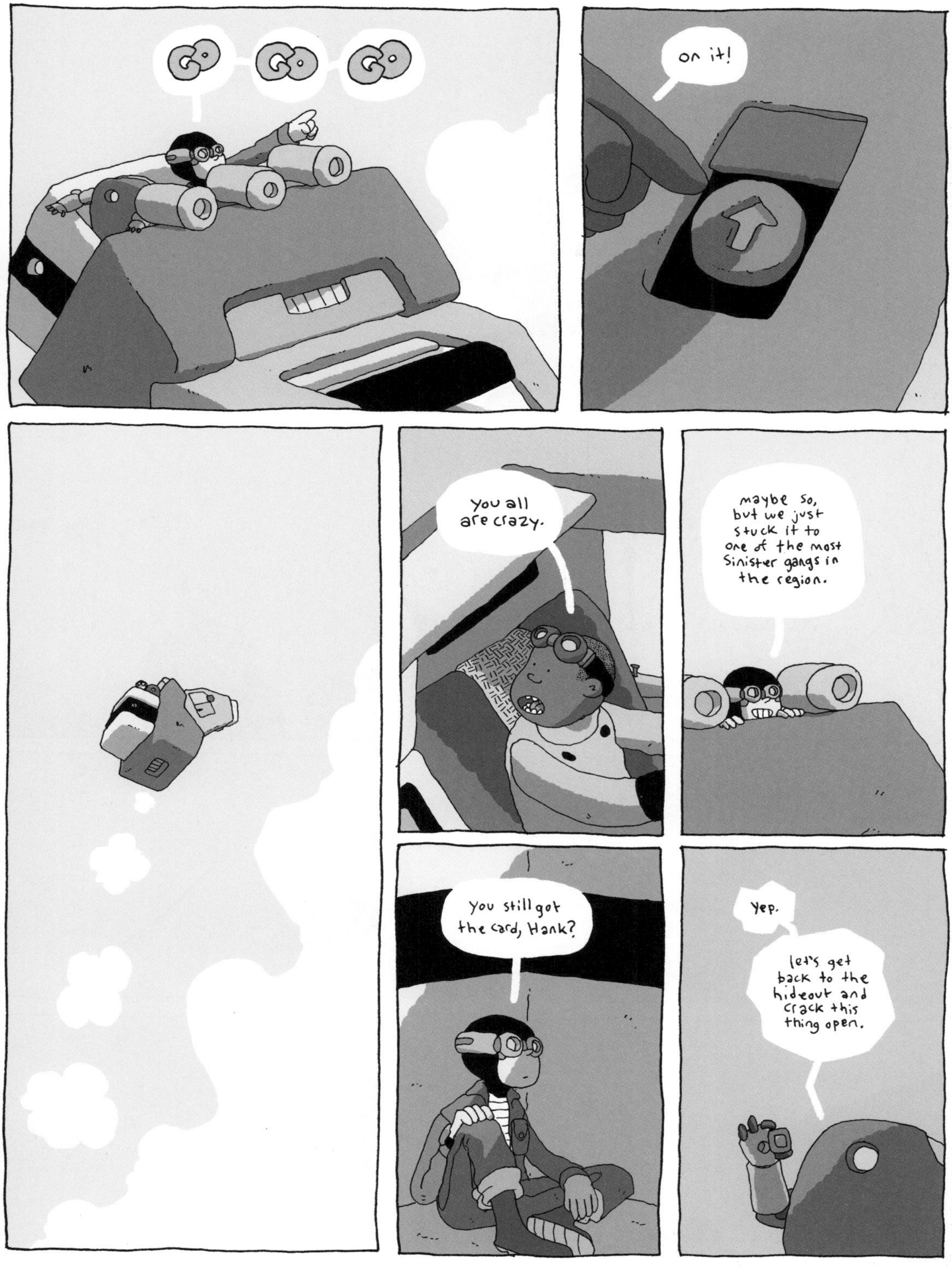
GO GO GO
on it!
you all are crazy.
maybe so, but we just stuck it to one of the most sinister gangs in the region.
you still got the card, Hank?
yep.
let's get back to the hideout and crack this thing open.

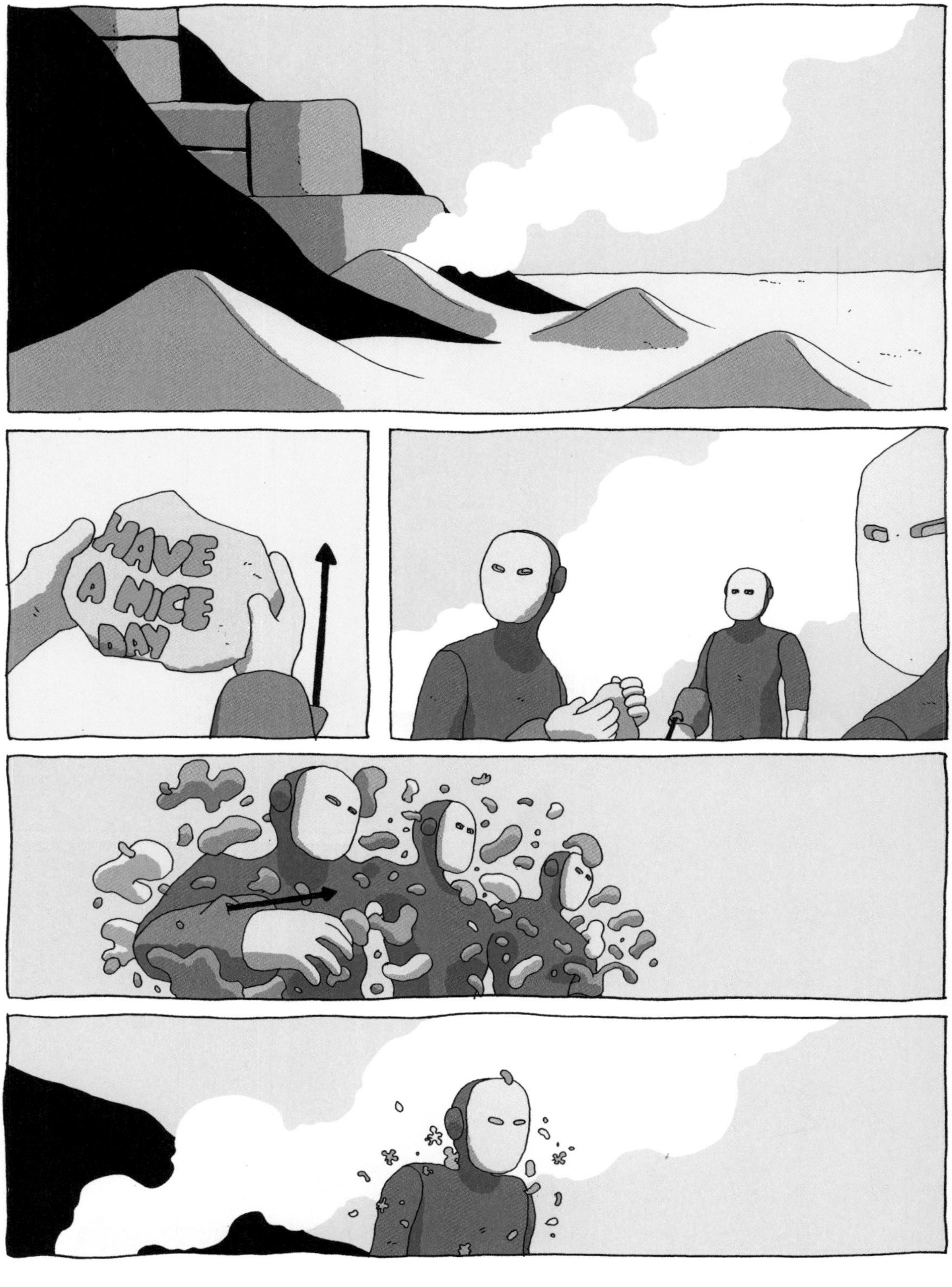
HAVE A NICE DAY

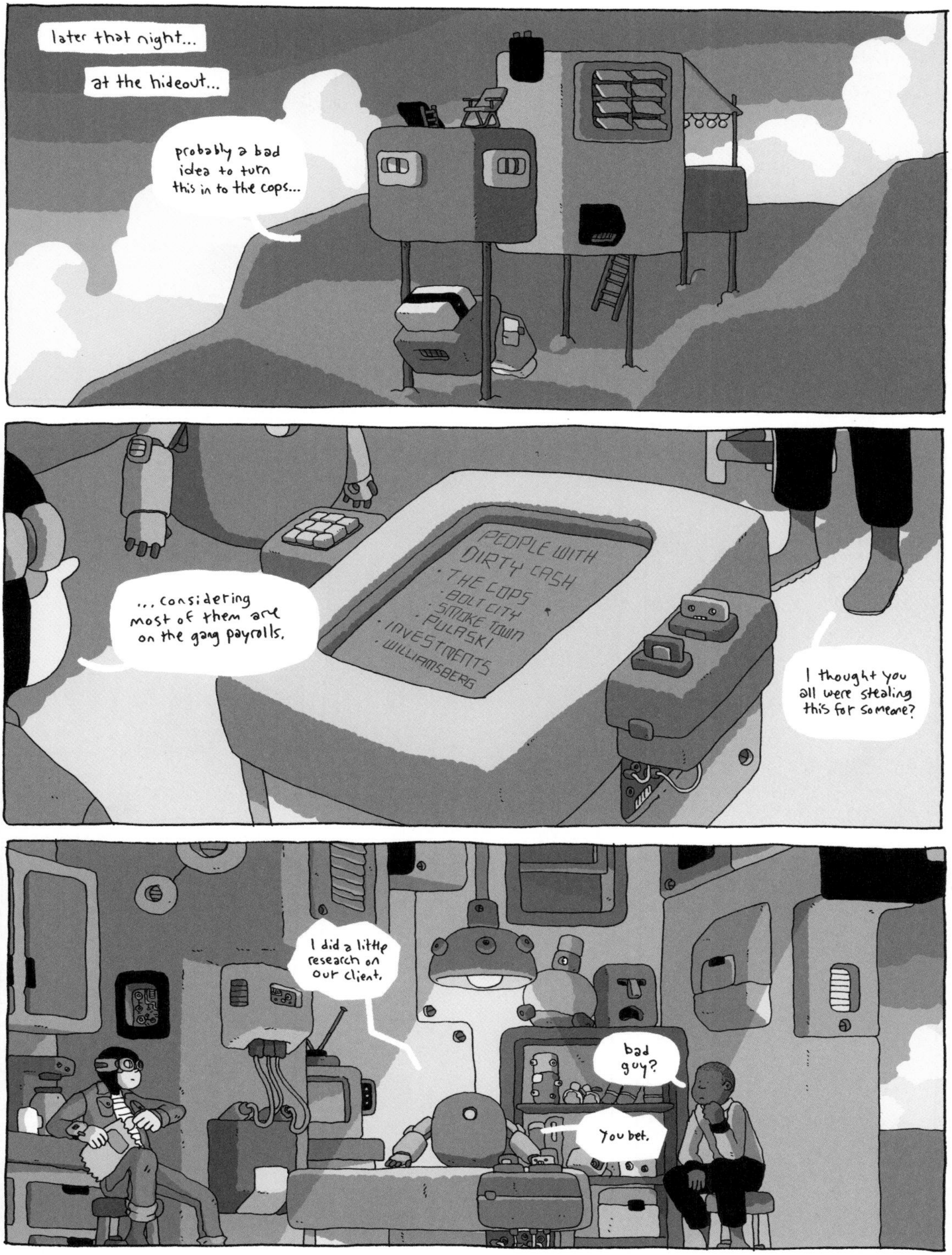
later that night...
at the hideout...
probably a bad idea to turn this in to the cops...
...considering most of them are on the gang payrolls.
PEOPLE WITH DIRTY CASH
• THE COPS
• BOLT CITY
• SMOKE TOWN
• PULASKI
• INVESTMENTS
• WILLIAMSBERG
I thought you all were stealing this for someone?
I did a little research on our client.
bad guy?
You bet.

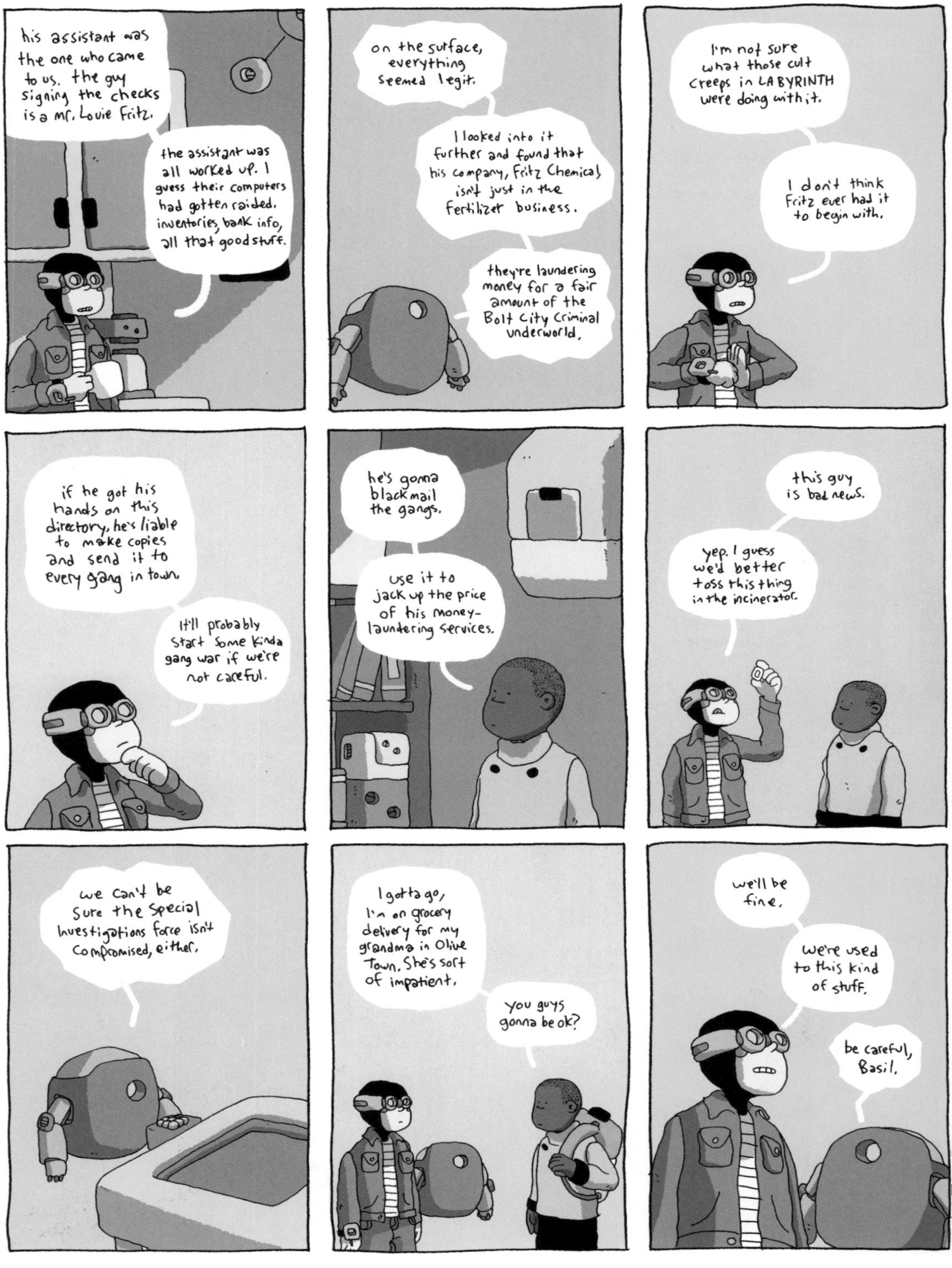
his assistant was the one who came to us. the guy signing the checks is a mr. Louie Fritz.
the assistant was all worked up. I guess their computers had gotten raided. inventories, bank info, all that good stuff.
on the surface, everything seemed legit.
I looked into it further and found that his company, Fritz Chemical, isn't just in the fertilizer business.
they're laundering money for a fair amount of the Bolt City criminal underworld.
I'm not sure what those cult creeps in LABYRINTH were doing with it.
I don't think Fritz ever had it to begin with.
if he got his hands on this directory, he's liable to make copies and send it to every gang in town.
It'll probably start some kinda gang war if we're not careful.
he's gonna blackmail the gangs.
use it to jack up the price of his money-laundering services.
this guy is bad news.
yep. I guess we'd better toss this thing in the incinerator.
we can't be sure the Special Investigations Force isn't compromised, either.
I gotta go, I'm on grocery delivery for my grandma in Olive Town. She's sort of impatient.
you guys gonna be ok?
we'll be fine.
We're used to this kind of stuff.
be careful, Basil.

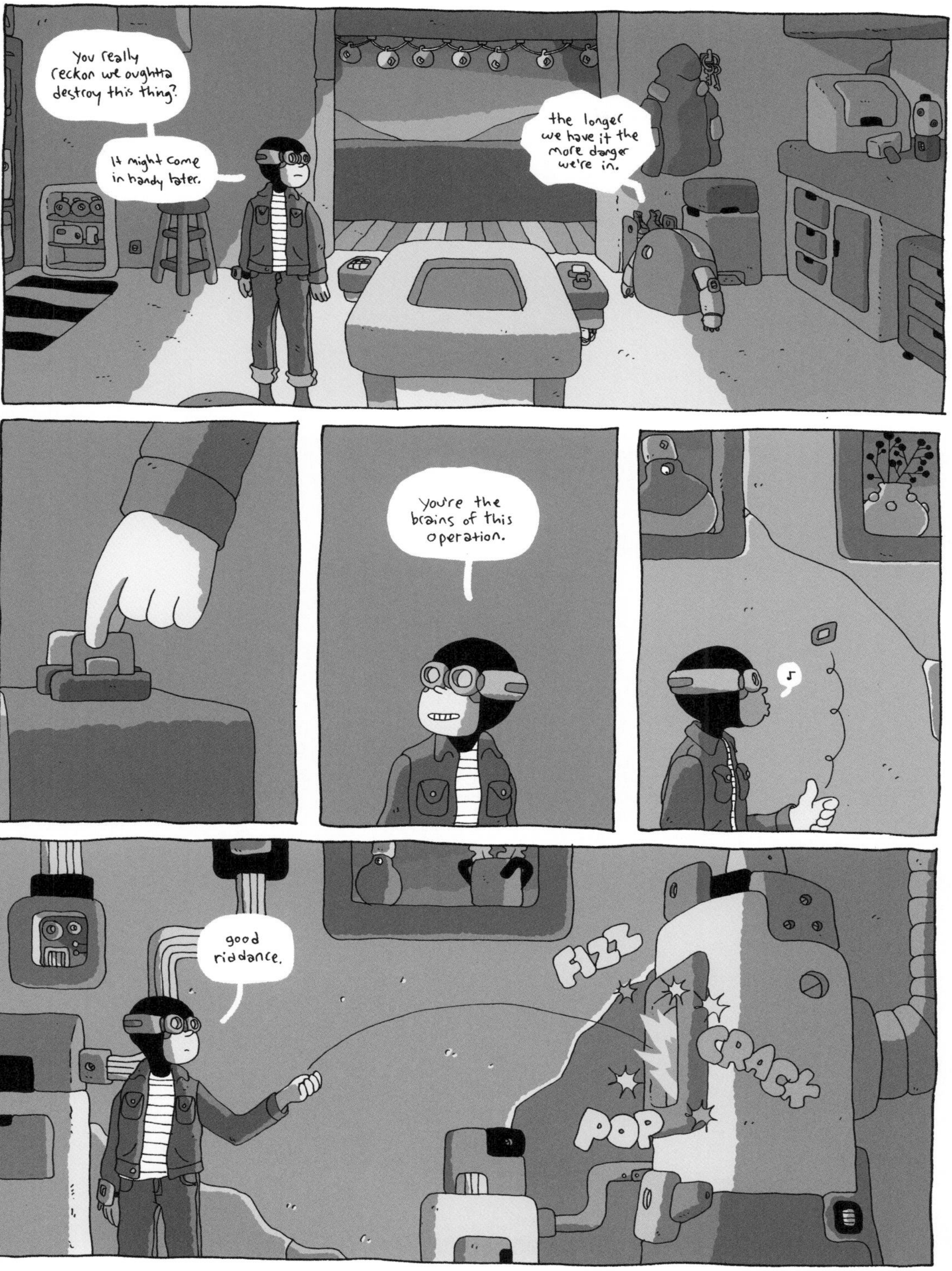

You really reckon we oughtta destroy this thing?
It might come in handy later.
the longer we have it the more danger we're in.
You're the brains of this operation.
good riddance.
FIZZ
CRACK
POP

PART 2

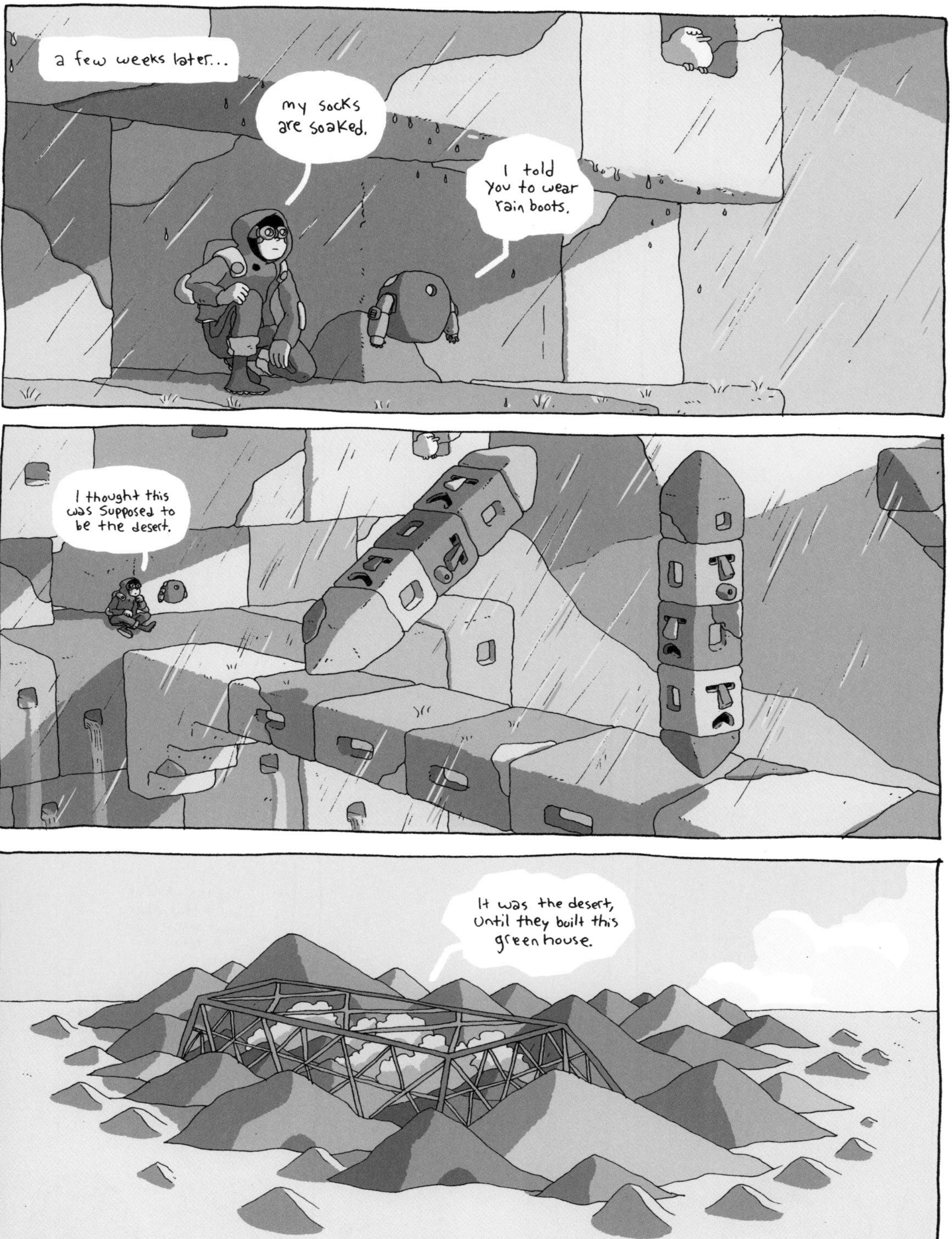
a few weeks later...
my socks are soaked.
I told you to wear rain boots.
I thought this was supposed to be the desert.
It was the desert, until they built this greenhouse.

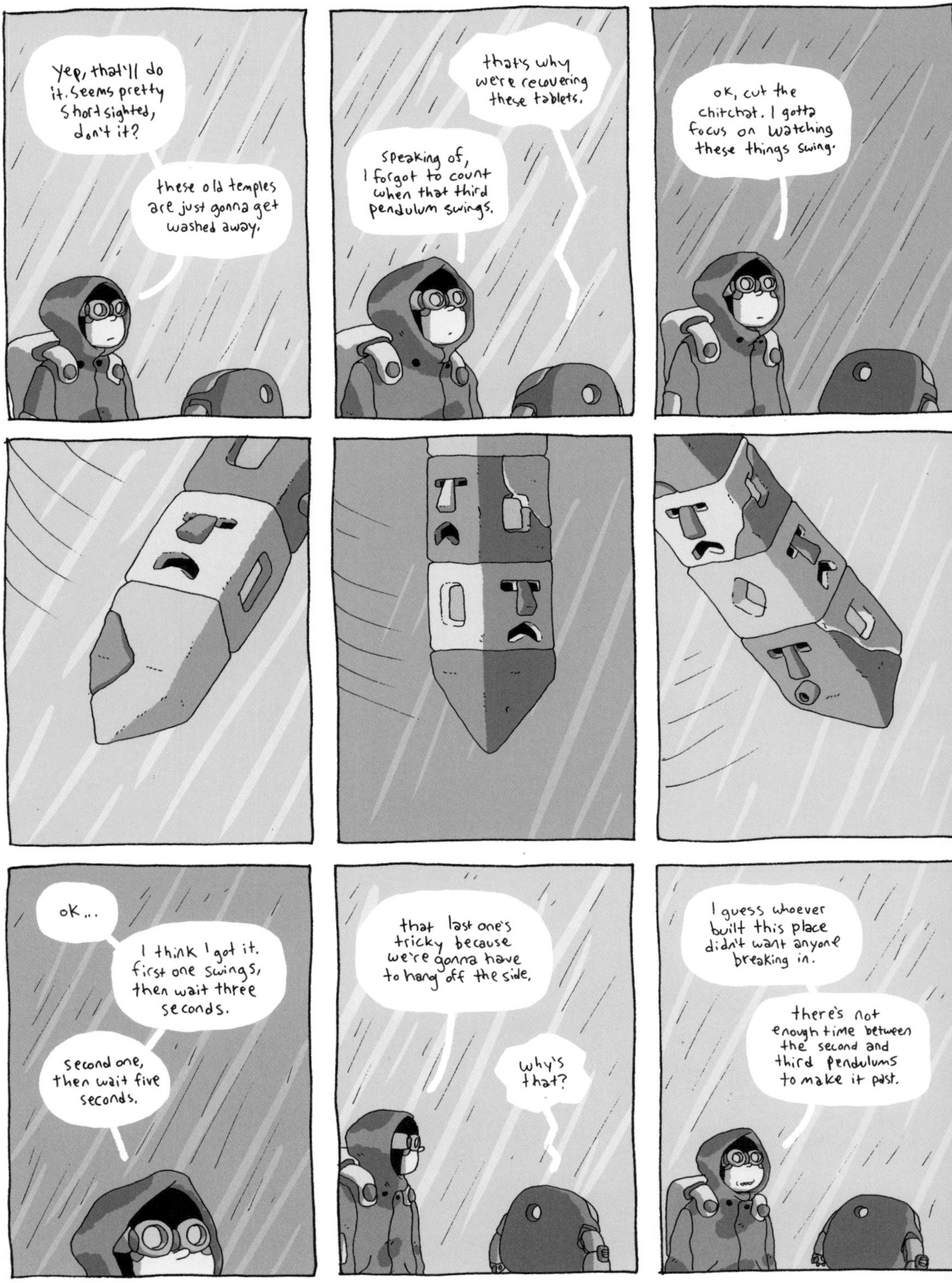
yep, that'll do it. Seems pretty Short sighted, don't it?
these old temples are just gonna get washed away.
that's why we're recovering these tablets.
Speaking of, I forgot to count when that third pendulum swings.
ok, cut the chitchat. I gotta focus on watching these things swing.
ok...
I think I got it. first one swings, then wait three seconds.
second one, then wait five seconds.
that last one's tricky because we're gonna have to hang off the side.
why's that?
I guess whoever built this place didn't want anyone breaking in.
there's not enough time between the second and third pendulums to make it past.

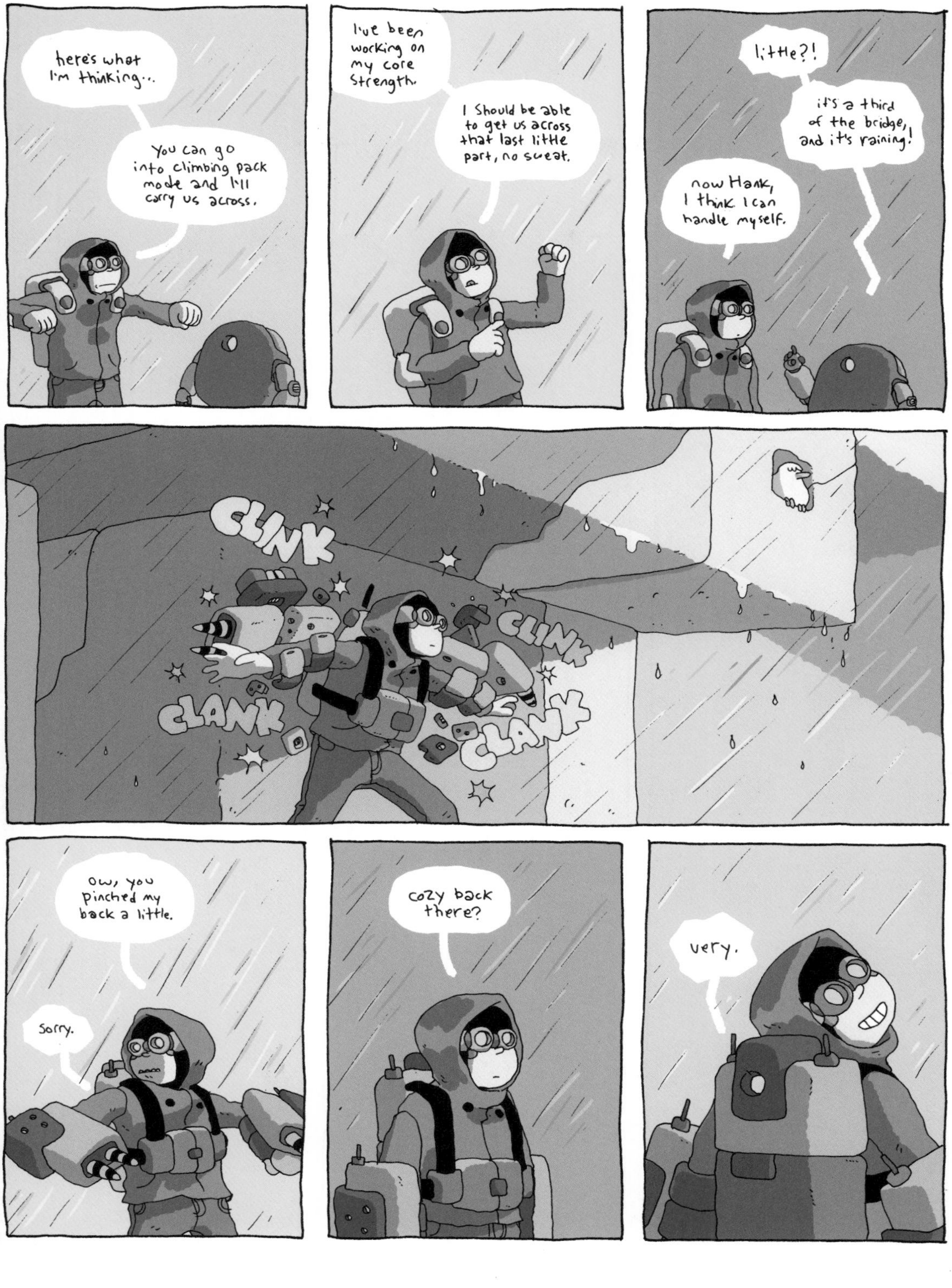
here's what I'm thinking...
You can go into climbing pack mode and I'll carry us across.
I've been working on my core strength.
I should be able to get us across that last little part, no sweat.
little?!
it's a third of the bridge, and it's raining!
now Hank, I think I can handle myself.
CLINK
CLINK
CLANK
CLANK
ow, you pinched my back a little.
sorry.
cozy back there?
very.

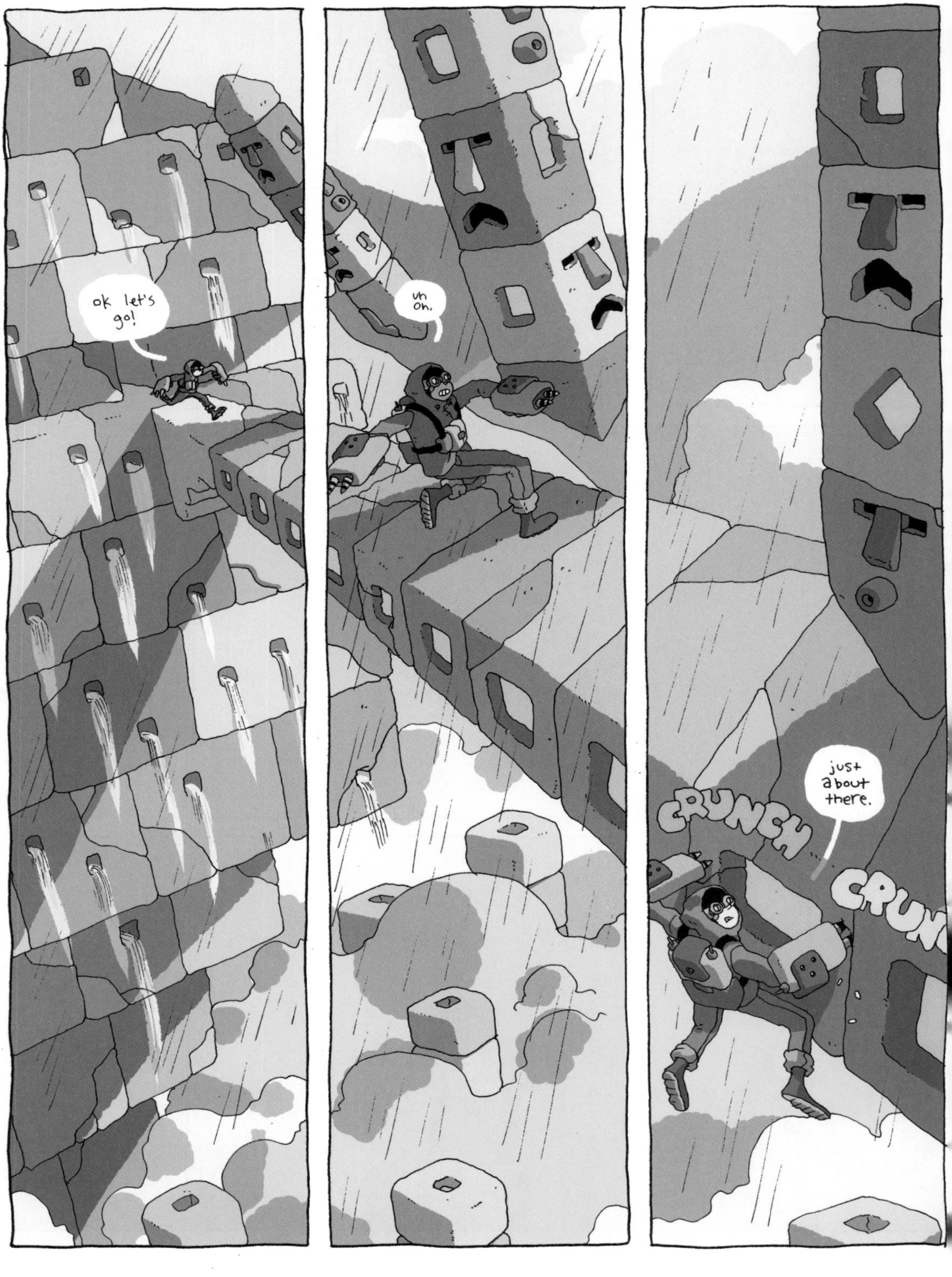
ok let's go!
uh oh.
CRUNCH
just about there.
CRUN

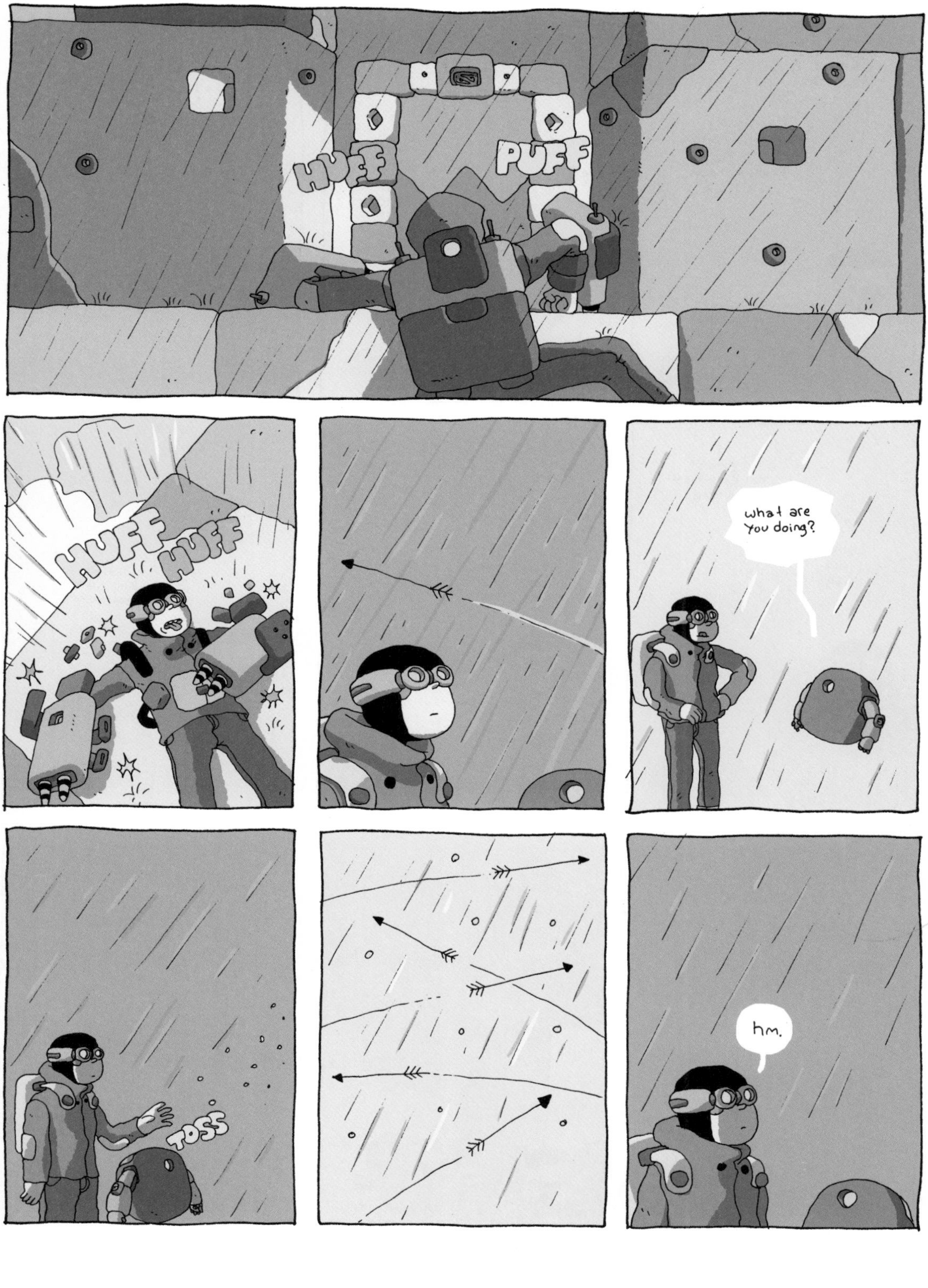
HUFF
PUFF
HUFF
HUFF
what are you doing?
TOSS
hm.

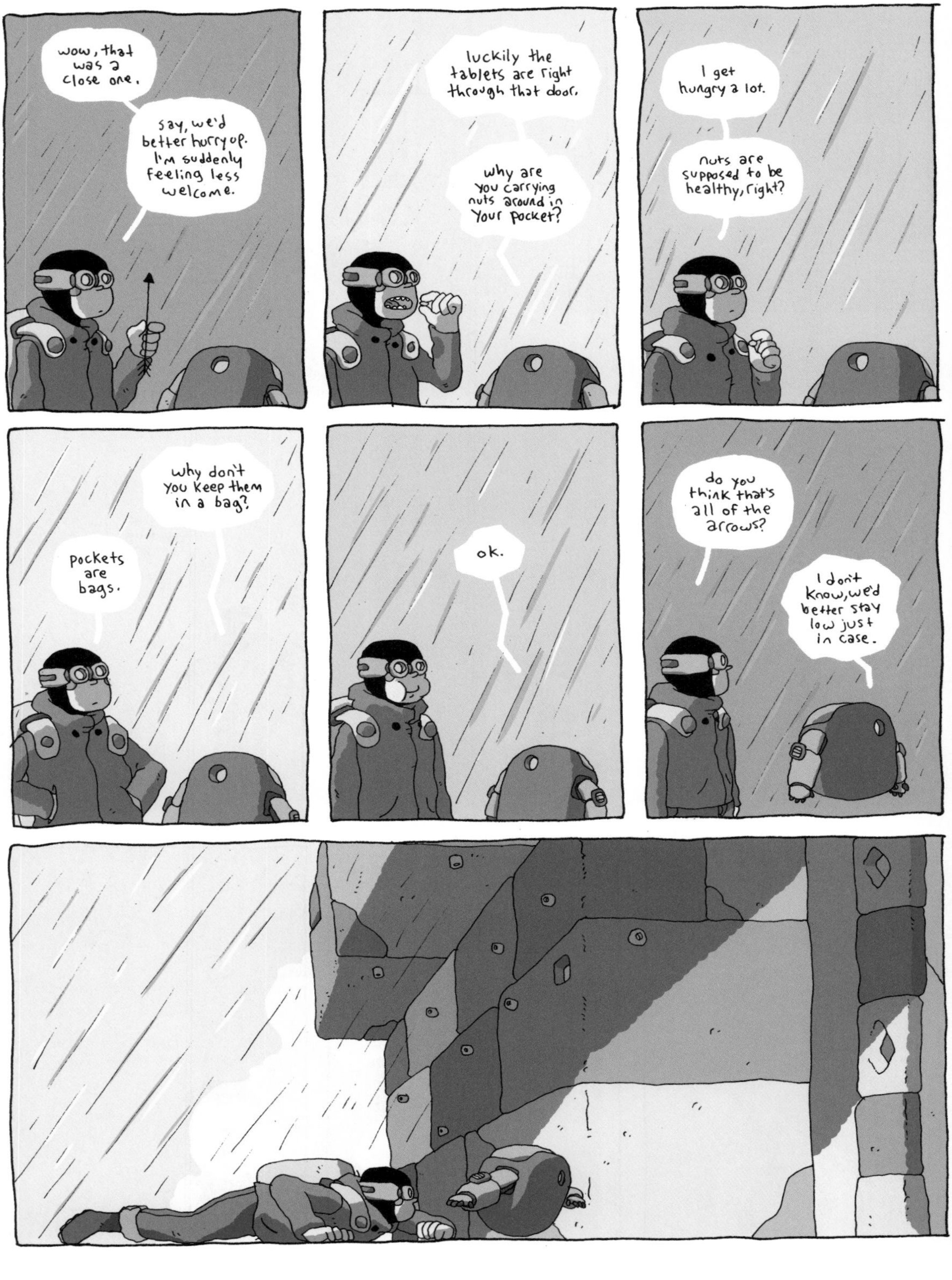
wow, that was a close one.
say, we'd better hurry up. I'm suddenly feeling less welcome.
luckily the tablets are right through that door.
why are you carrying nuts around in your pocket?
I get hungry a lot.
nuts are supposed to be healthy, right?
why don't you keep them in a bag?
pockets are bags.
ok.
do you think that's all of the arrows?
I don't know, we'd better stay low just in case.

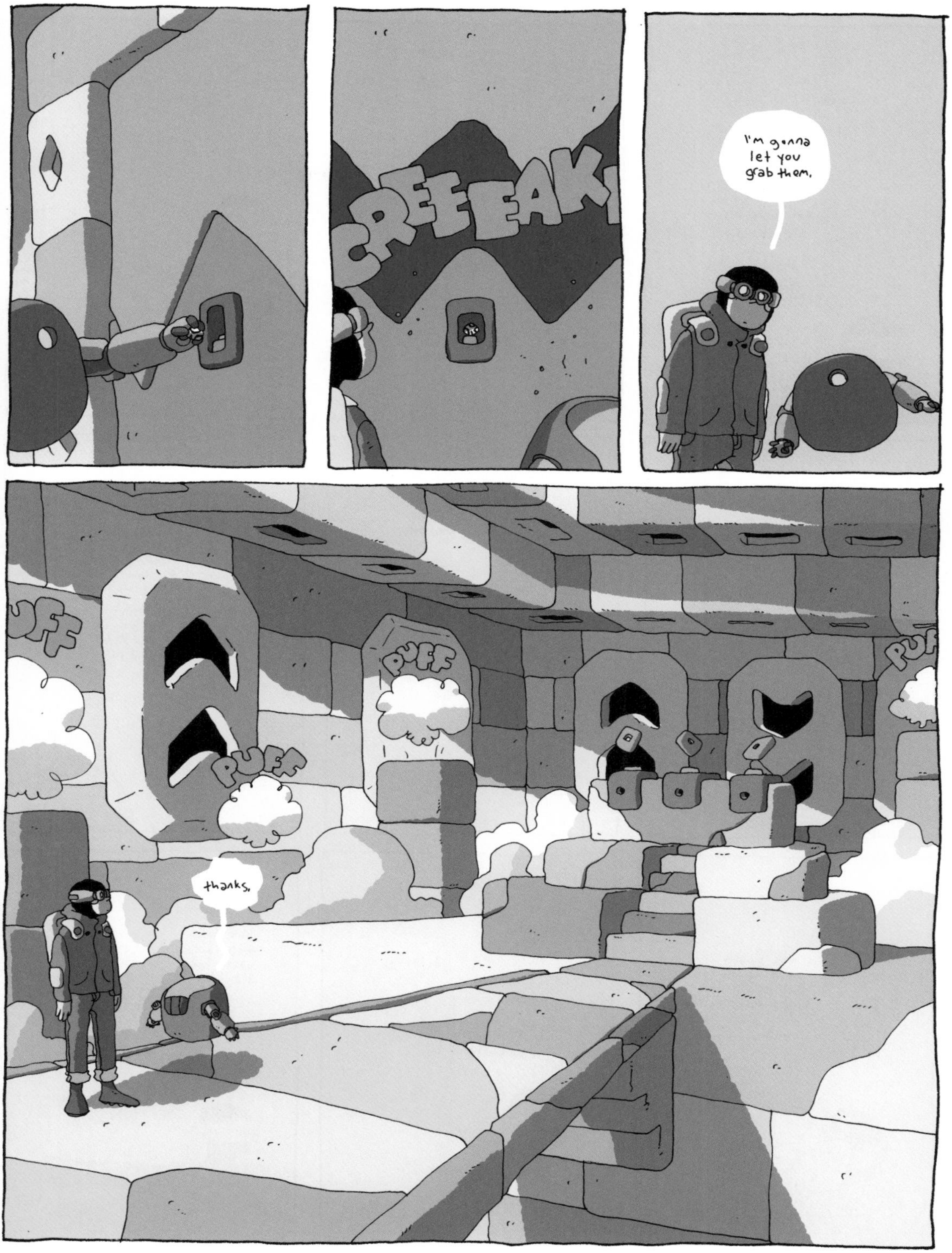
CREEEAK!
I'm gonna let you grab them.
PUFF
PUFF
PUFF
PUFF
thanks.

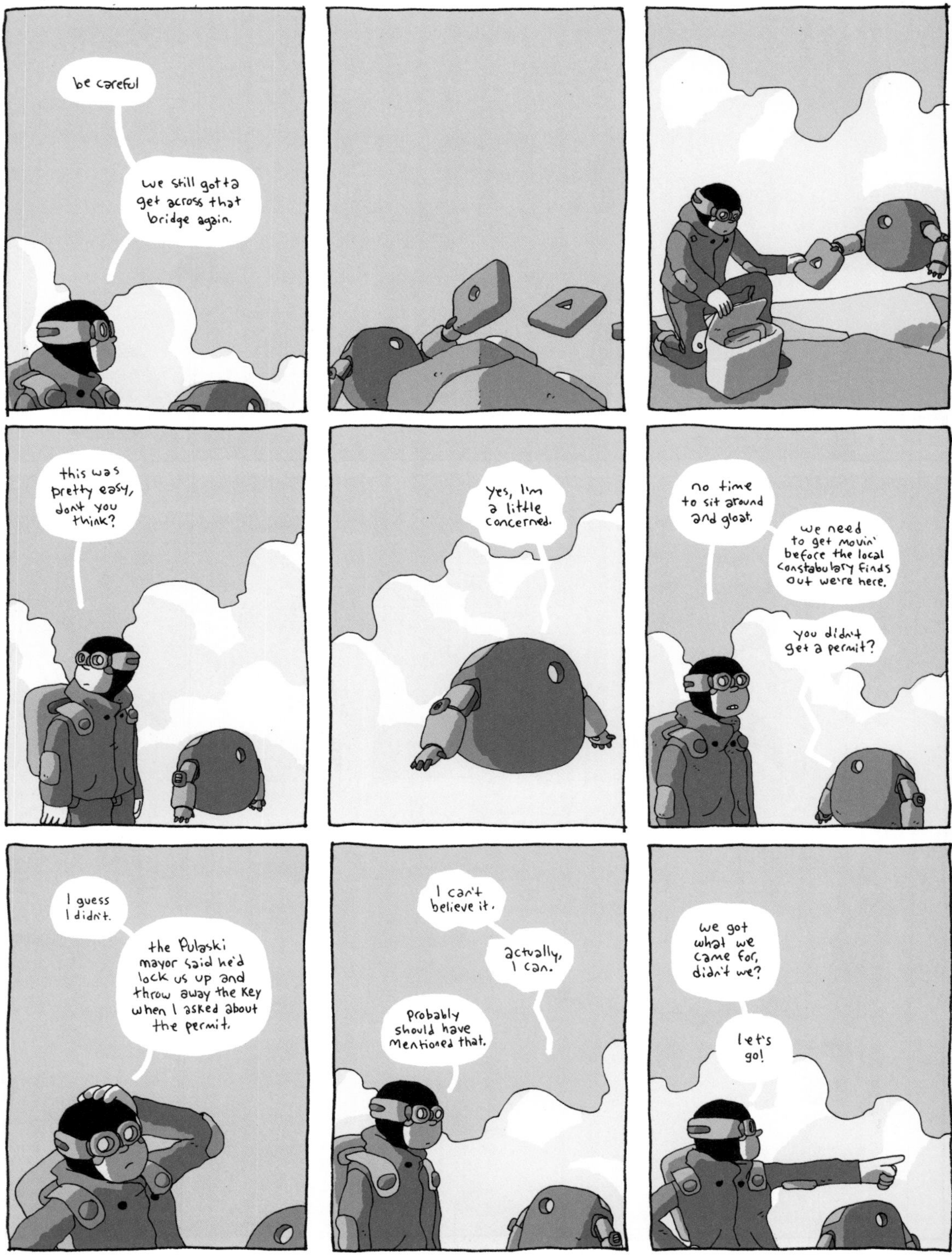
be careful
we still gotta get across that bridge again.
this was pretty easy, don't you think?
Yes, I'm a little concerned.
no time to sit around and gloat.
we need to get movin' before the local constabulary finds out we're here.
you didn't get a permit?
I guess I didn't.
the Pulaski mayor said he'd lock us up and throw away the key when I asked about the permit.
I can't believe it.
actually, I can.
Probably should have mentioned that.
we got what we came for, didn't we?
let's go!

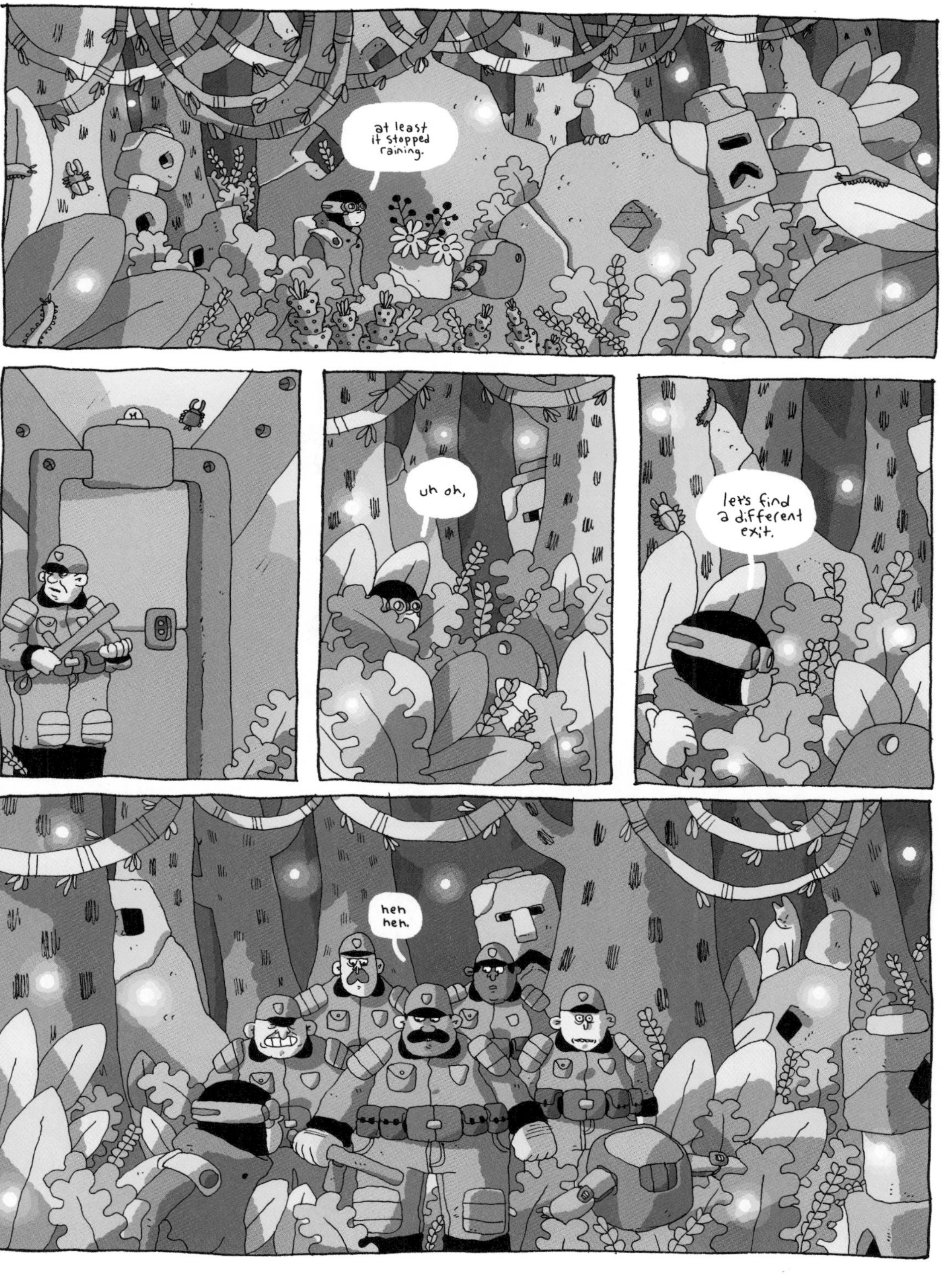
at least it stopped raining.
uh oh,
let's find a different exit.
heh heh.

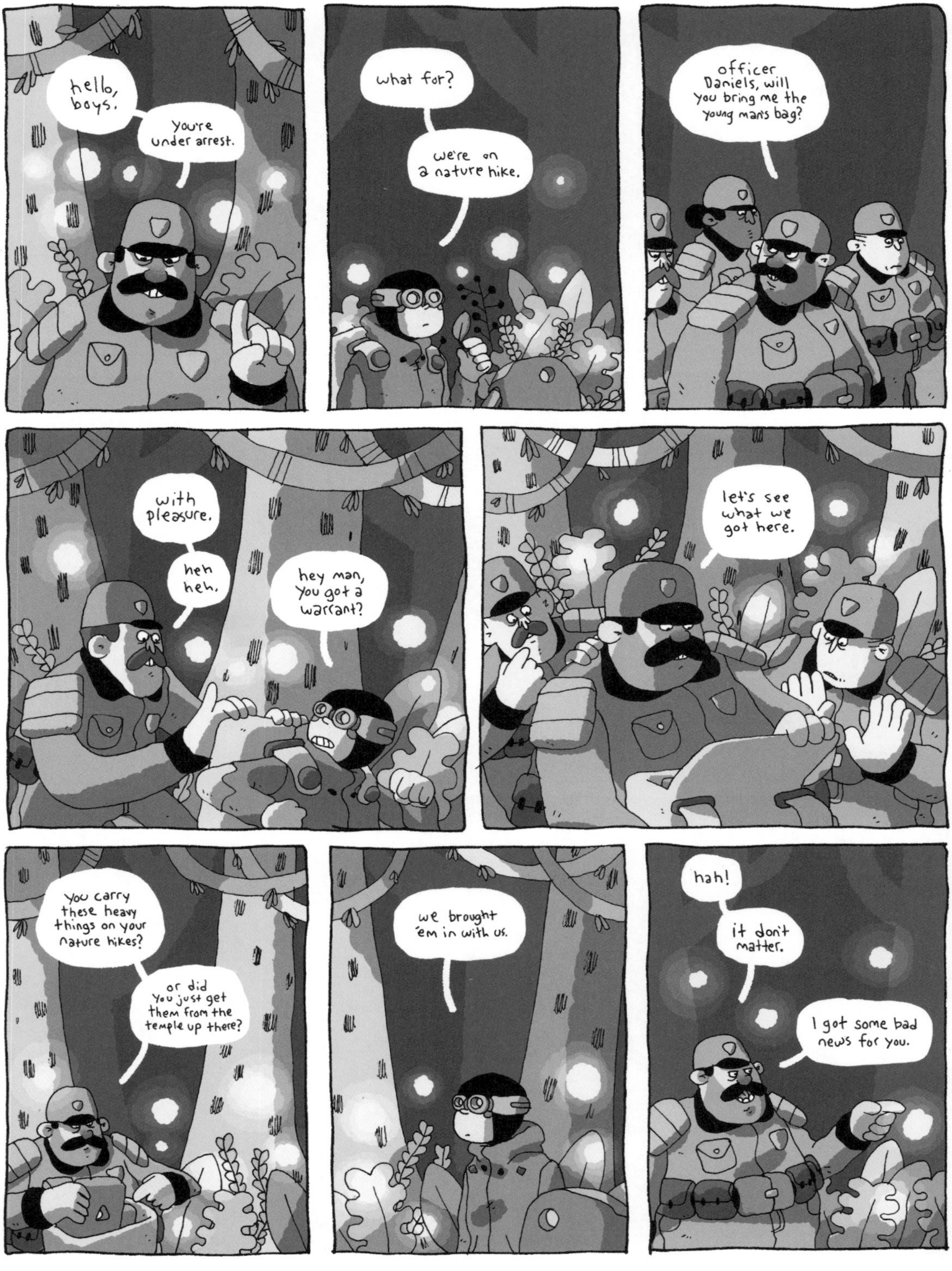
hello, boys.
you're under arrest.
what for?
we're on a nature hike.
officer Daniels, will you bring me the young man's bag?
with pleasure.
heh heh.
hey man, you got a warrant?
let's see what we got here.
you carry these heavy things on your nature hikes?
or did you just get them from the temple up there?
we brought 'em in with us.
hah!
it don't matter.
I got some bad news for you.

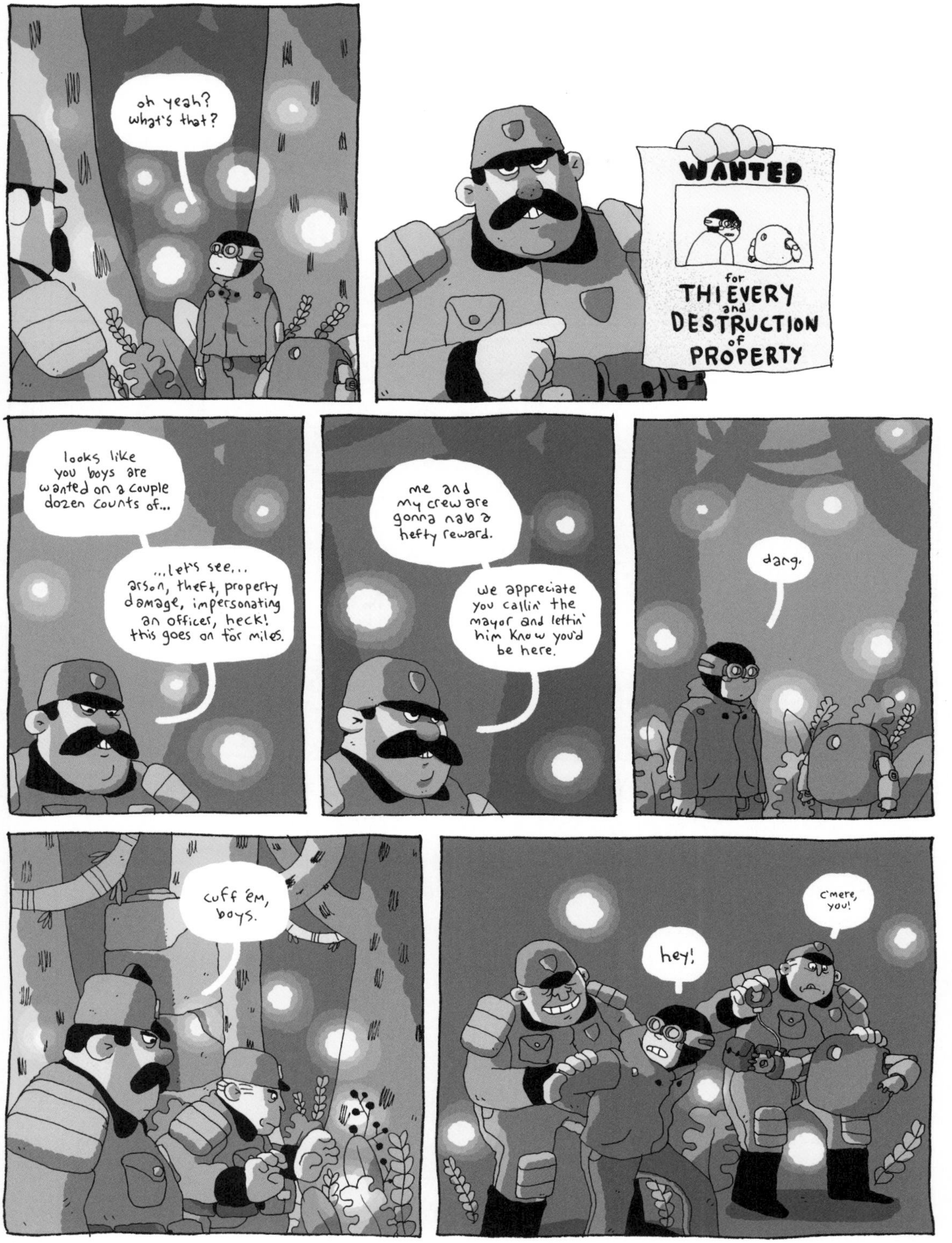
oh yeah? what's that?
WANTED
for THIEVERY and DESTRUCTION of PROPERTY
looks like you boys are wanted on a couple dozen counts of...
...let's see... arson, theft, property damage, impersonating an officer, heck! this goes on for miles.
me and my crew are gonna nab a hefty reward.
we appreciate you callin' the mayor and lettin' him know you'd be here.
dang.
cuff 'em, boys.
hey!
c'mere, you!

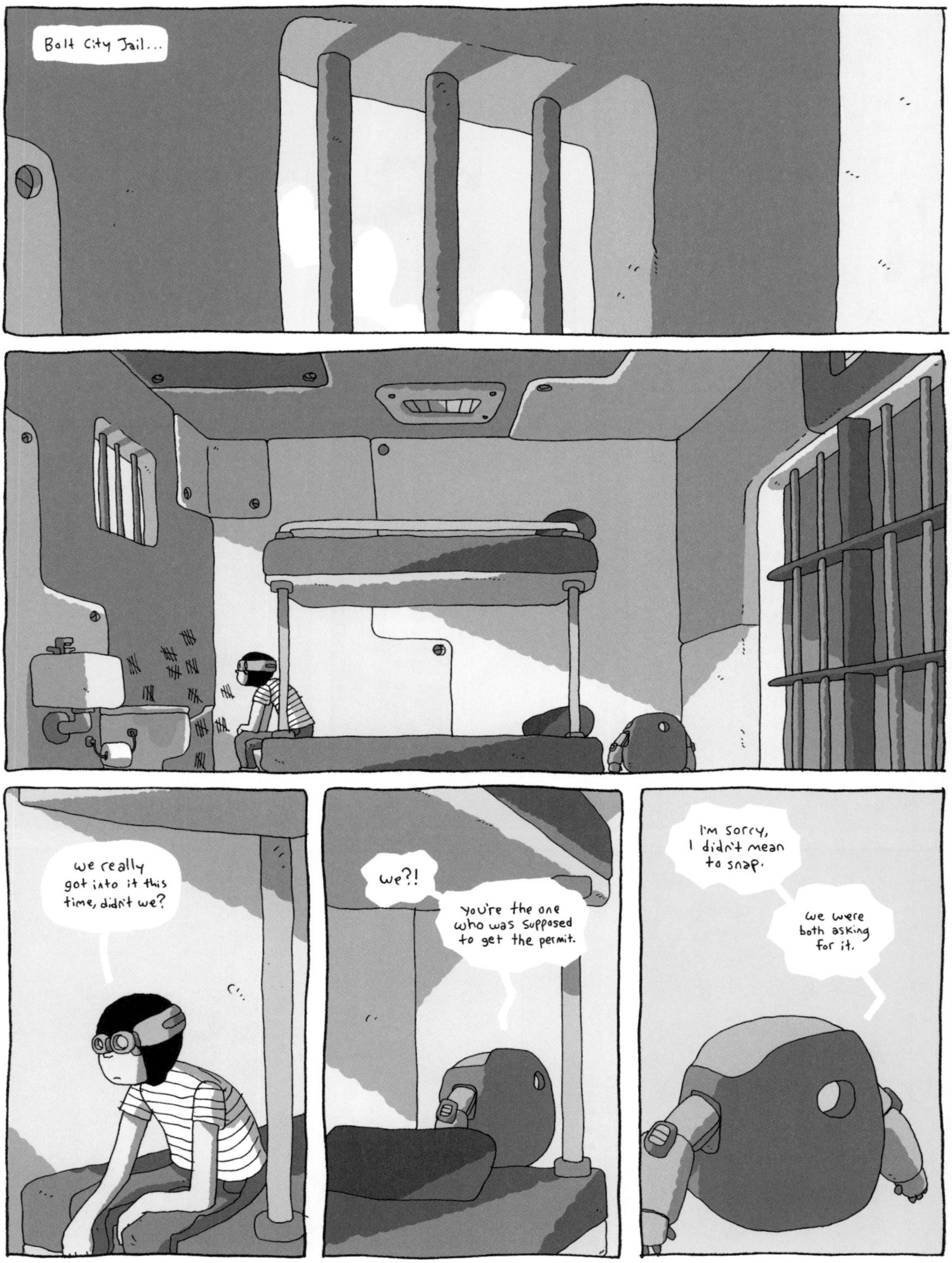
Bolt City Jail...
we really got into it this time, didn't we?
we?!
you're the one who was supposed to get the permit.
I'm sorry, I didn't mean to snap.
we were both asking for it.

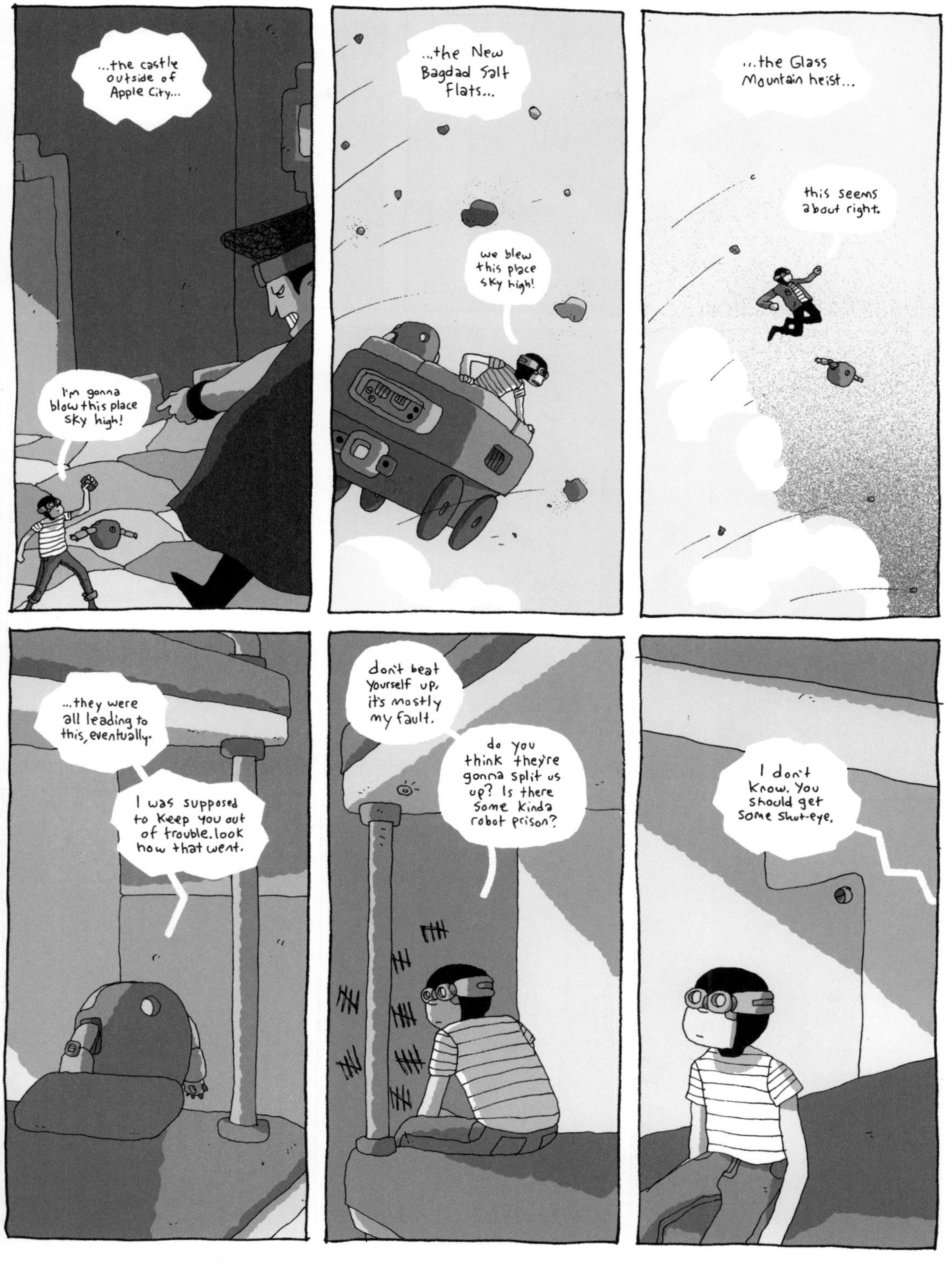
...the castle outside of Apple City...
I'm gonna blow this place sky high!
...the New Bagdad Salt Flats...
we blew this place sky high!
...the Glass Mountain heist...
this seems about right.
...they were all leading to this, eventually.
I was supposed to keep you out of trouble. look how that went.
don't beat yourself up, it's mostly my fault.
do you think they're gonna split us up? Is there some kinda robot prison?
I don't know. You should get some shut-eye.

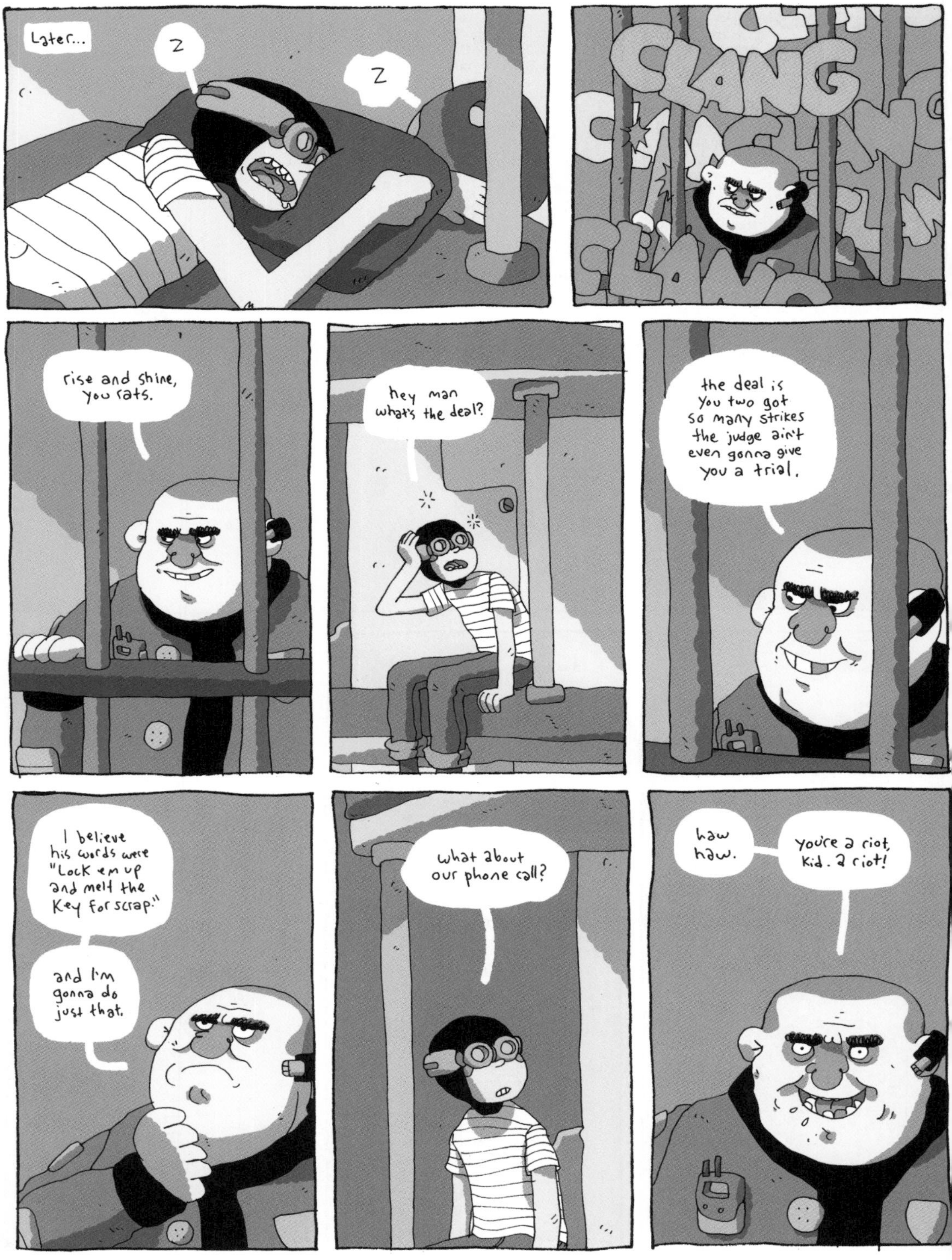
Later...
Z
Z
CLANG
CLANG
CLANG
CLANG
CLANG
rise and shine, you rats.
hey man what's the deal?
the deal is you two got so many strikes the judge ain't even gonna give you a trial.
I believe his words were "Lock em up and melt the Key for scrap."
and I'm gonna do just that.
what about our phone call?
haw haw.
you're a riot, kid. a riot!

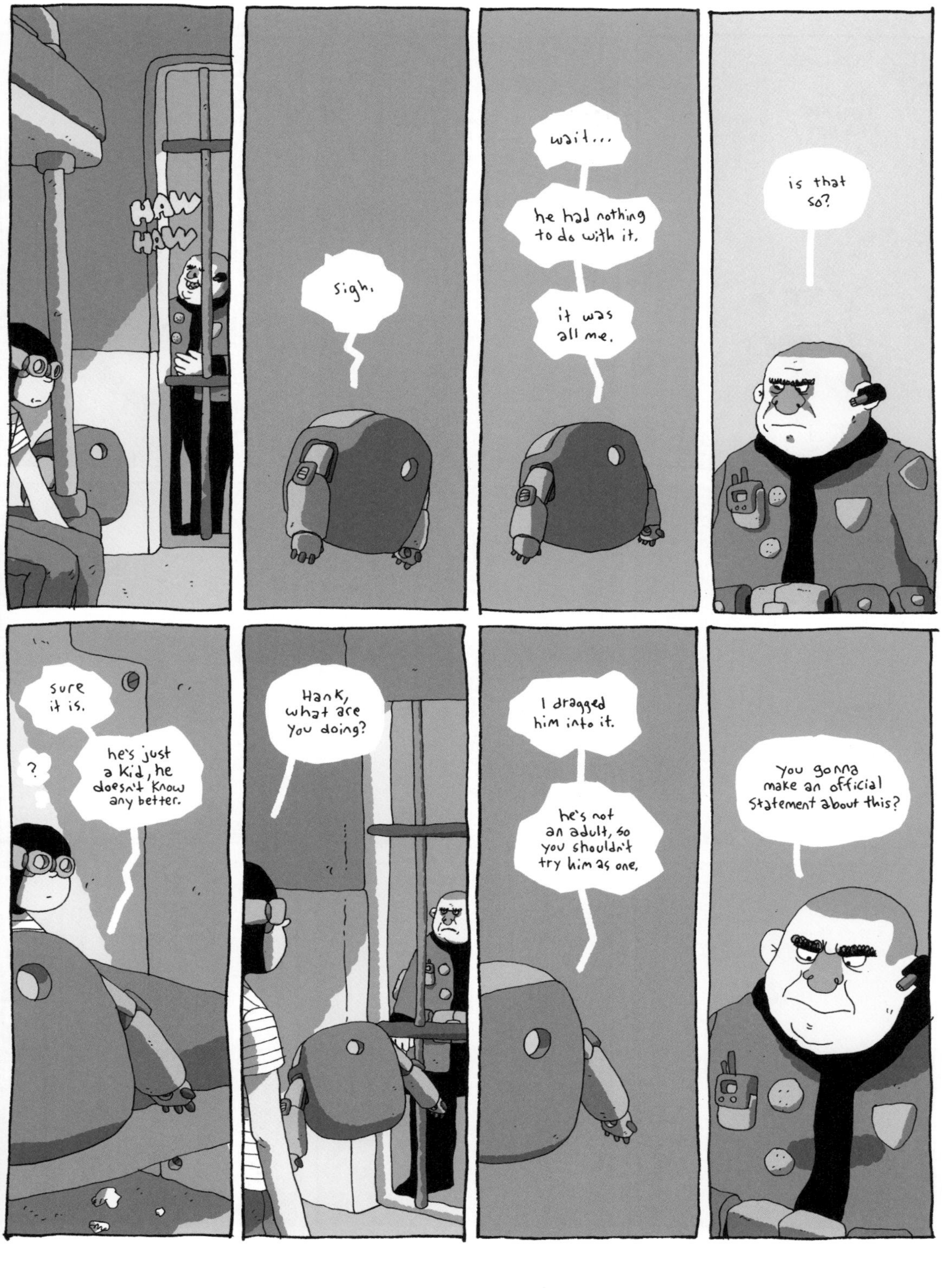
HAW
HAW
sigh.
wait...
he had nothing to do with it.
it was all me.
is that so?
sure it is.
?
he's just a kid, he doesn't know any better.
Hank, what are you doing?
I dragged him into it.
he's not an adult, so you shouldn't try him as one.
you gonna make an official statement about this?

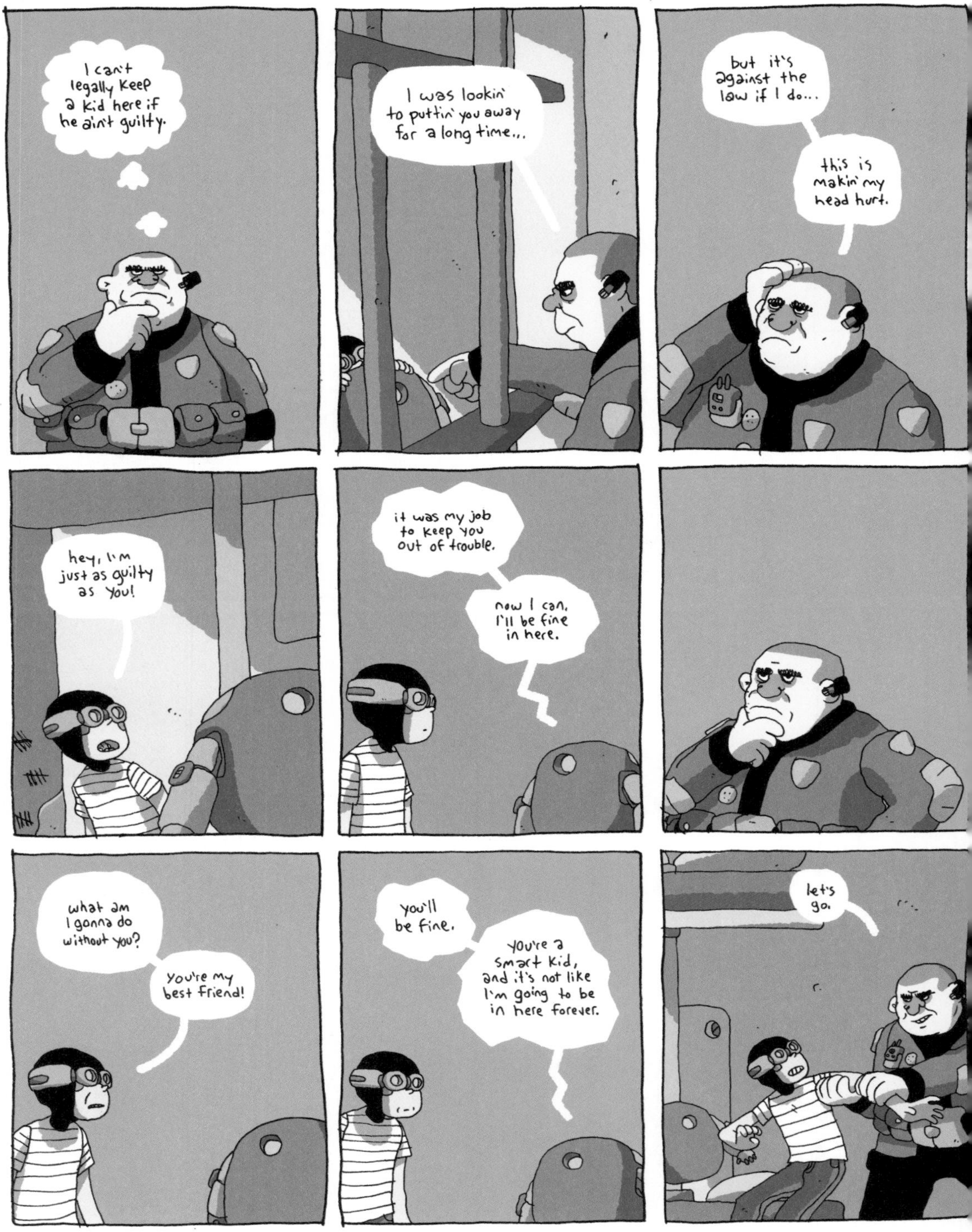
I can't legally keep a kid here if he ain't guilty.
I was lookin' to puttin' you away for a long time...
but it's against the law if I do...
this is makin' my head hurt.
hey, I'm just as guilty as you!
...
it was my job to keep you out of trouble.
now I can. I'll be fine in here.
what am I gonna do without you?
you're my best friend!
you'll be fine.
you're a smart kid, and it's not like I'm going to be in here forever.
let's go.
...

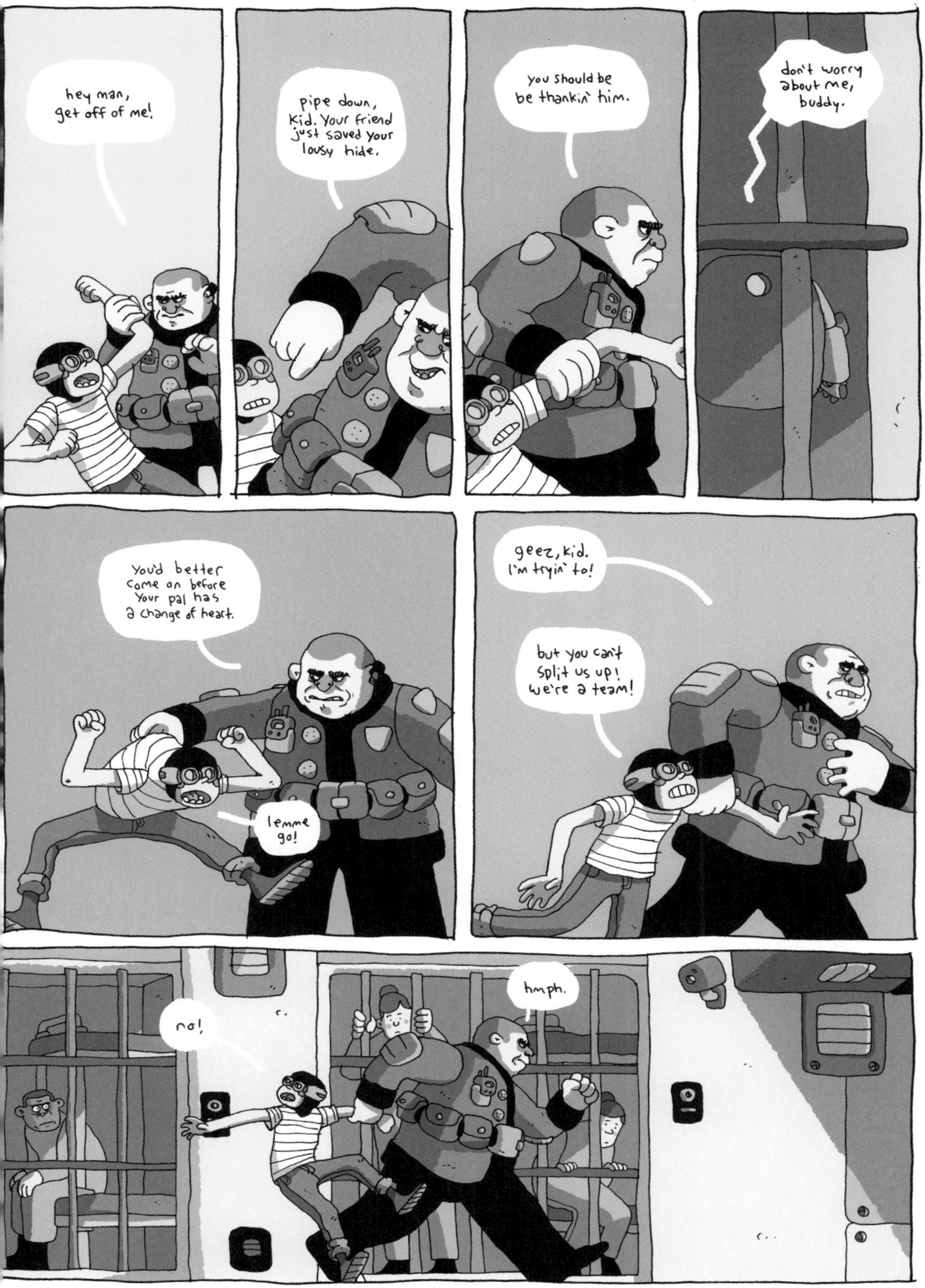
hey man, get off of me!
pipe down, kid. Your friend just saved your lousy hide.
you should be be thankin' him.
don't worry about me, buddy.
You'd better come on before your pal has a change of heart.
lemme go!
geez, kid. I'm tryin' to!
but you can't split us up! we're a team!
no!
hmph.

PART 3

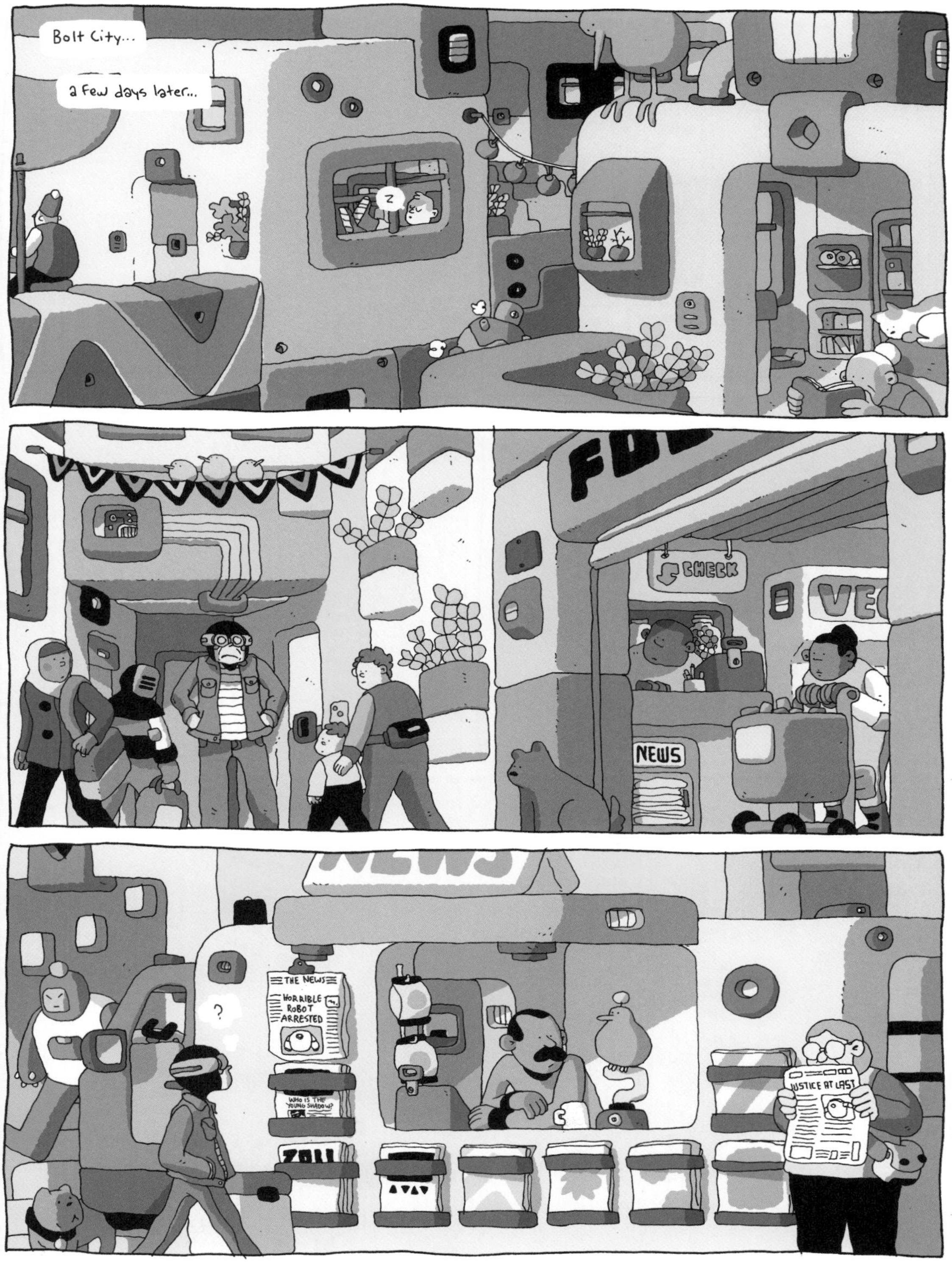
Bolt City...
a few days later...
z
CHECK
NEWS
?
THE NEWS
HORRIBLE ROBOT ARRESTED
WHO IS THE YOUNG SHADOW?
JUSTICE AT LAST

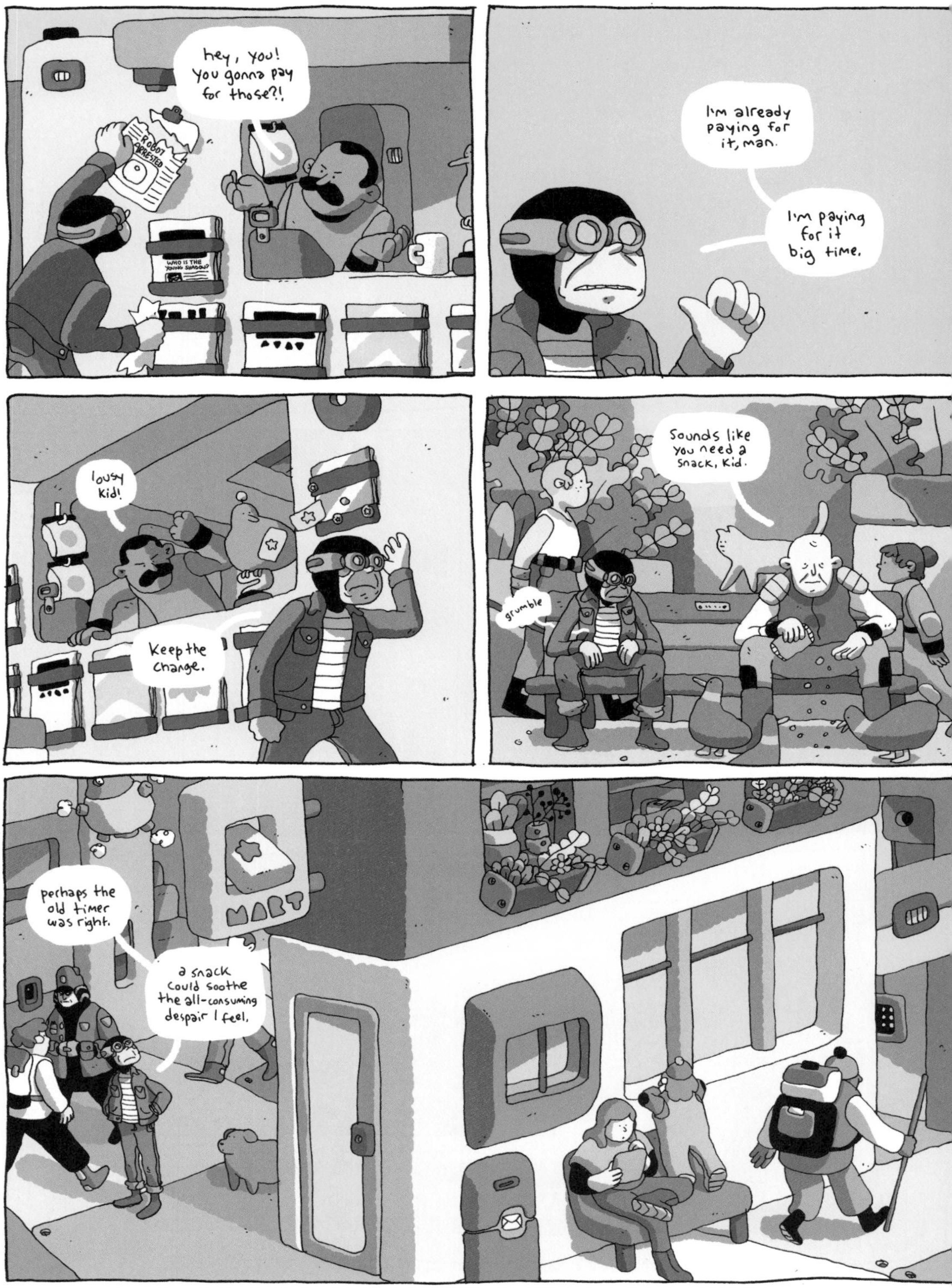
hey, you!
you gonna pay
for those?!
ROBOT ARRESTED
WHO IS THE YOUNG SHADOW?
I'm already
paying for
it, man.
I'm paying
for it
big time.
lousy
kid!
Keep the
change.
Sounds like
you need a
snack, kid.
grumble
MART
perhaps the
old timer
was right.
a snack
could soothe
the all-consuming
despair I feel.

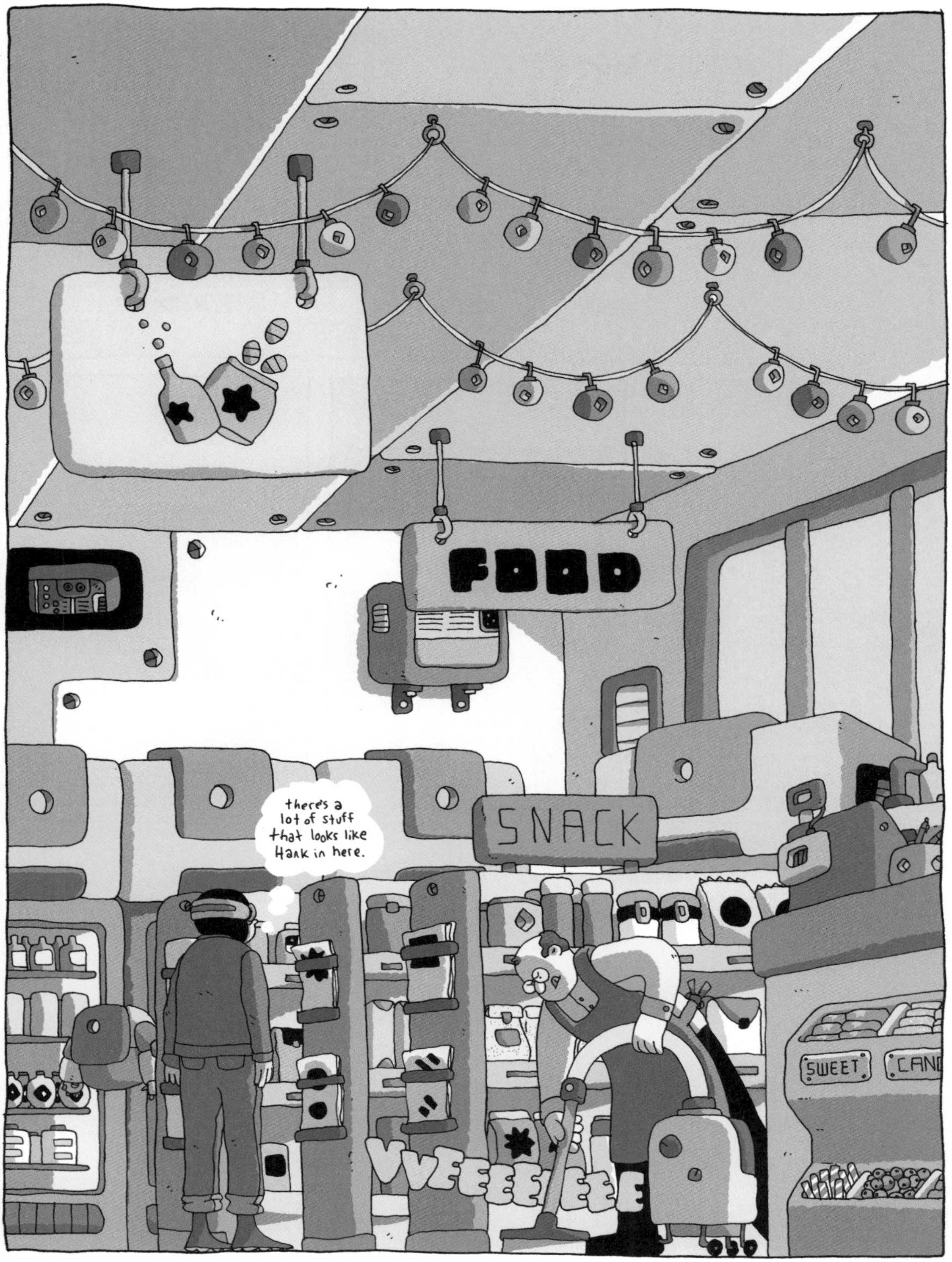
FOOD
SNACK
there's a lot of stuff that looks like Hank in here.
SWEET
CAND
VVEEEEEEEE

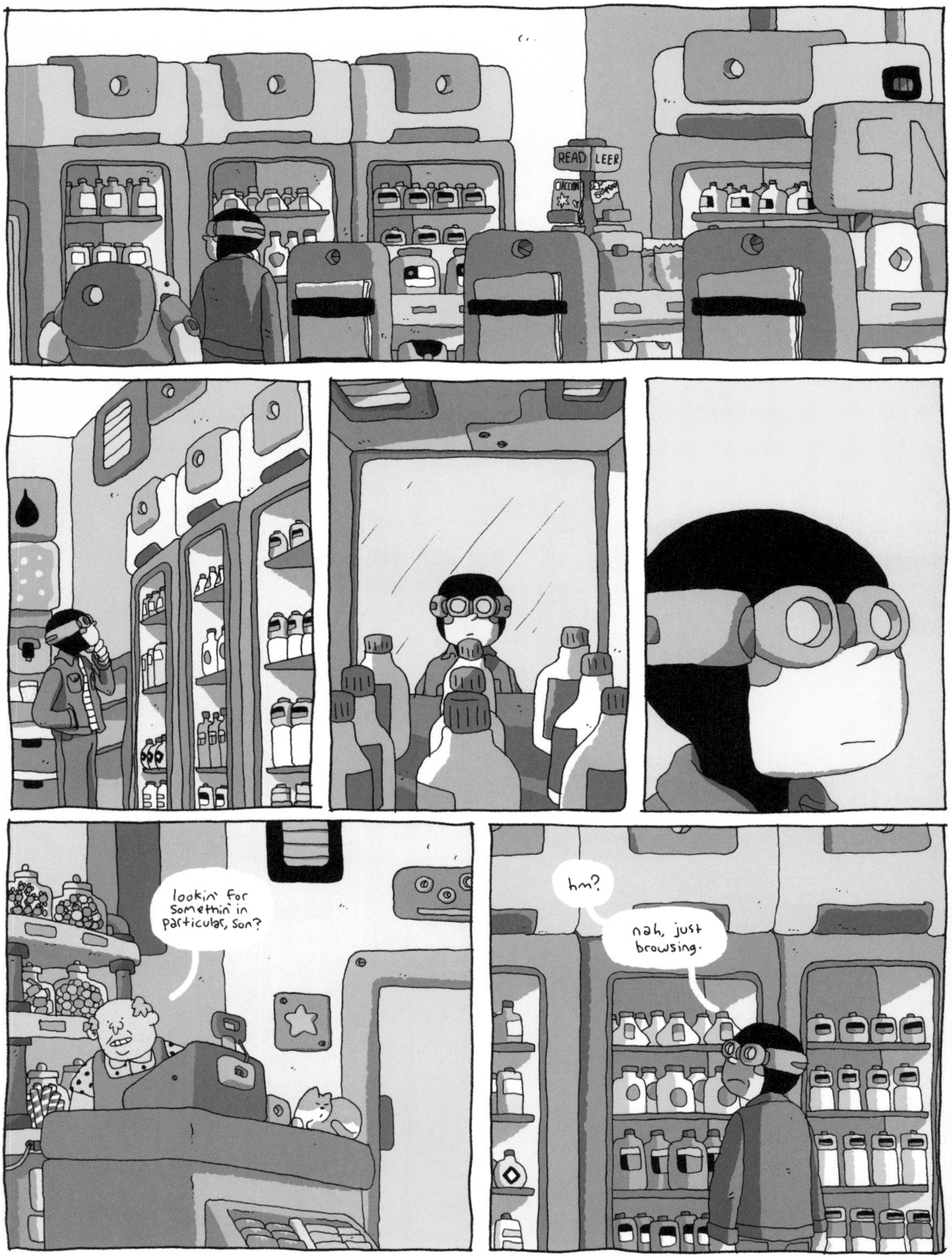
READ
LEER
lookin' for somethin' in particular, son?
hm?
nah, just browsing.

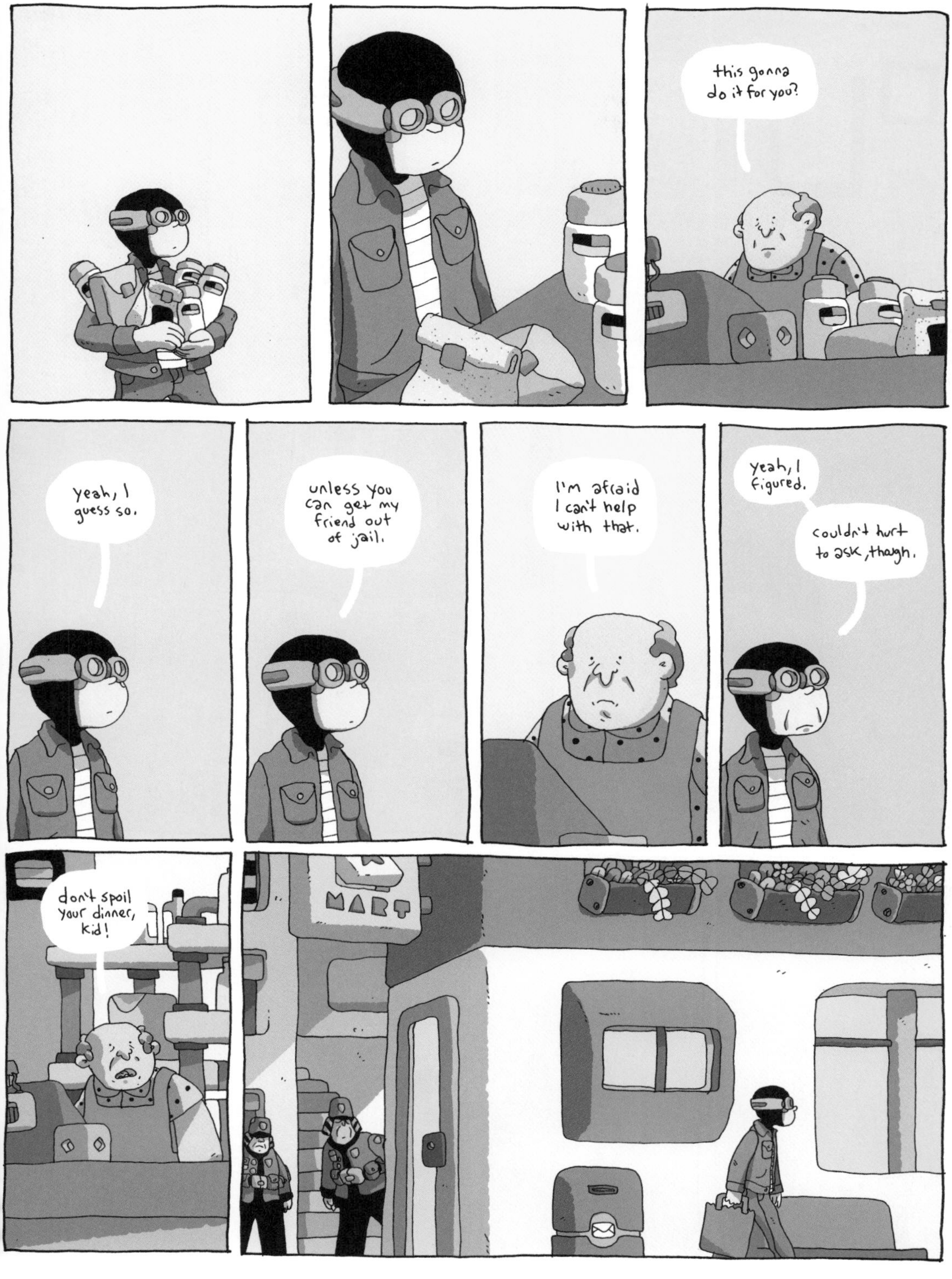
this gonna do it for you?
yeah, I guess so.
unless you can get my friend out of jail.
I'm afraid I can't help with that.
yeah, I figured.
couldn't hurt to ask, though.
don't spoil your dinner, kid!
MART

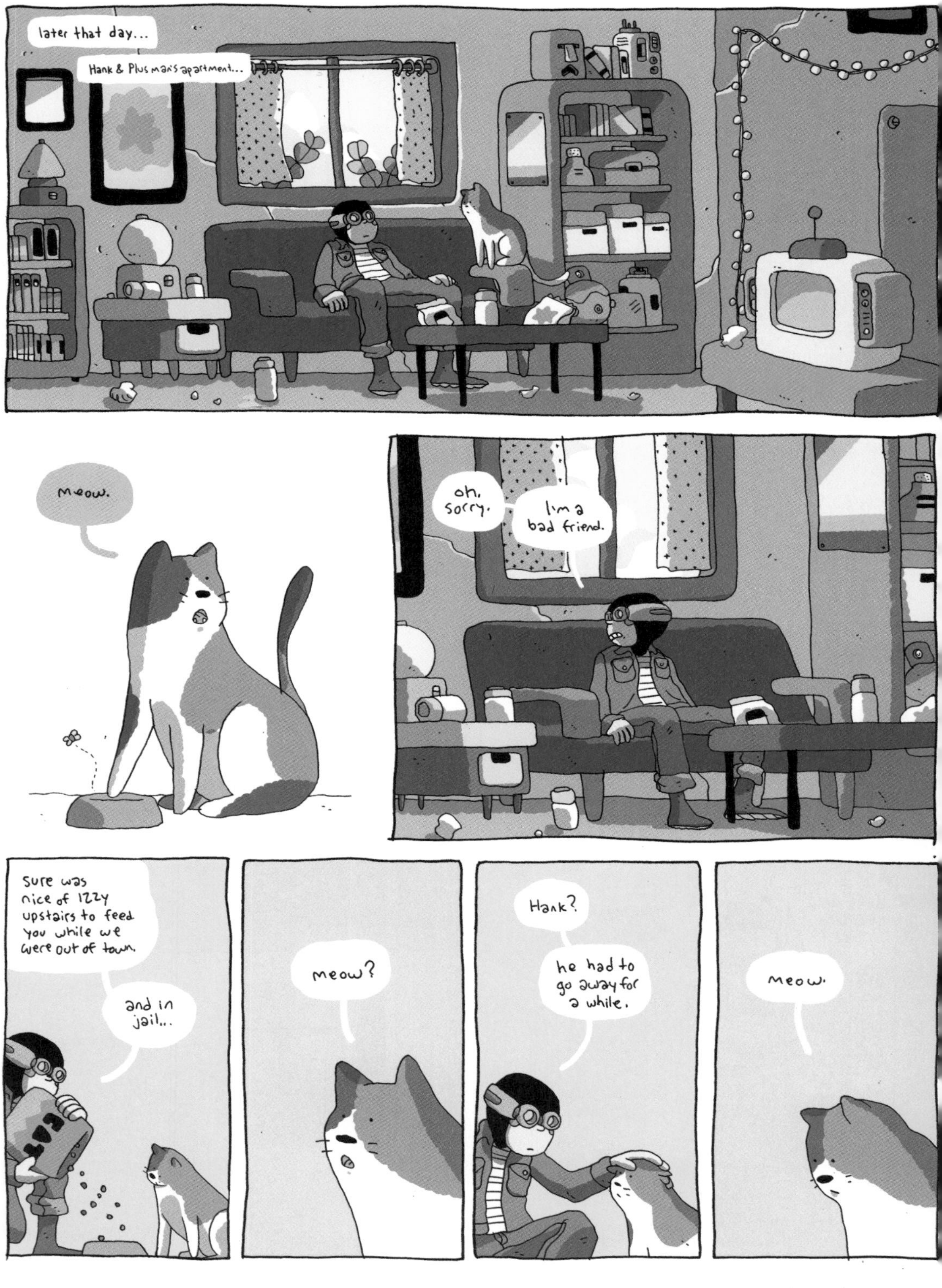

later that day...
Hank & Plus man's apartment...
meow.
oh, sorry.
I'm a bad friend.
sure was nice of Izzy upstairs to feed you while we were out of town.
and in jail...
meow?
Hank?
he had to go away for a while.
meow.

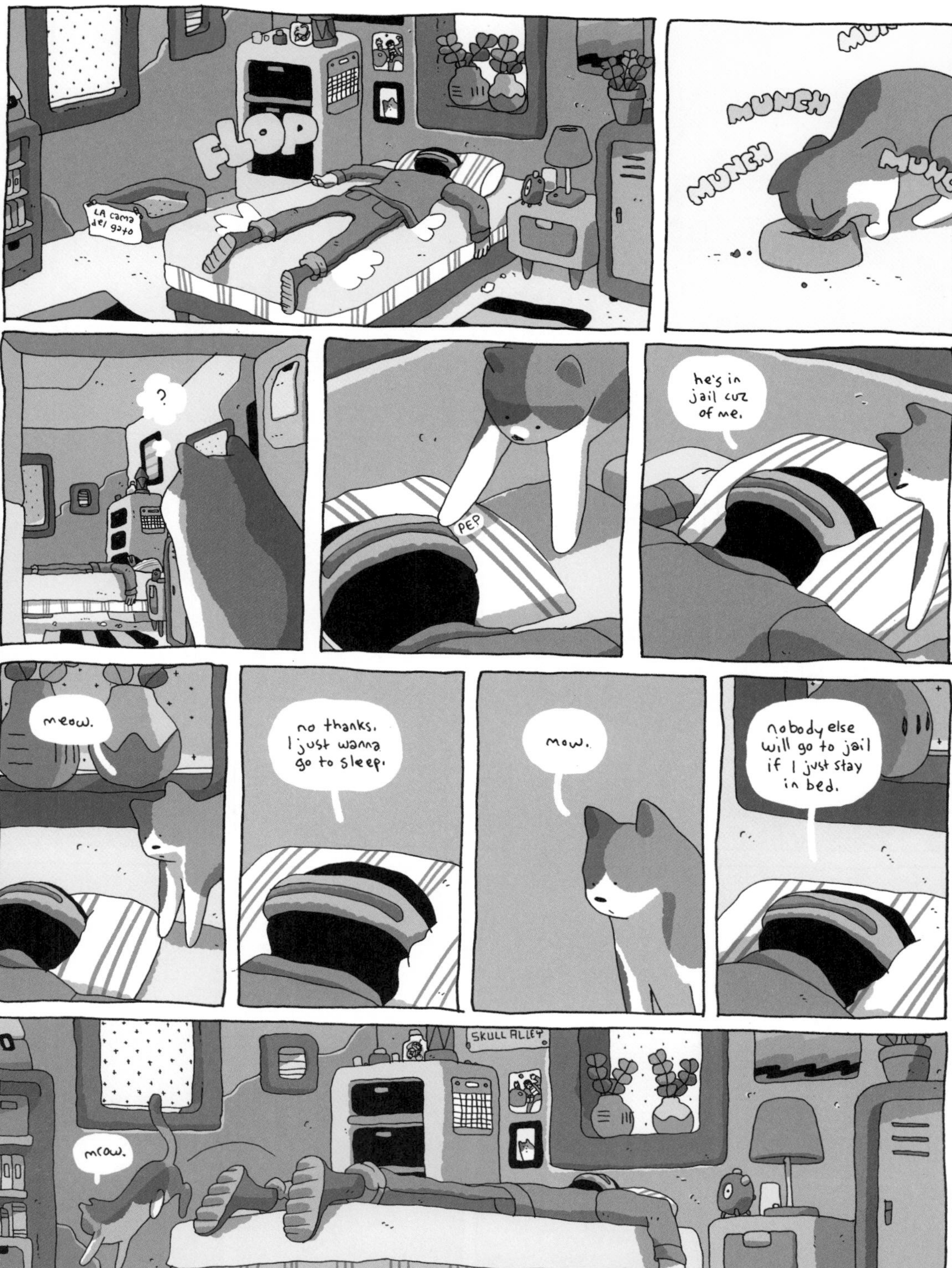
FLOP
LA cama del gato
MUNCH
MUNCH
MUNCH
MUNCH
?
PEP
he's in jail cuz of me.
meow.
no thanks. I just wanna go to sleep.
mow.
nobody else will go to jail if I just stay in bed.
SKULL ALLEY
mrow.

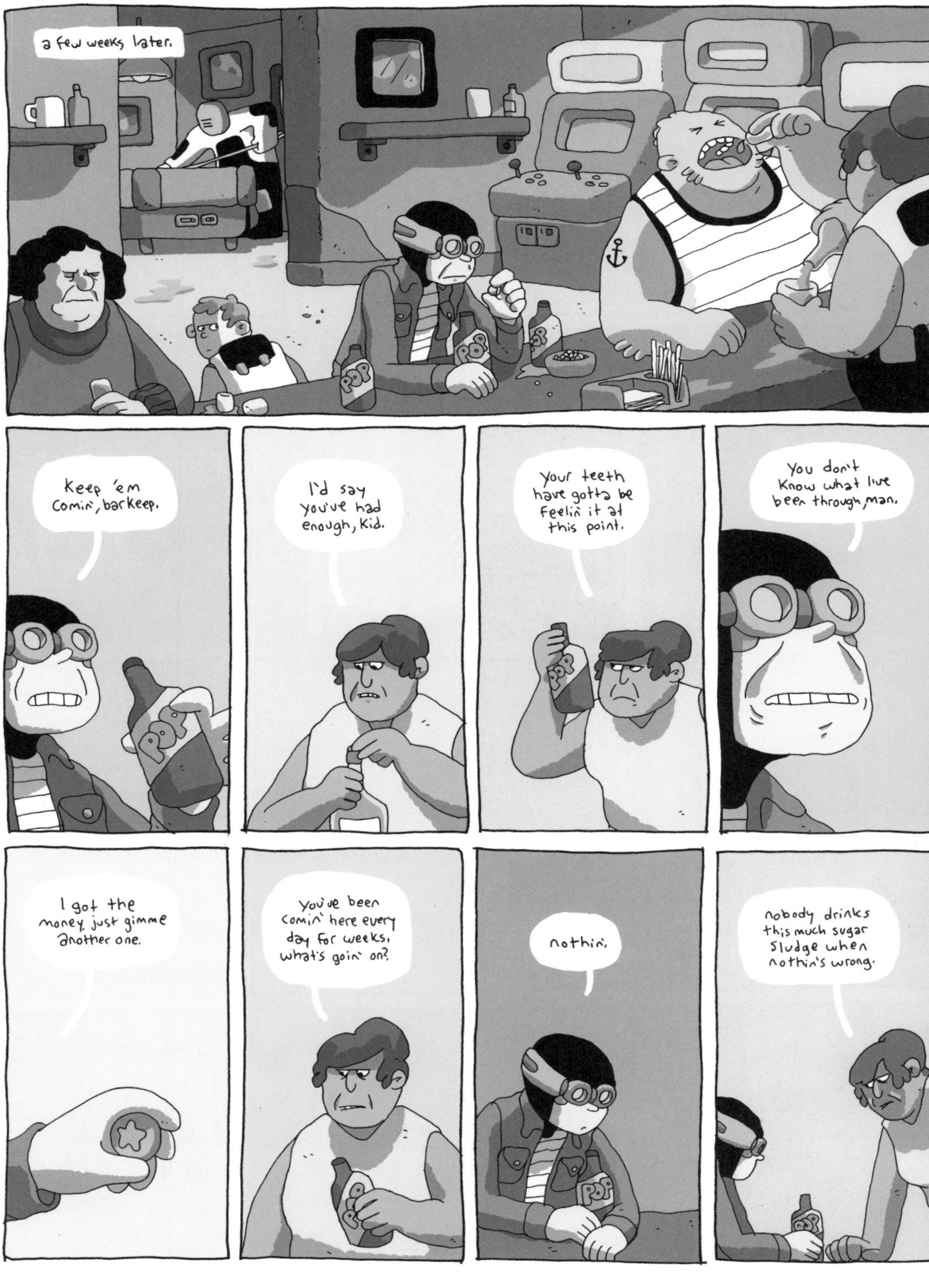
a few weeks later.
Keep 'em comin', barkeep.
I'd say you've had enough, kid.
Your teeth have gotta be feelin' it at this point.
You don't know what I've been through, man.
I got the money, just gimme another one.
You've been comin' here every day for weeks, what's goin' on?
nothin'.
nobody drinks this much sugar sludge when nothin's wrong.

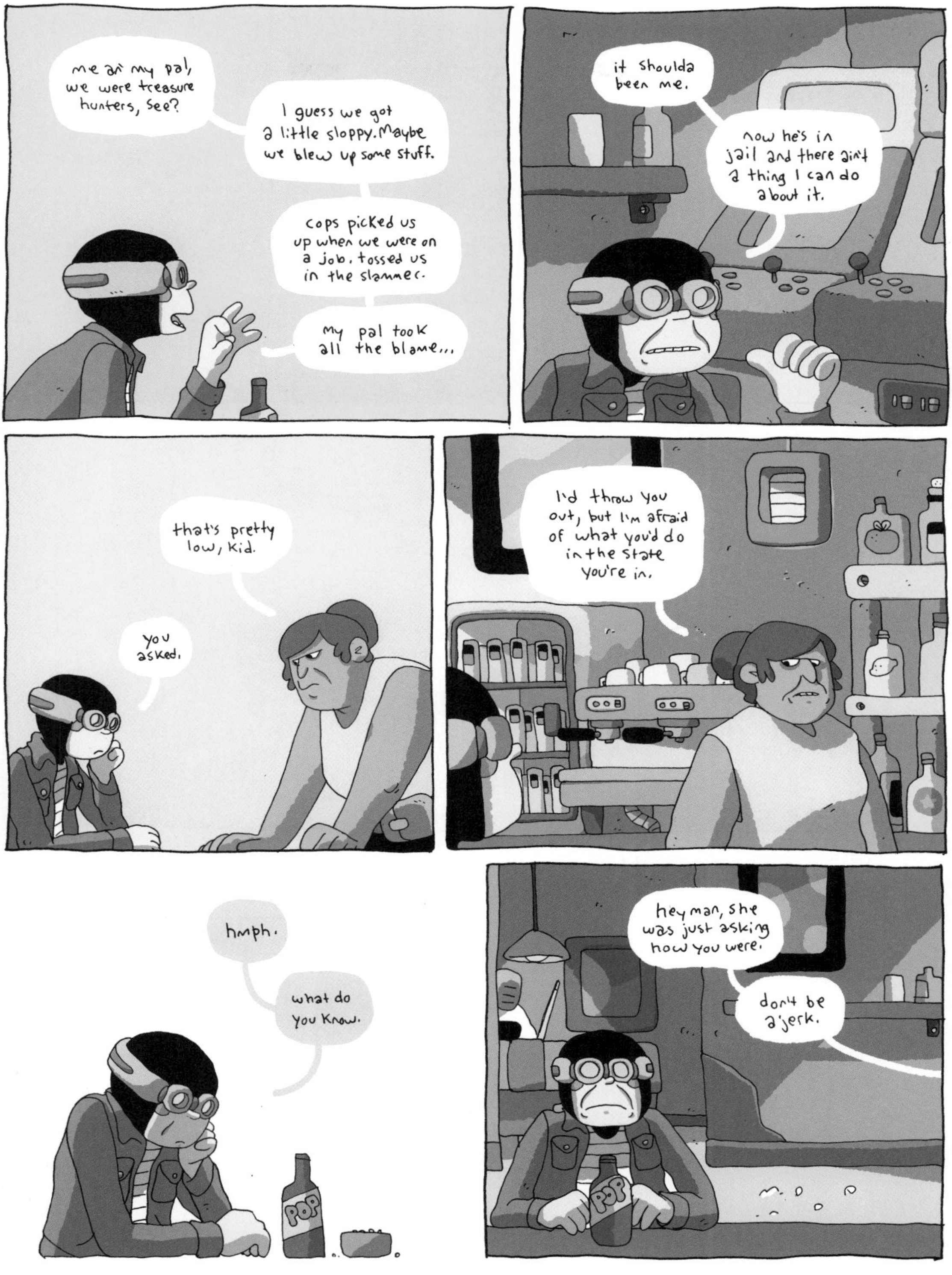
me an my pal, we were treasure hunters, see?
I guess we got a little sloppy. Maybe we blew up some stuff.
cops picked us up when we were on a job. tossed us in the slammer.
My pal took all the blame...
it shoulda been me.
now he's in jail and there ain't a thing I can do about it.
that's pretty low, kid.
you asked.
I'd throw you out, but I'm afraid of what you'd do in the state you're in.
hmph.
what do you know.
hey man, she was just asking how you were.
don't be a jerk.
POP
POP

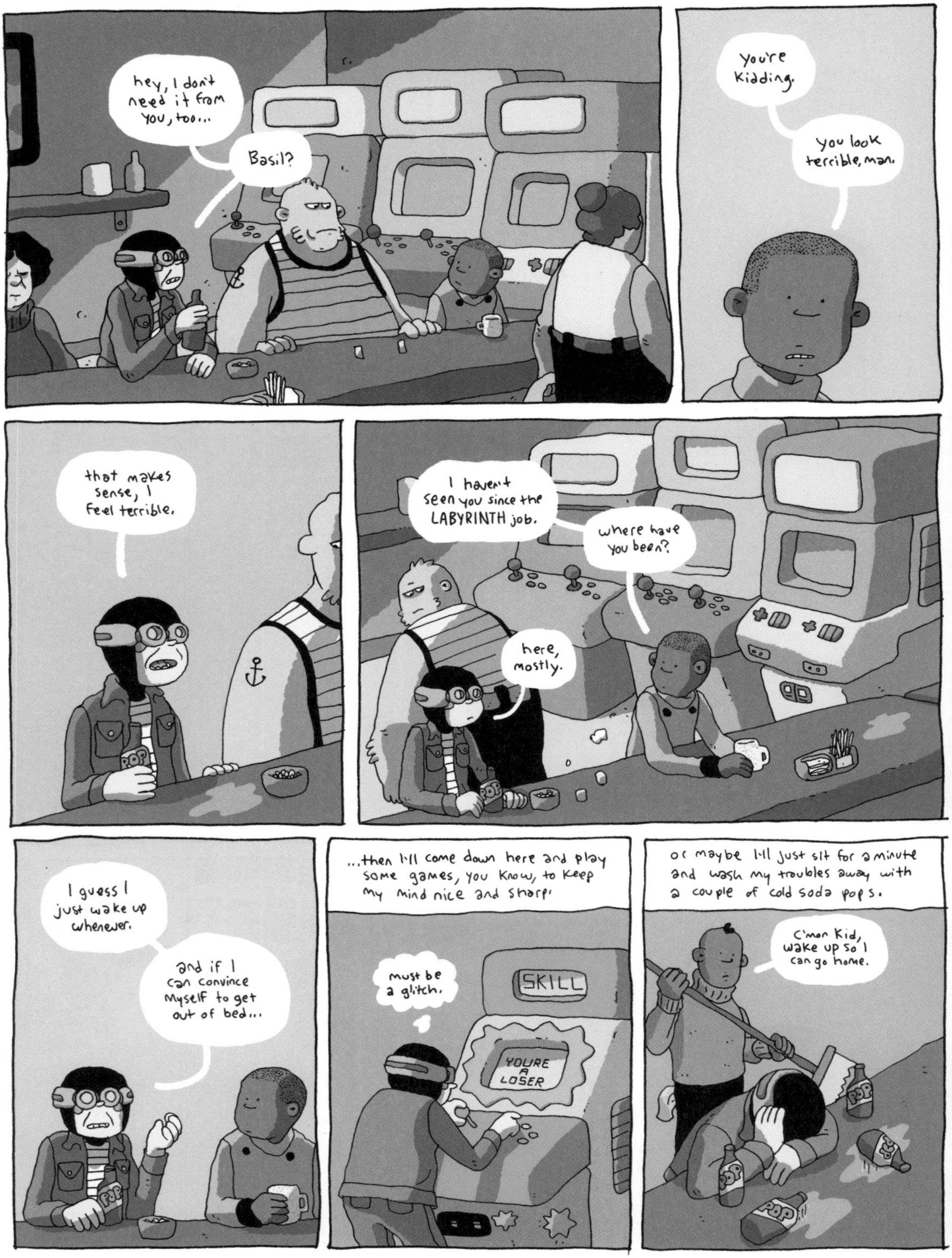
hey, I don't need it from you, too...
Basil?
You're kidding.
you look terrible, man.
that makes sense, I feel terrible.
I haven't seen you since the LABYRINTH job.
where have you been?
here, mostly.
I guess I just wake up whenever.
and if I can convince myself to get out of bed...
...then I'll come down here and play some games, you know, to keep my mind nice and sharp.
SKILL
must be a glitch.
YOU'RE A LOSER
or maybe I'll just sit for a minute and wash my troubles away with a couple of cold soda pops.
C'mon kid, wake up so I can go home.
POP

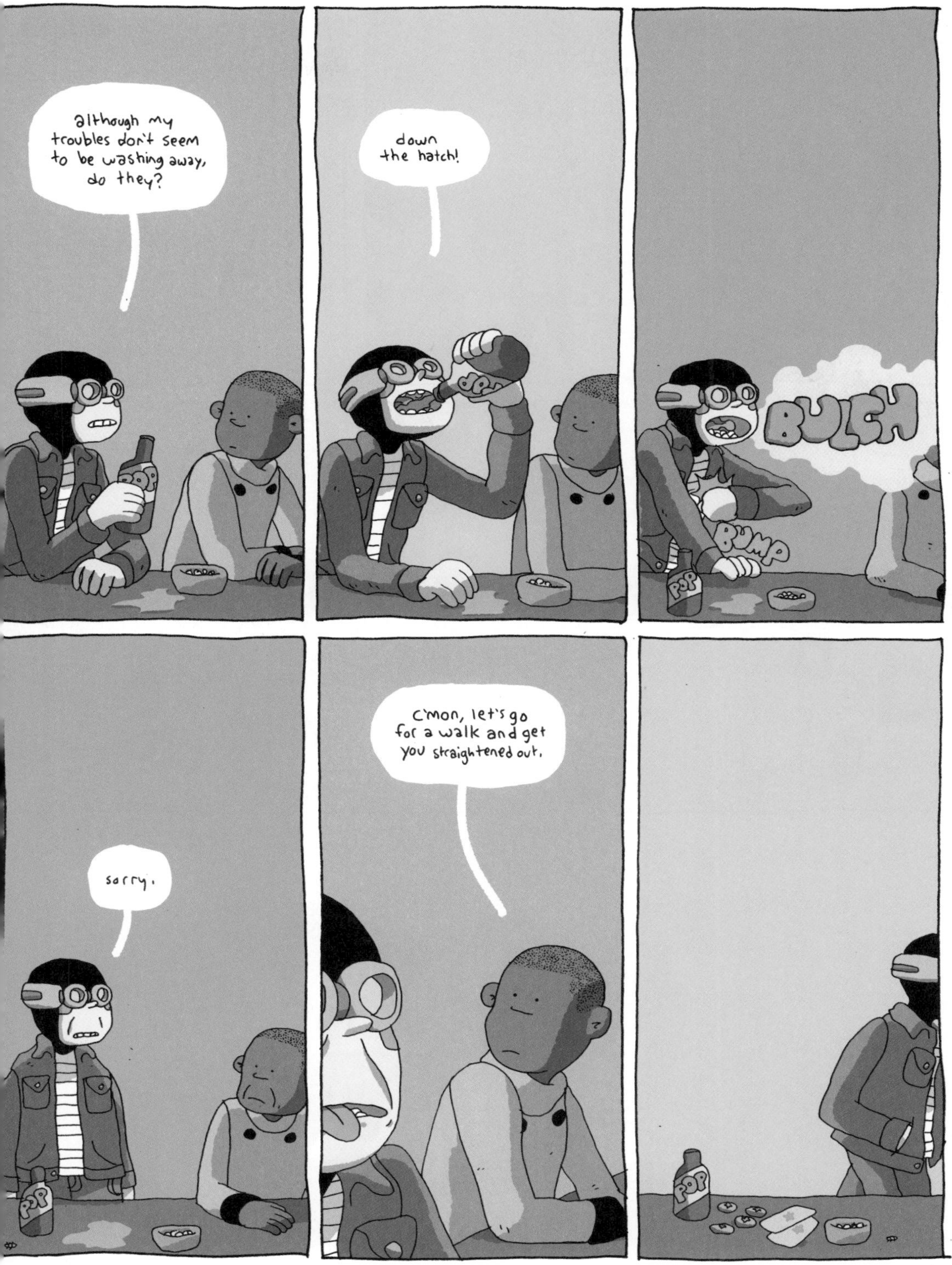
although my troubles don't seem to be washing away, do they?
POP
down the hatch!
POP
BULCH
BUMP
POP
sorry.
POP
C'mon, let's go for a walk and get you straightened out.
POP

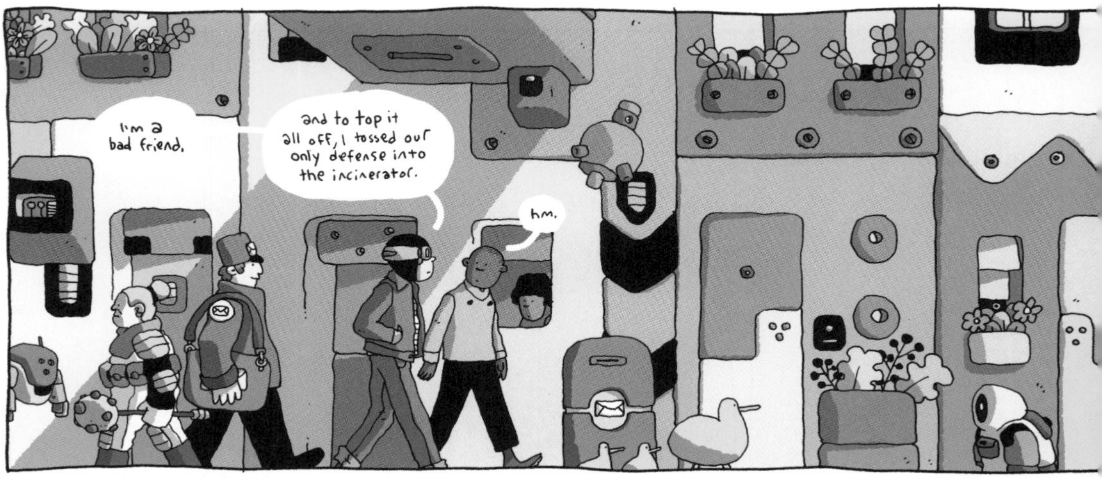
I'm a bad friend.
and to top it all off, I tossed our only defense into the incinerator.
hm.

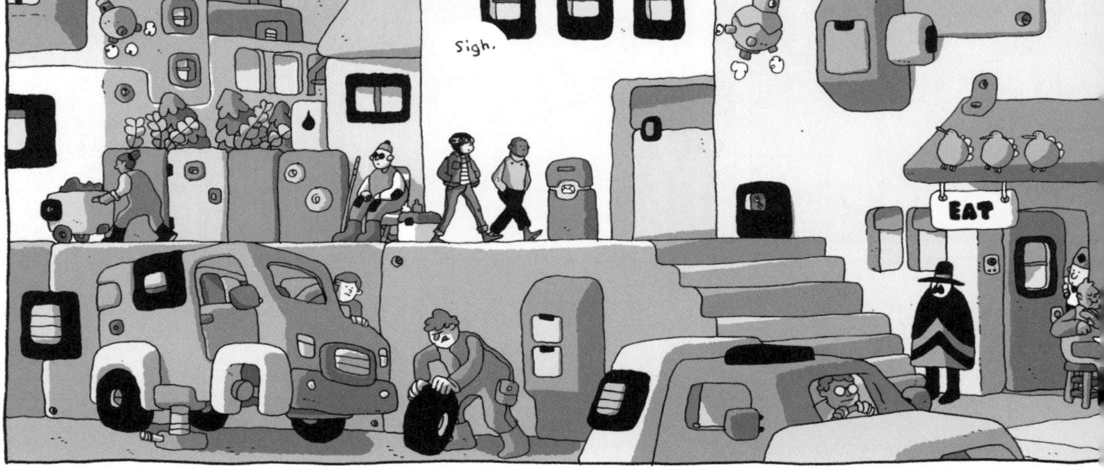
Sigh.
EAT

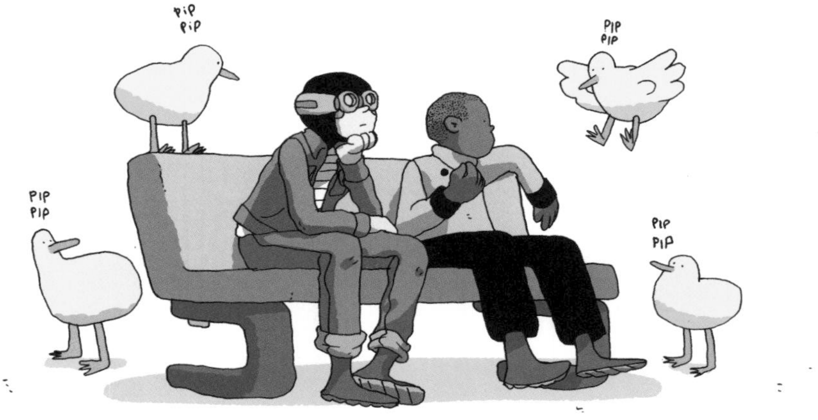
PIP PIP
PIP PIP
PIP PIP
PIP PIP

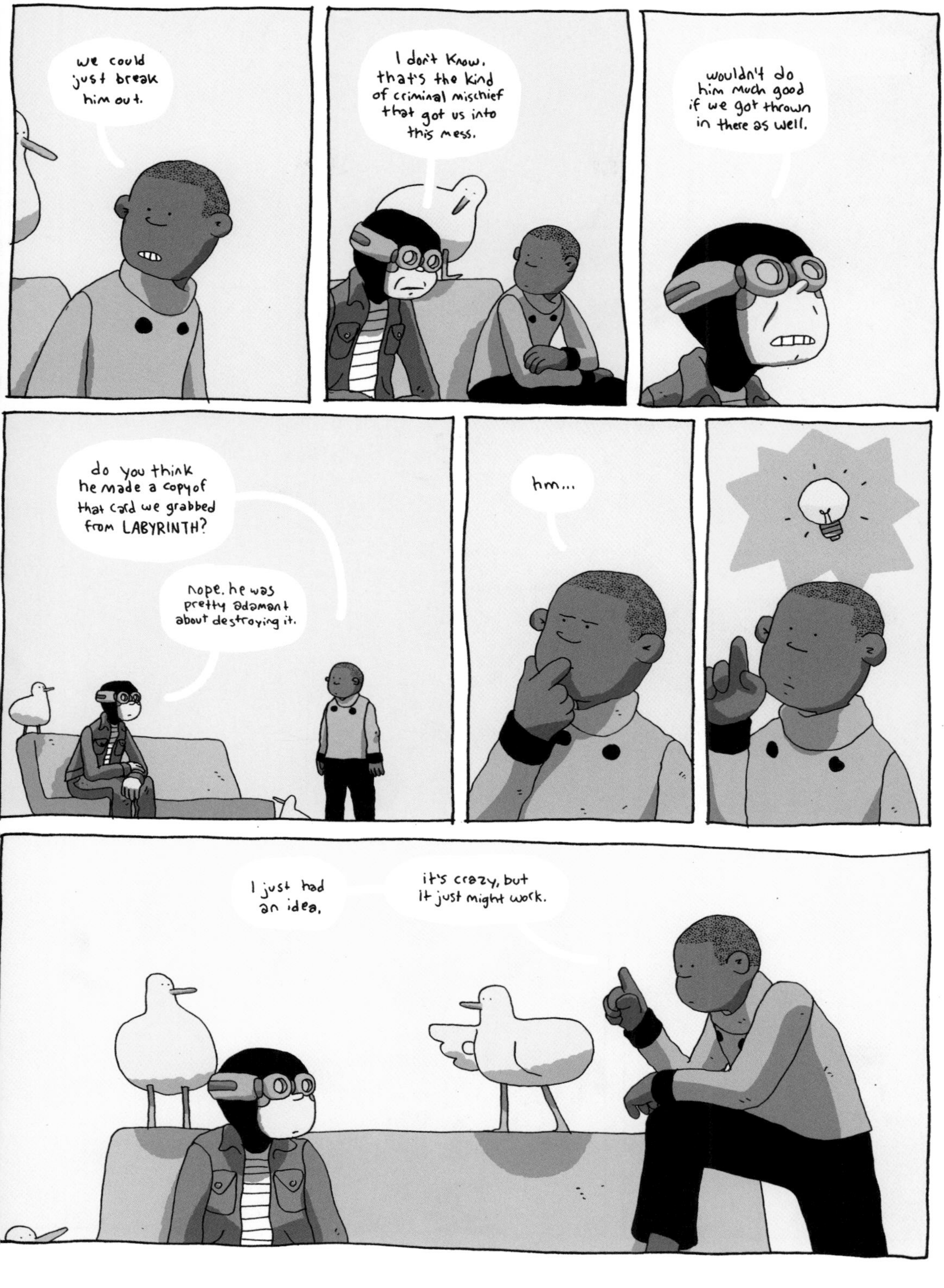
we could just break him out.
I don't know. that's the kind of criminal mischief that got us into this mess.
wouldn't do him much good if we got thrown in there as well.
do you think he made a copy of that card we grabbed from LABYRINTH?
nope. he was pretty adamant about destroying it.
hm...
I just had an idea.
it's crazy, but it just might work.

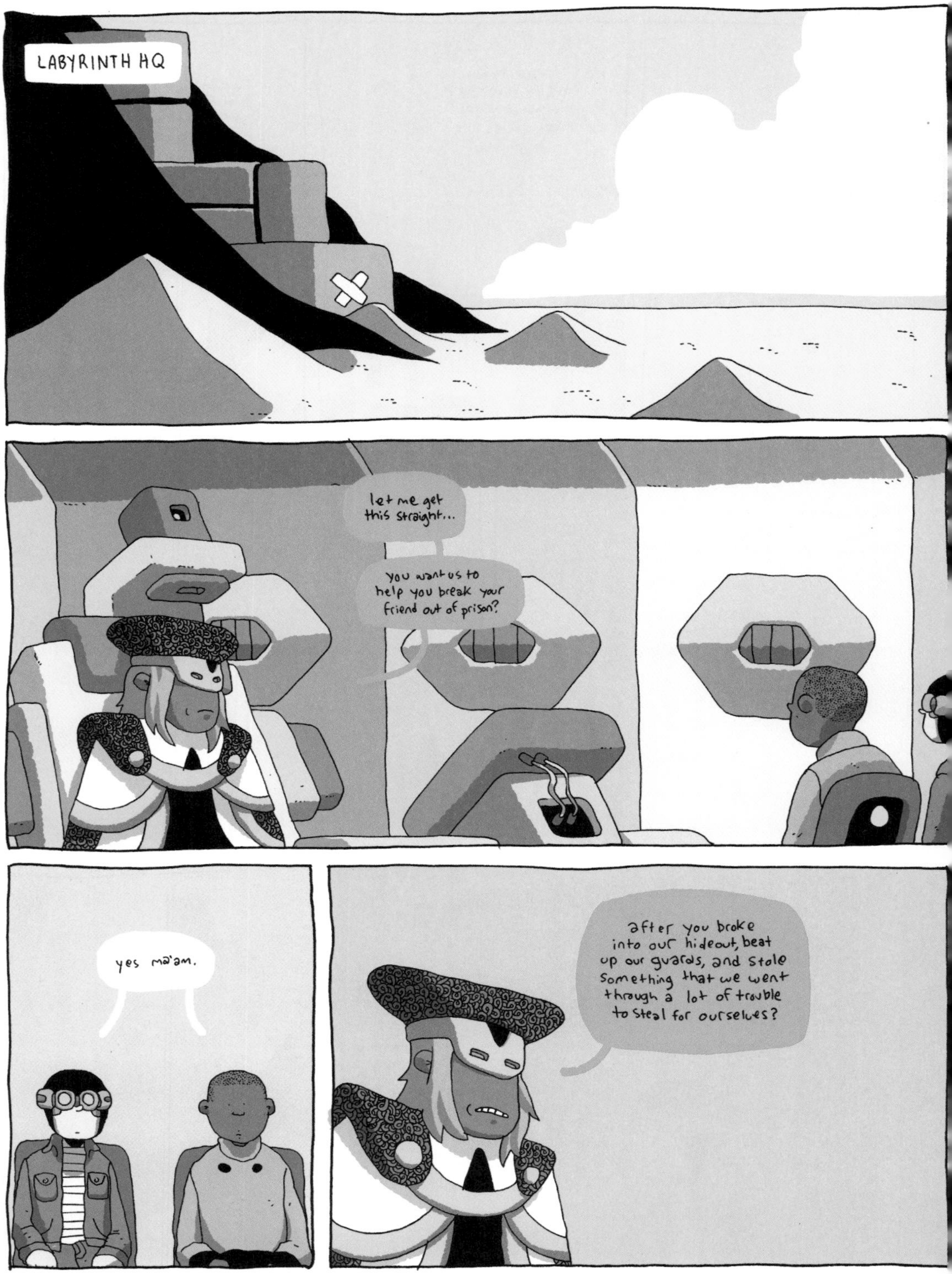
LABYRINTH HQ
let me get this straight...
you want us to help you break your friend out of prison?
yes ma'am.
after you broke into our hideout, beat up our guards, and stole something that we went through a lot of trouble to steal for ourselves?

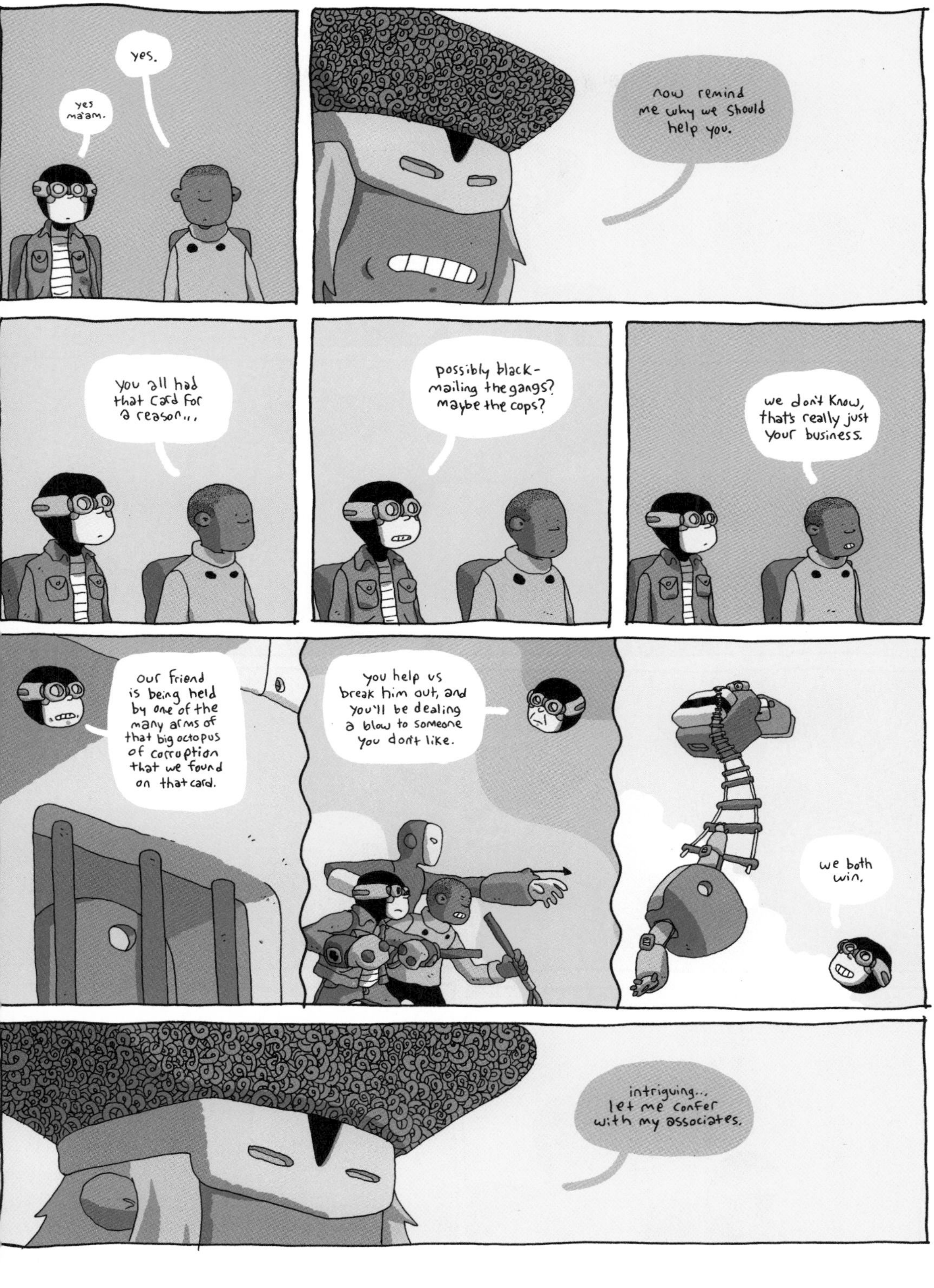
yes ma'am.
yes.
now remind me why we should help you.
you all had that card for a reason...
possibly black-mailing the gangs? maybe the cops?
we don't know, that's really just your business.
our friend is being held by one of the many arms of that big octopus of corruption that we found on that card.
you help us break him out, and you'll be dealing a blow to someone you don't like.
we both win.
intriguing... let me confer with my associates.

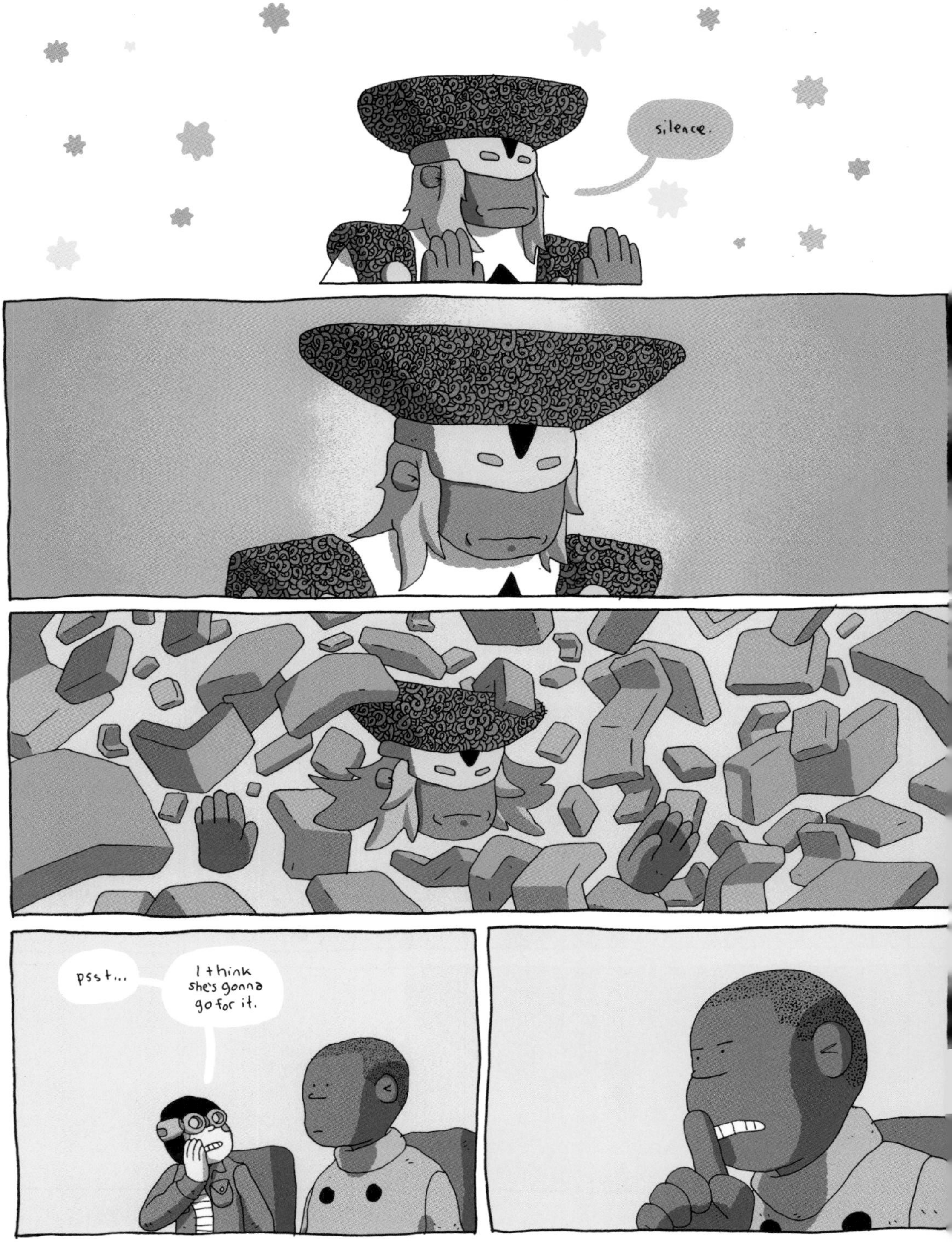
silence.
psst...
I think she's gonna go for it.

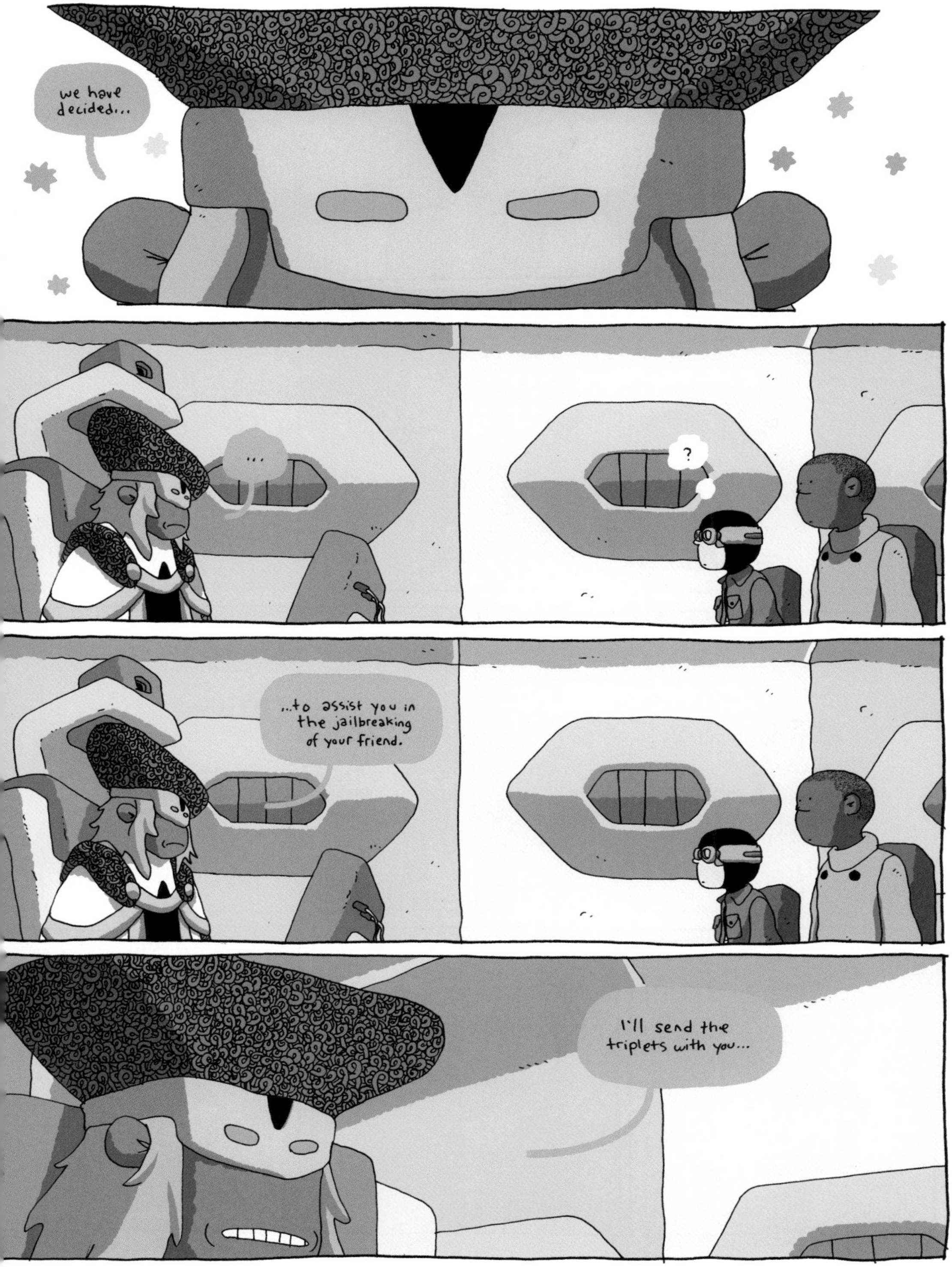
we have decided...
...
?
...to assist you in the jailbreaking of your friend.
I'll send the triplets with you...

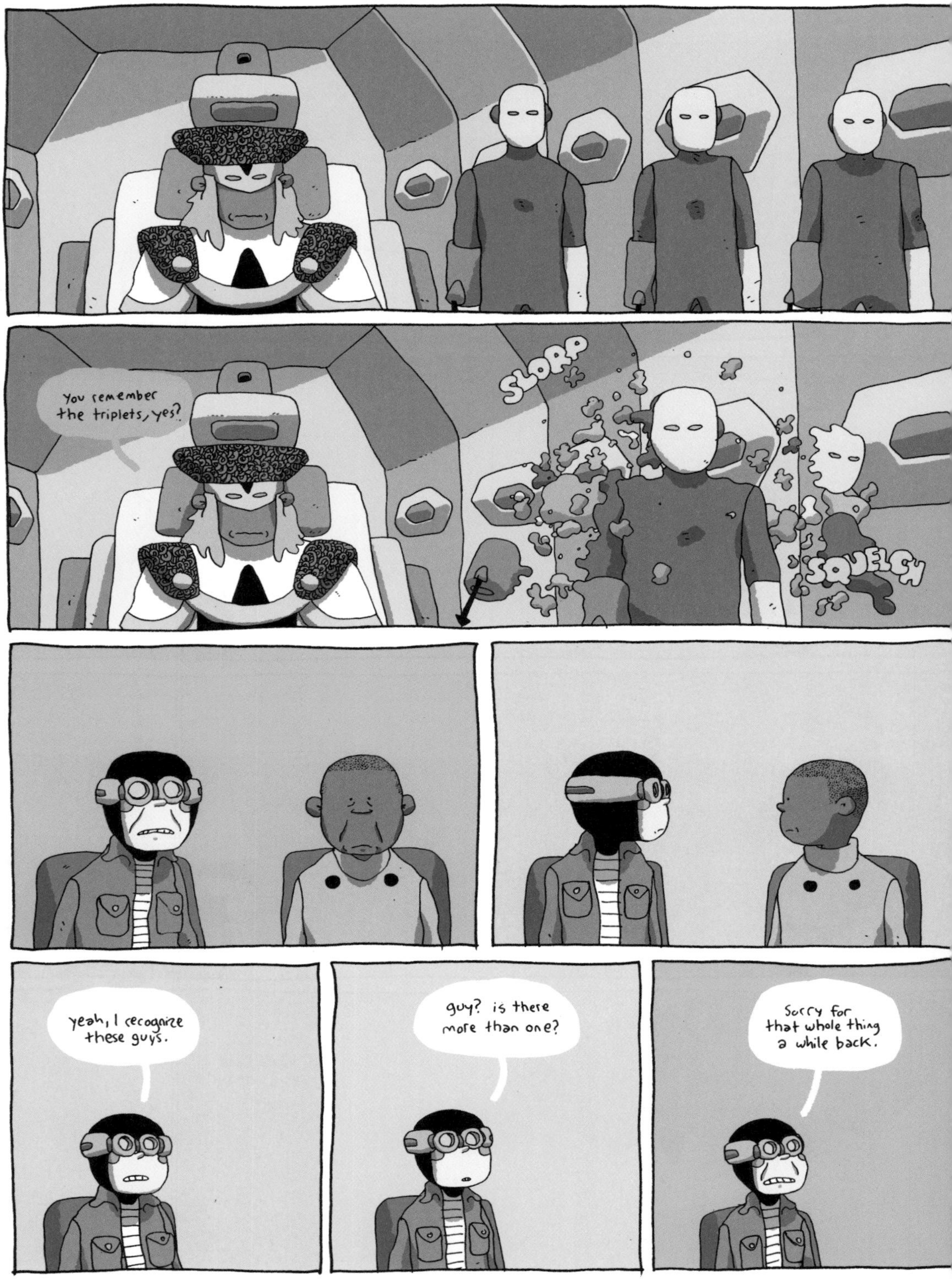
You remember the triplets, yes?
SLORP
SQUELCH
yeah, I recognize these guys.
guy? is there more than one?
Sorry for that whole thing a while back.

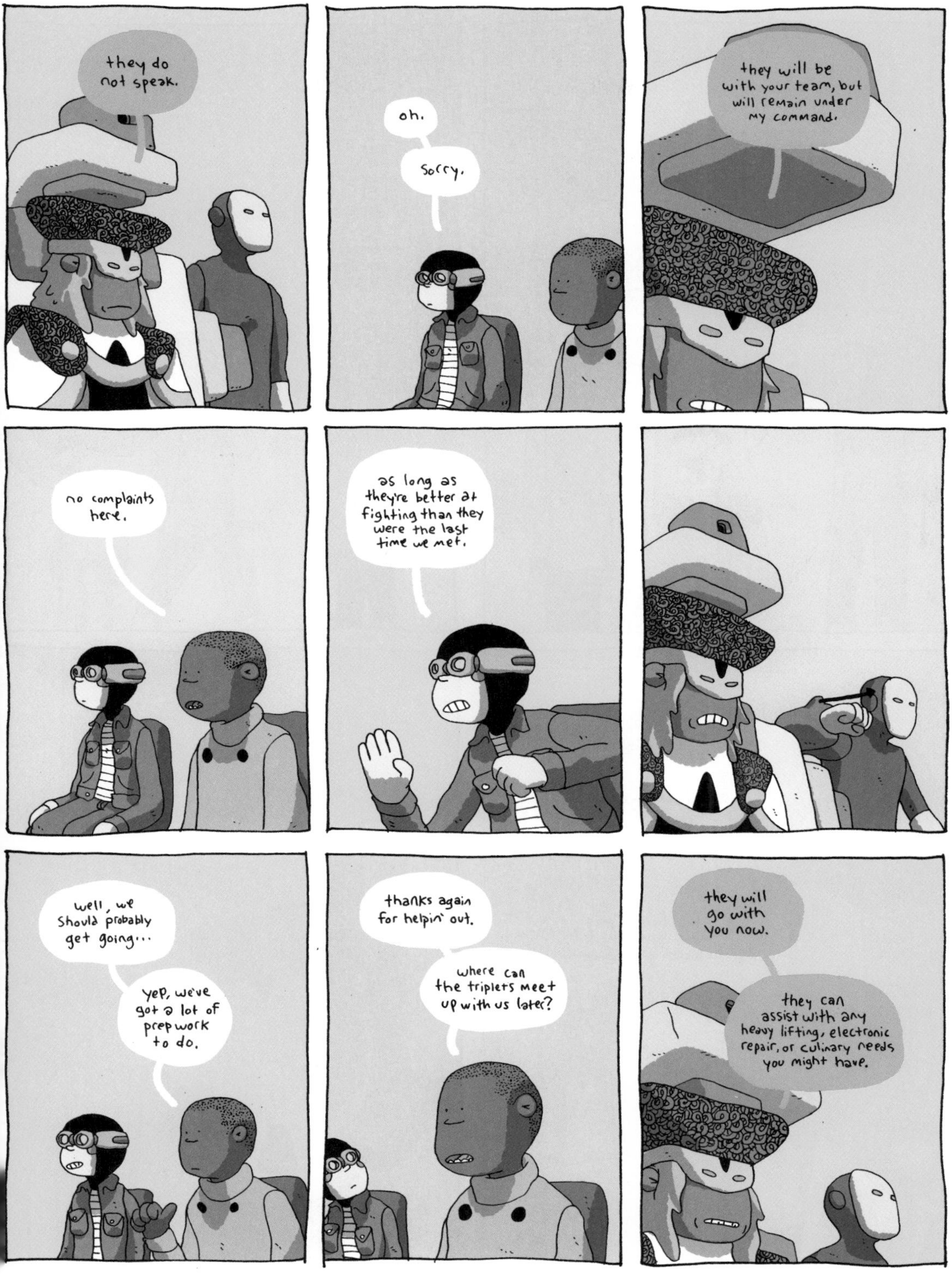
they do not speak.
oh.
sorry.
they will be with your team, but will remain under my command.
no complaints here.
as long as they're better at fighting than they were the last time we met.
well, we should probably get going...
yep, we've got a lot of prep work to do.
thanks again for helpin' out.
where can the triplets meet up with us later?
they will go with you now.
they can assist with any heavy lifting, electronic repair, or culinary needs you might have.

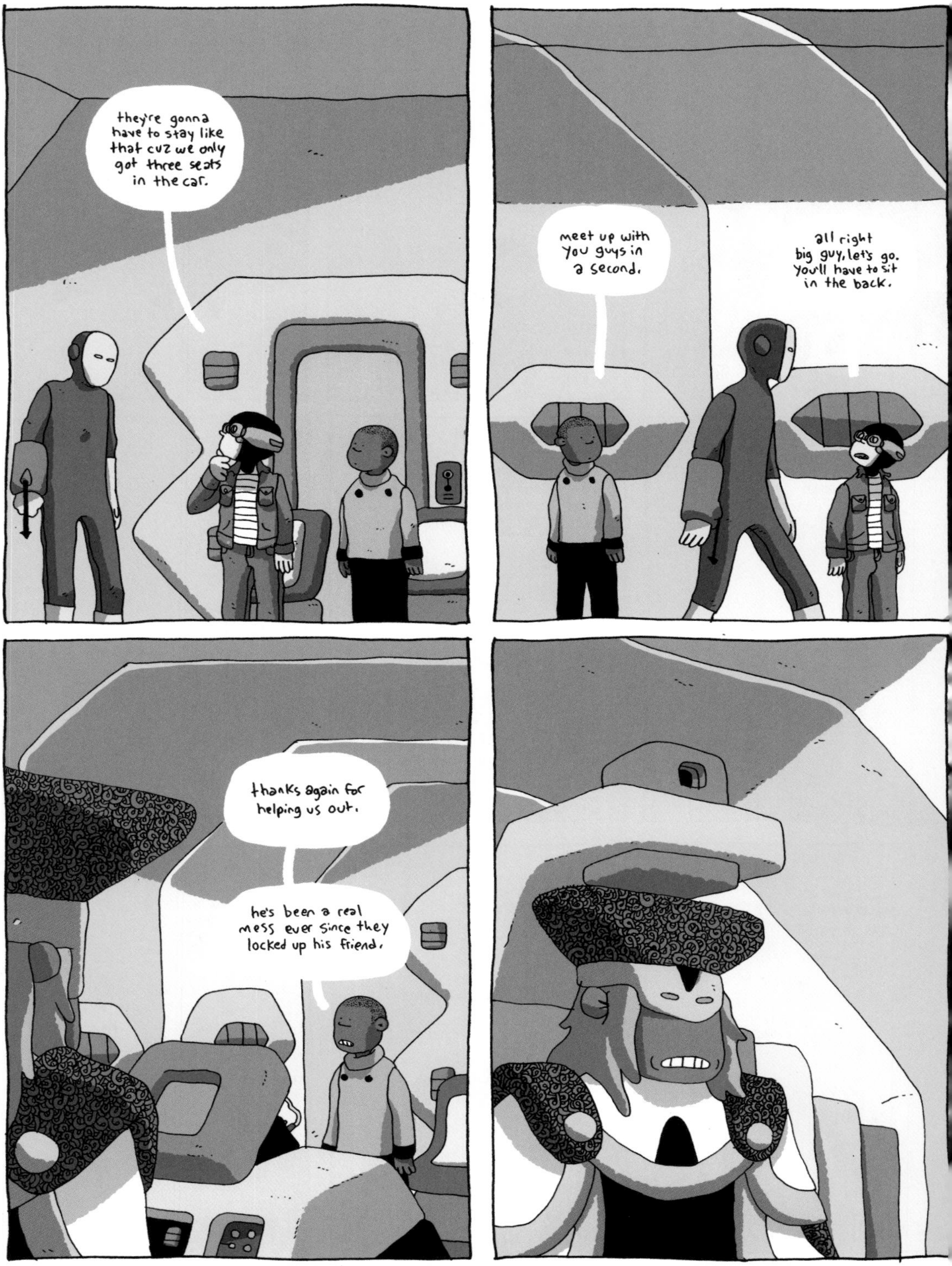
they're gonna have to stay like that cuz we only got three seats in the car.
meet up with you guys in a second.
all right big guy, let's go. you'll have to sit in the back.
thanks again for helping us out.
he's been a real mess ever since they locked up his friend.

PART 4

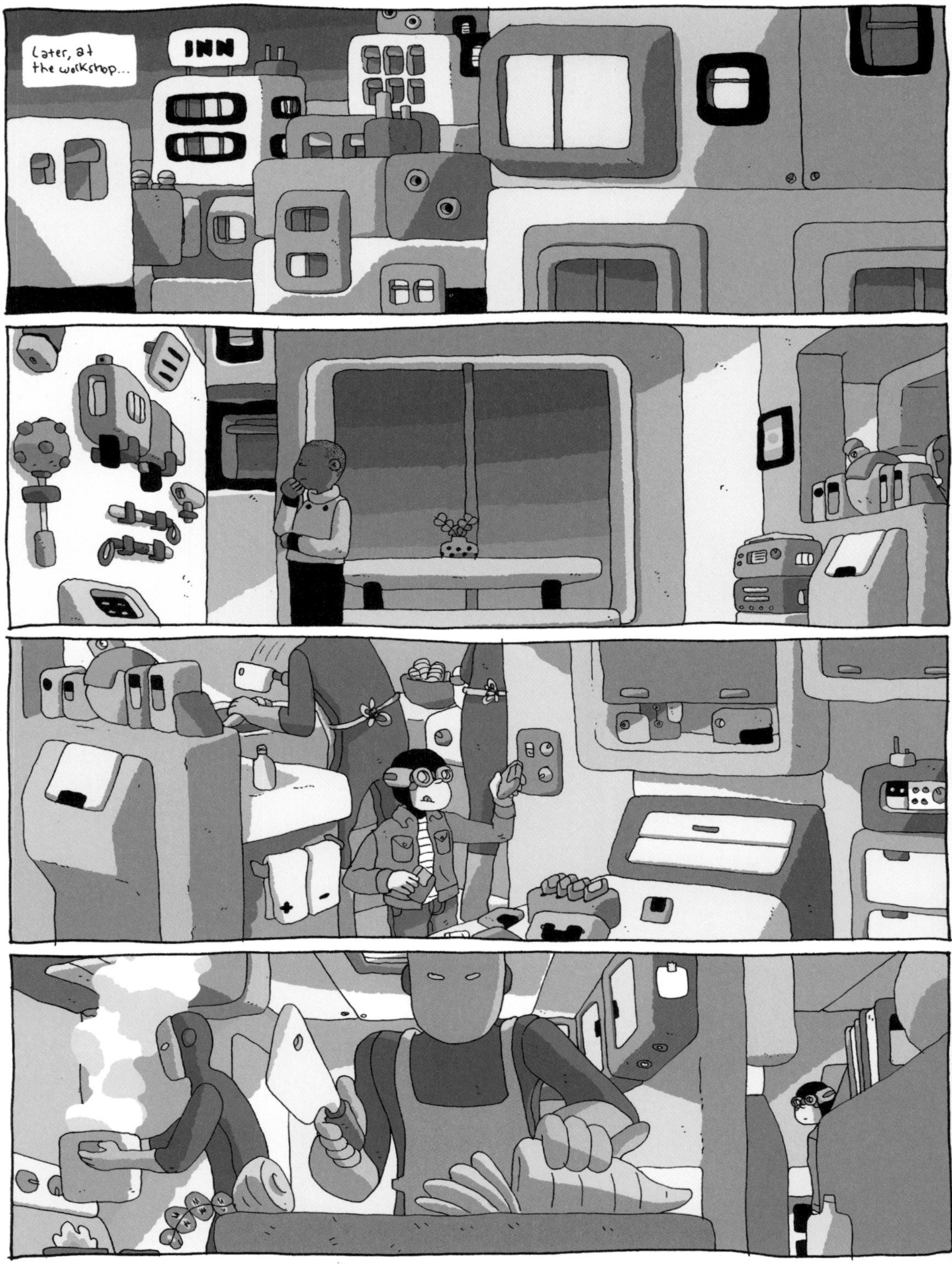
Later, at the workshop...
INN

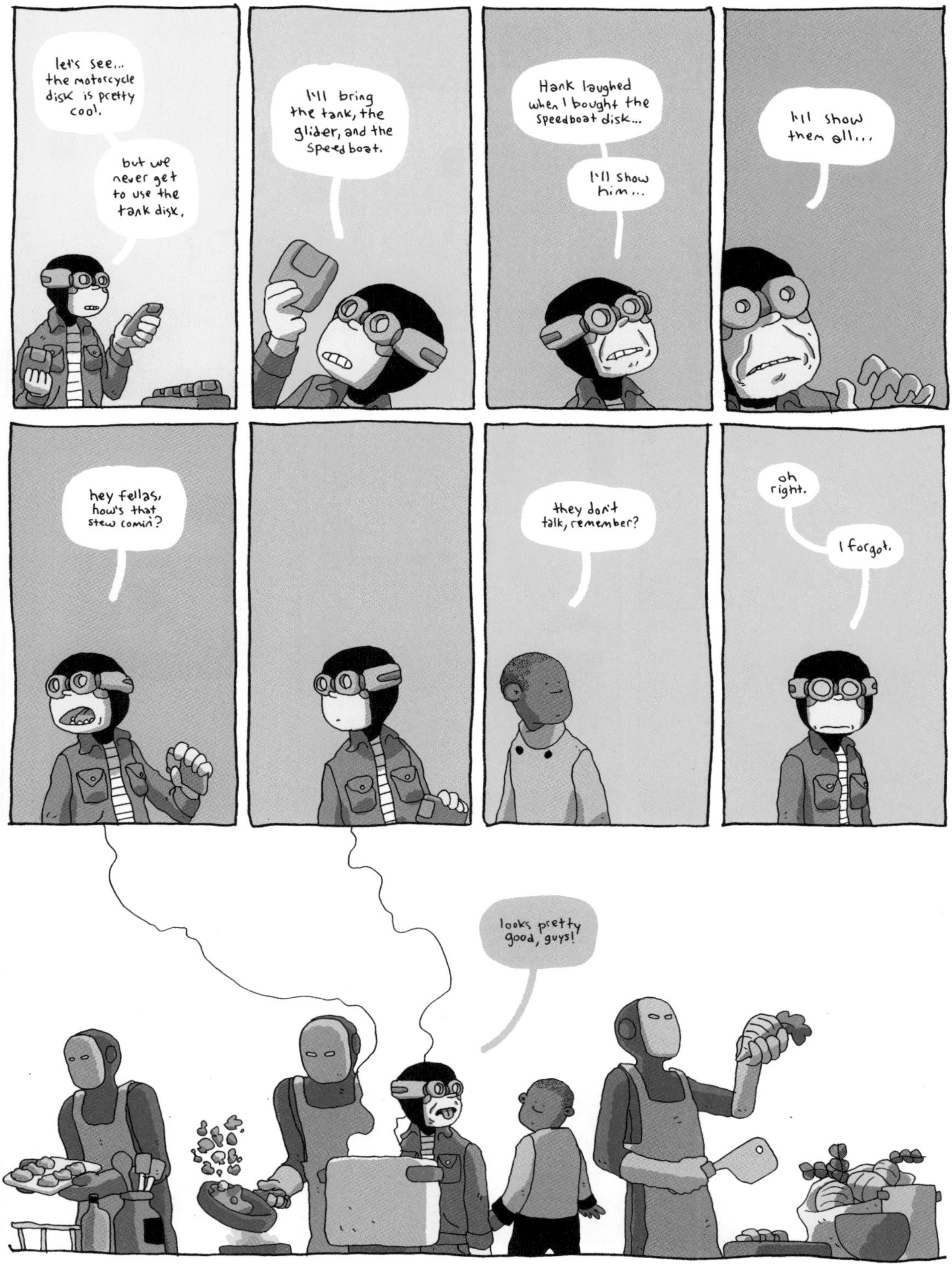
let's see... the motorcycle disk is pretty cool.
but we never get to use the tank disk.
I'll bring the tank, the glider, and the speedboat.
Hank laughed when I bought the speedboat disk...
I'll show him...
I'll show them all...
hey fellas, how's that stew comin?
they don't talk, remember?
oh right.
I forgot.
looks pretty good, guys!

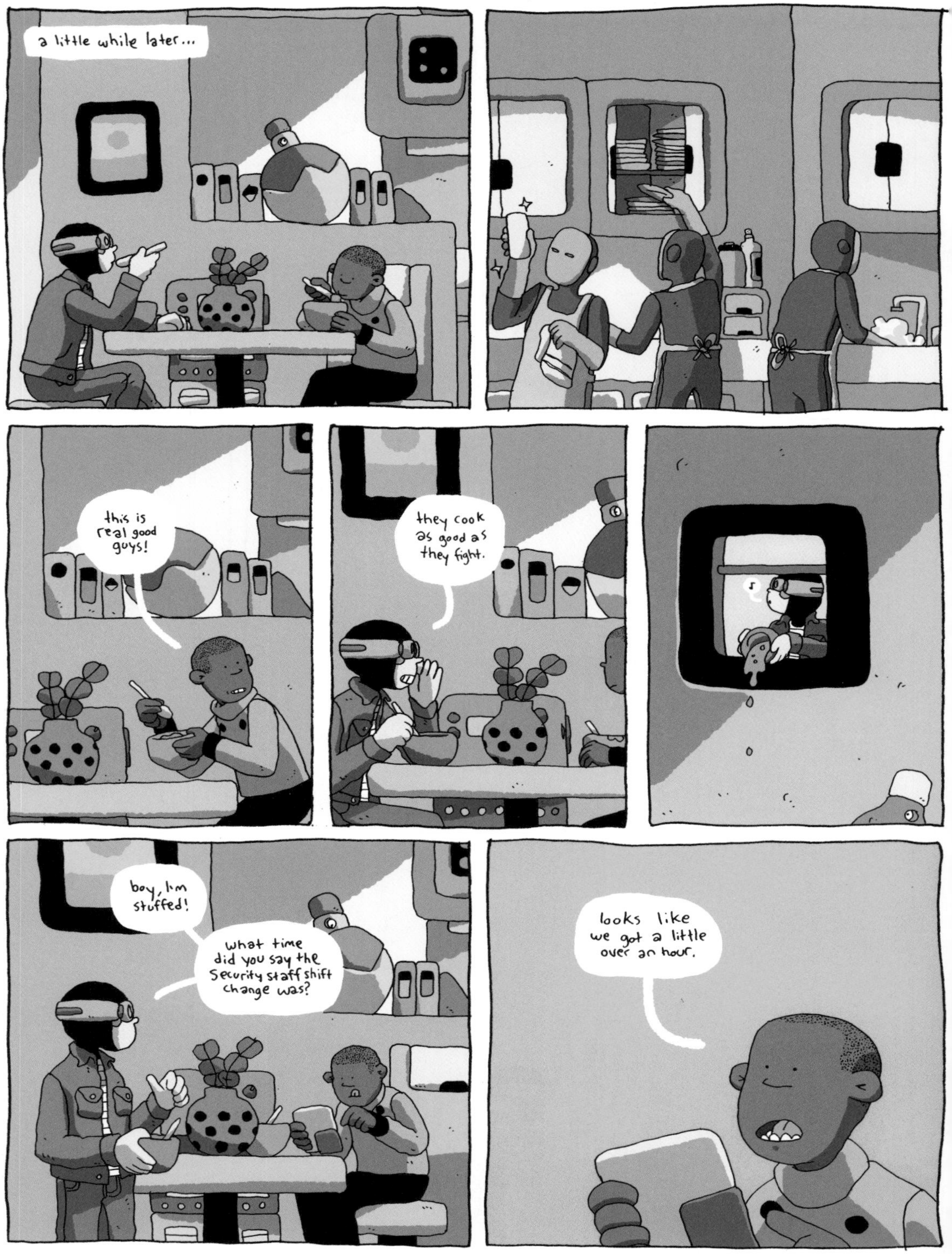
a little while later...
this is real good guys!
they cook as good as they fight.
boy, I'm stuffed!
what time did you say the security staff shift change was?
looks like we got a little over an hour.

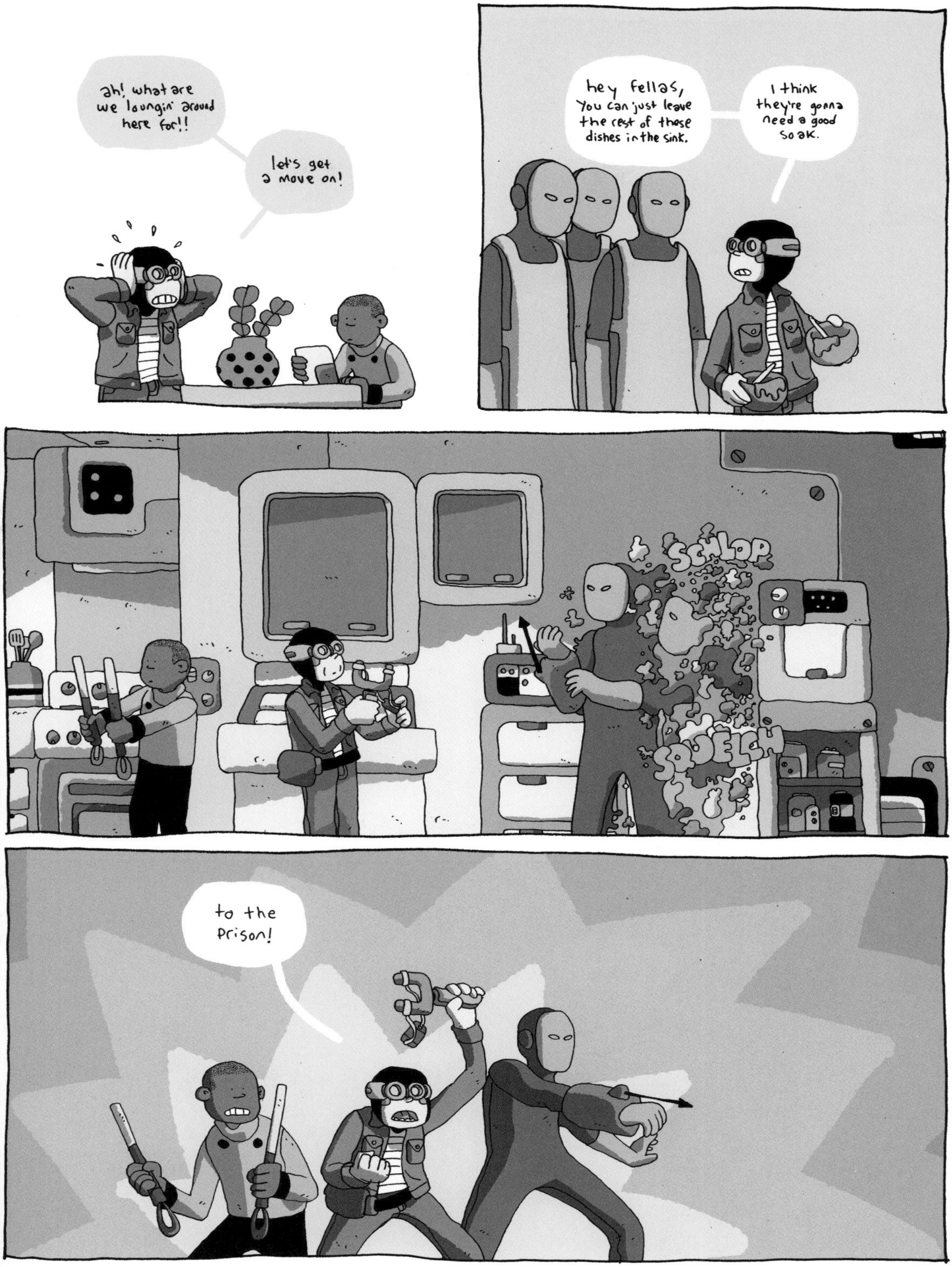
ah! what are we loungin' around here for!!
let's get a move on!
hey fellas, you can just leave the rest of these dishes in the sink.
I think they're gonna need a good soak.
SCHLOP
SQUELCH
to the prison!

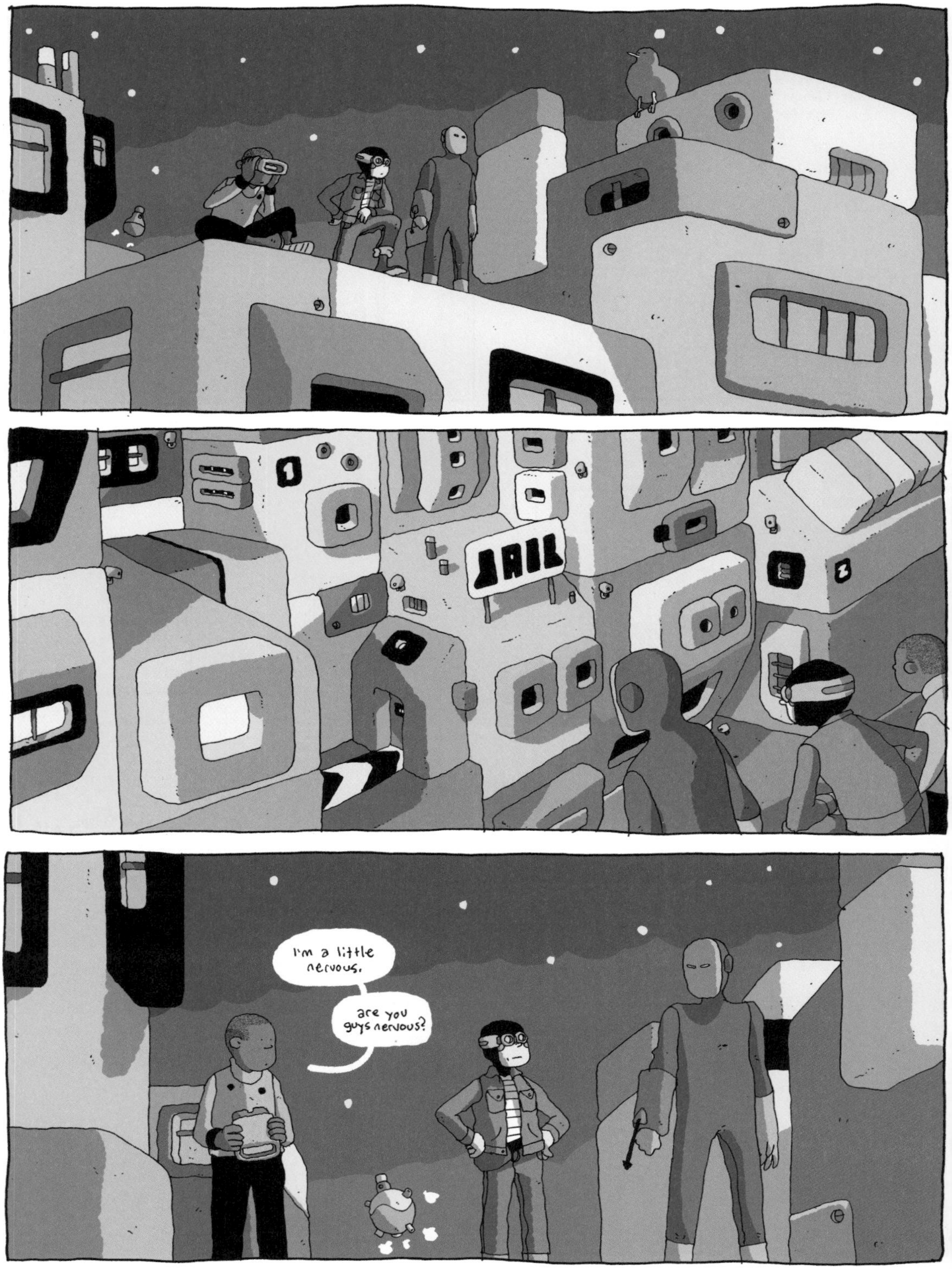
JAIL
I'm a little nervous.
are you guys nervous?

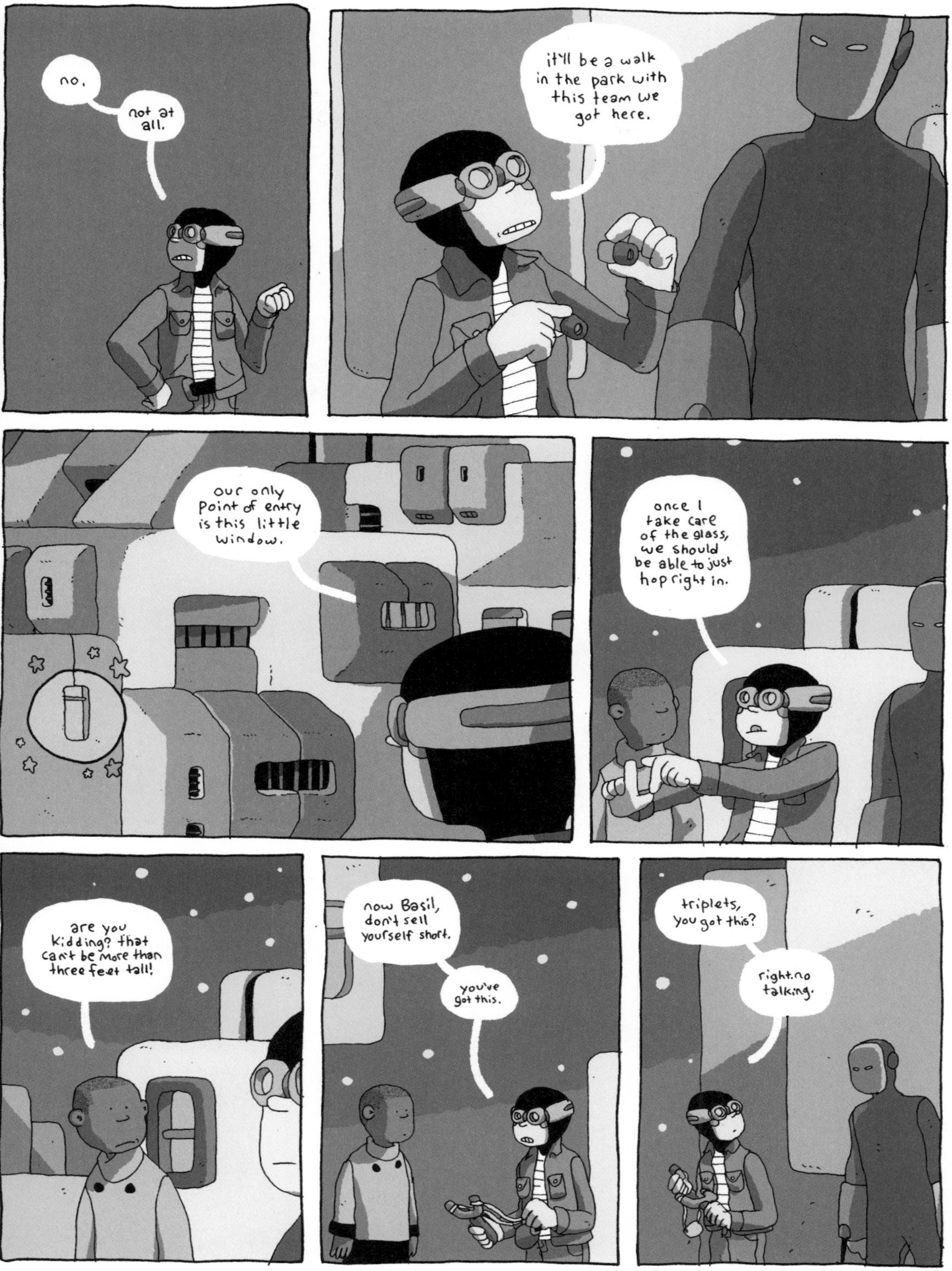
no.
not at all.
it'll be a walk in the park with this team we got here.
our only point of entry is this little window.
once I take care of the glass, we should be able to just hop right in.
are you kidding? that can't be more than three feet tall!
now Basil, don't sell yourself short.
you've got this.
triplets, you got this?
right. no talking.

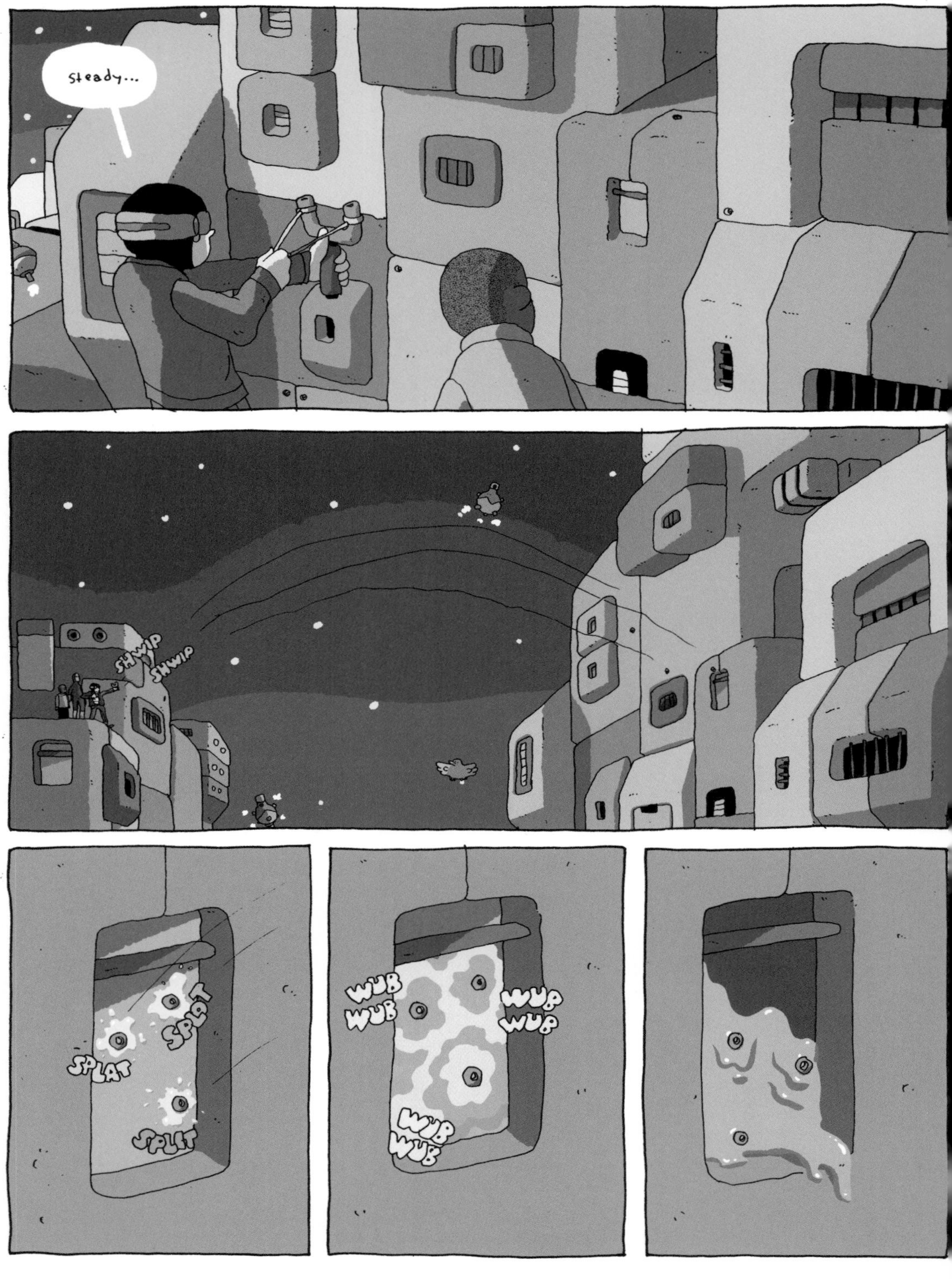
steady...
SHWIP
SHWIP
SPLAT
SPLOT
SPLIT
WUB WUB
WUB WUB
WUB WUB

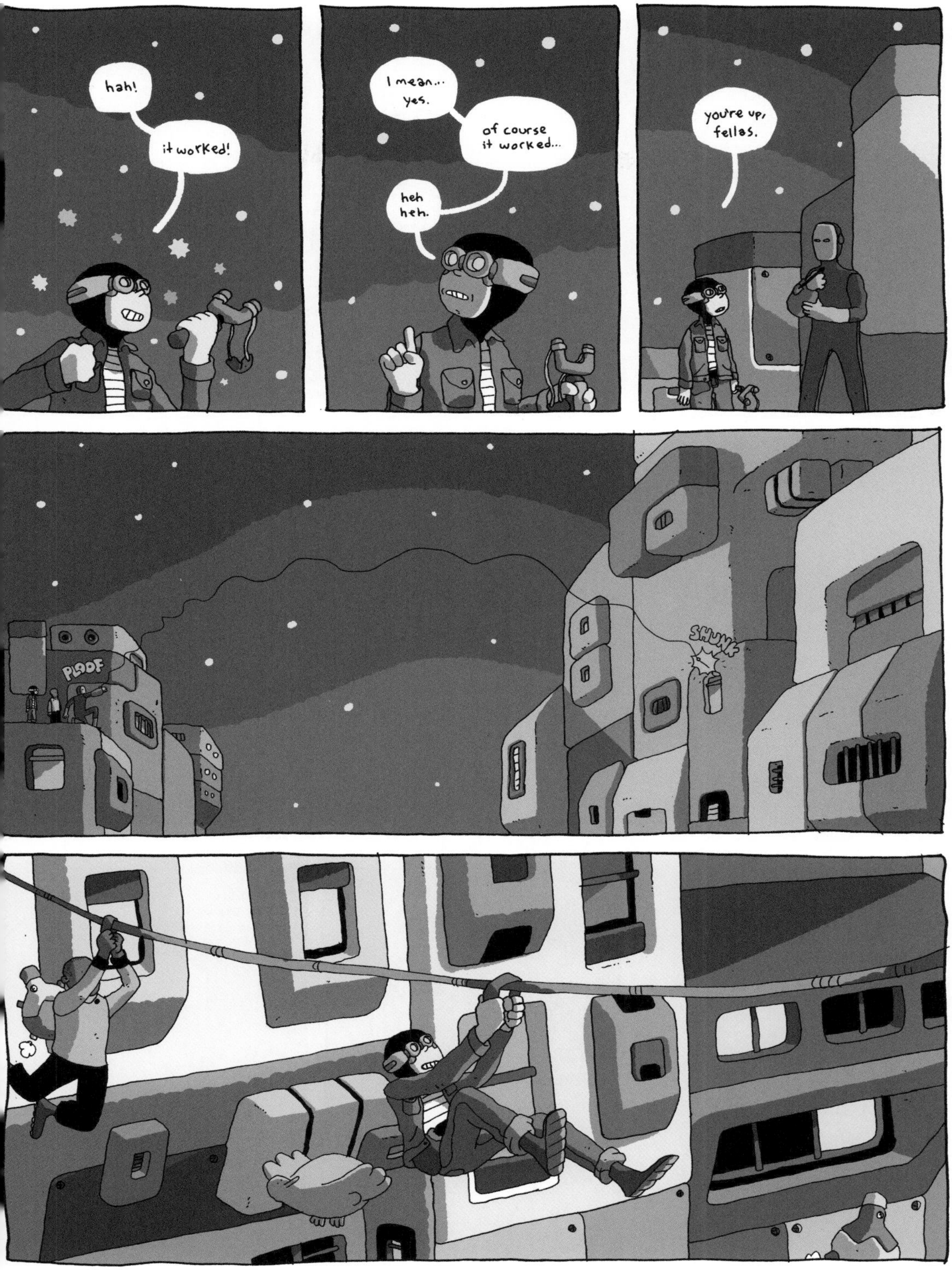
hah!
it worked!
I mean... yes.
of course it worked...
heh heh.
you're up, fellas.
PLOOF
SHUNK

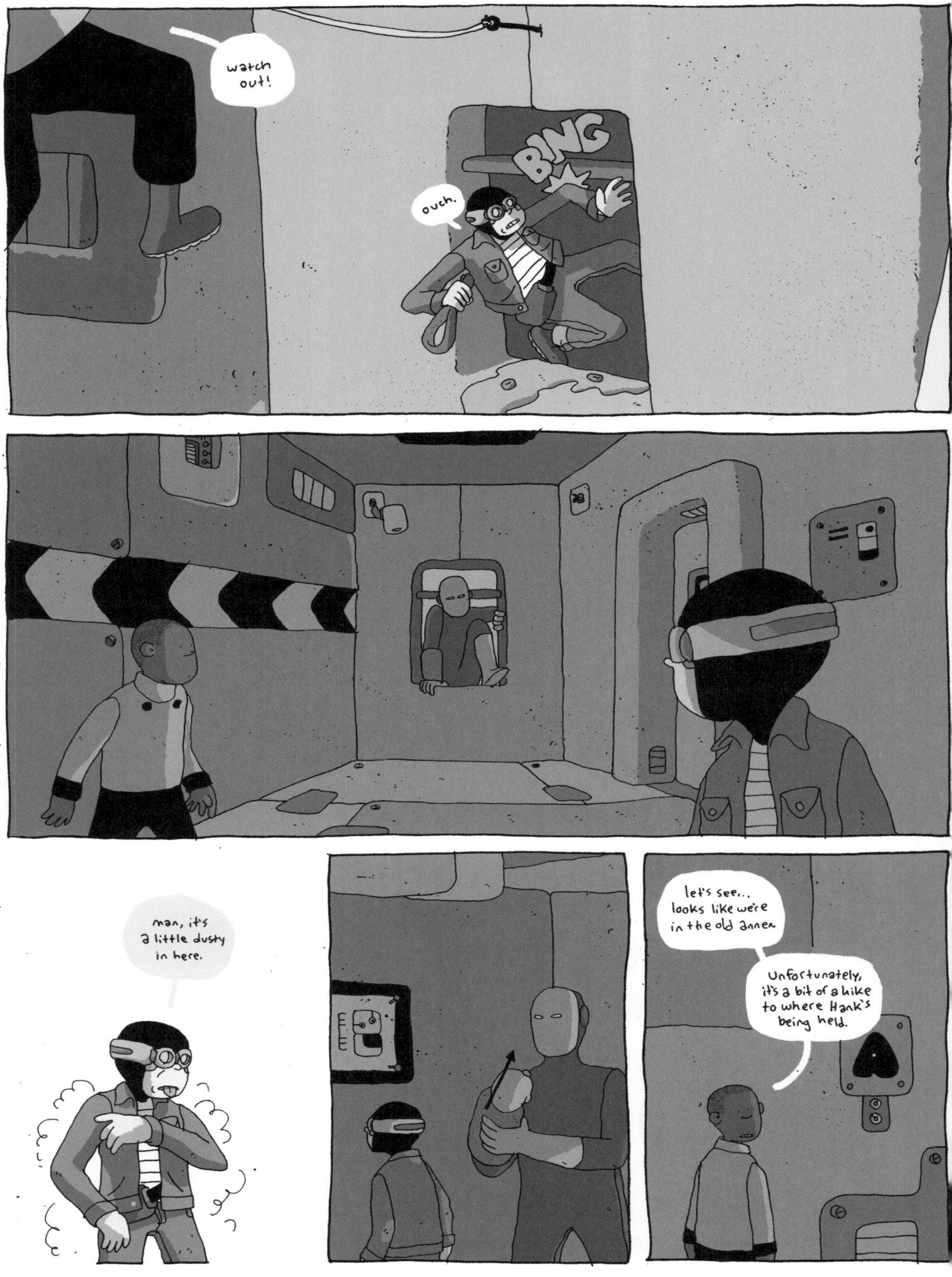
watch out!
BING
ouch.
man, it's a little dusty in here.
let's see... looks like we're in the old annex
Unfortunately, it's a bit of a hike to where Hank's being held.

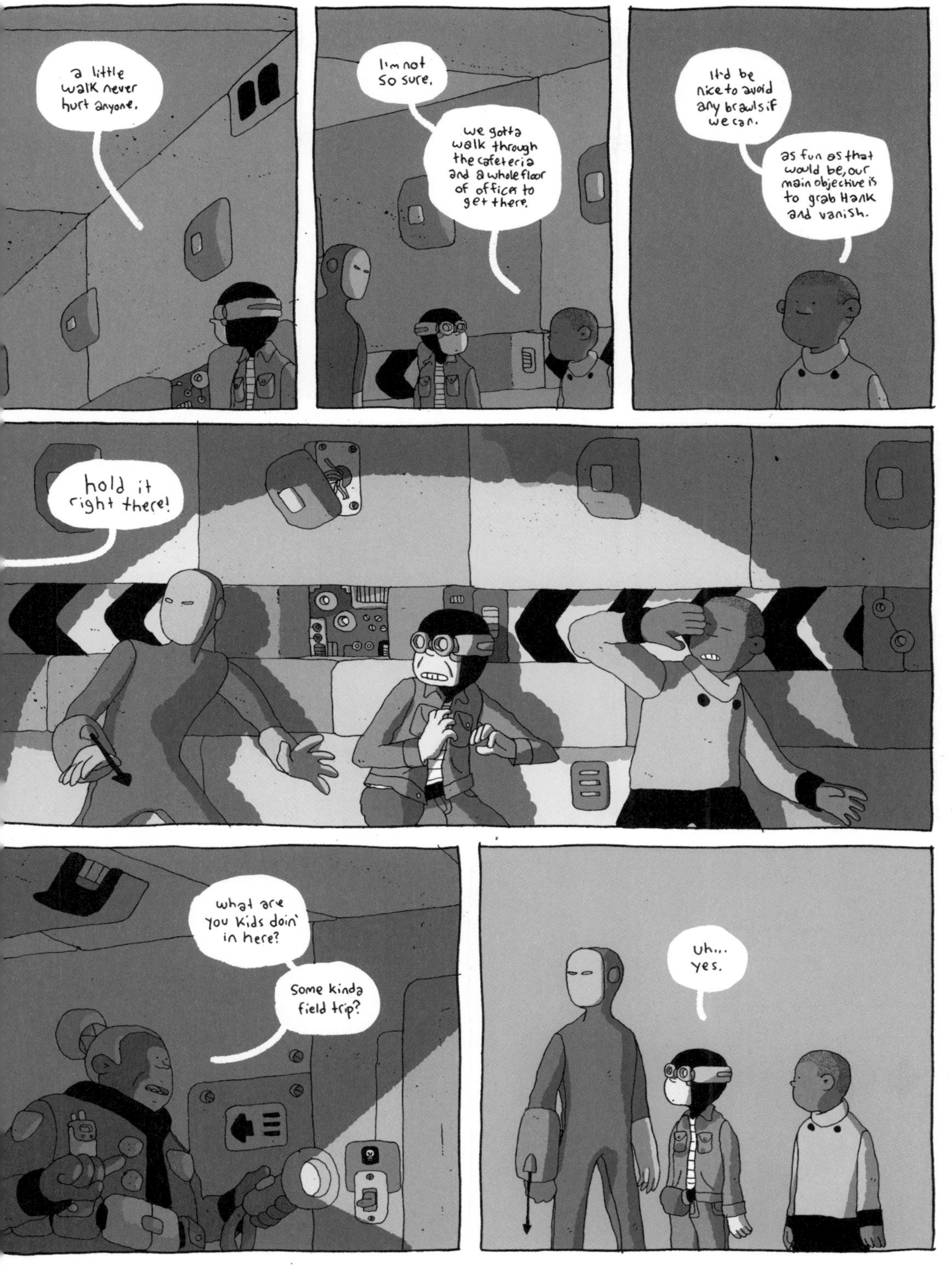
a little walk never hurt anyone.
I'm not so sure.
we gotta walk through the cafeteria and a whole floor of offices to get there.
It'd be nice to avoid any brawls if we can.
as fun as that would be, our main objective is to grab Hank and vanish.
hold it right there!
what are you kids doin' in here?
Some kinda field trip?
uh... yes.

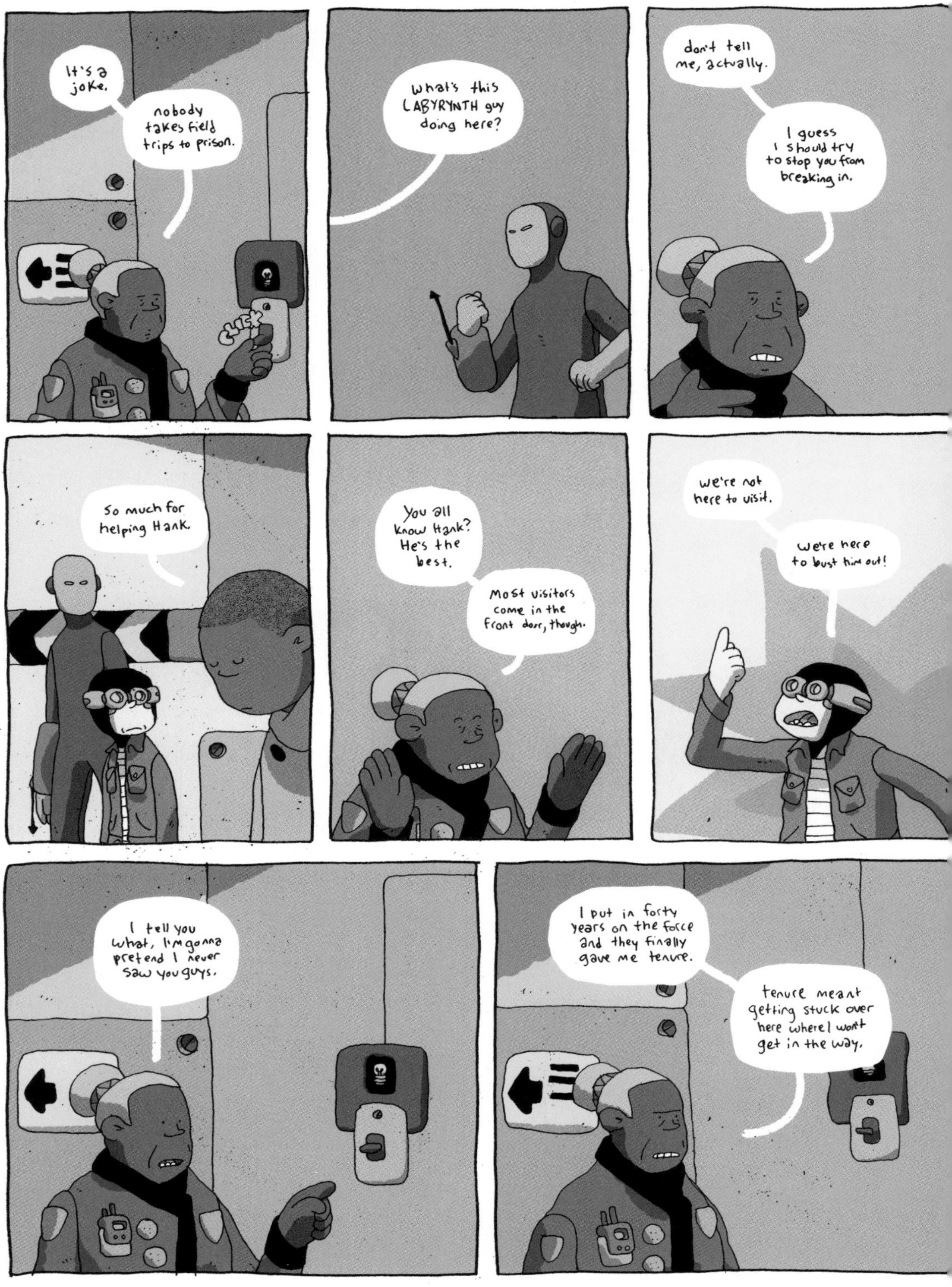
It's a joke.
nobody takes field trips to prison.
CLICK
what's this LABYRYNTH guy doing here?
don't tell me, actually.
I guess I should try to stop you from breaking in.
So much for helping Hank.
You all know Hank? He's the best.
Most visitors come in the front door, though.
we're not here to visit.
we're here to bust him out!
I tell you what, I'm gonna pretend I never saw you guys.
I put in forty years on the force and they finally gave me tenure.
tenure meant getting stuck over here where I won't get in the way.

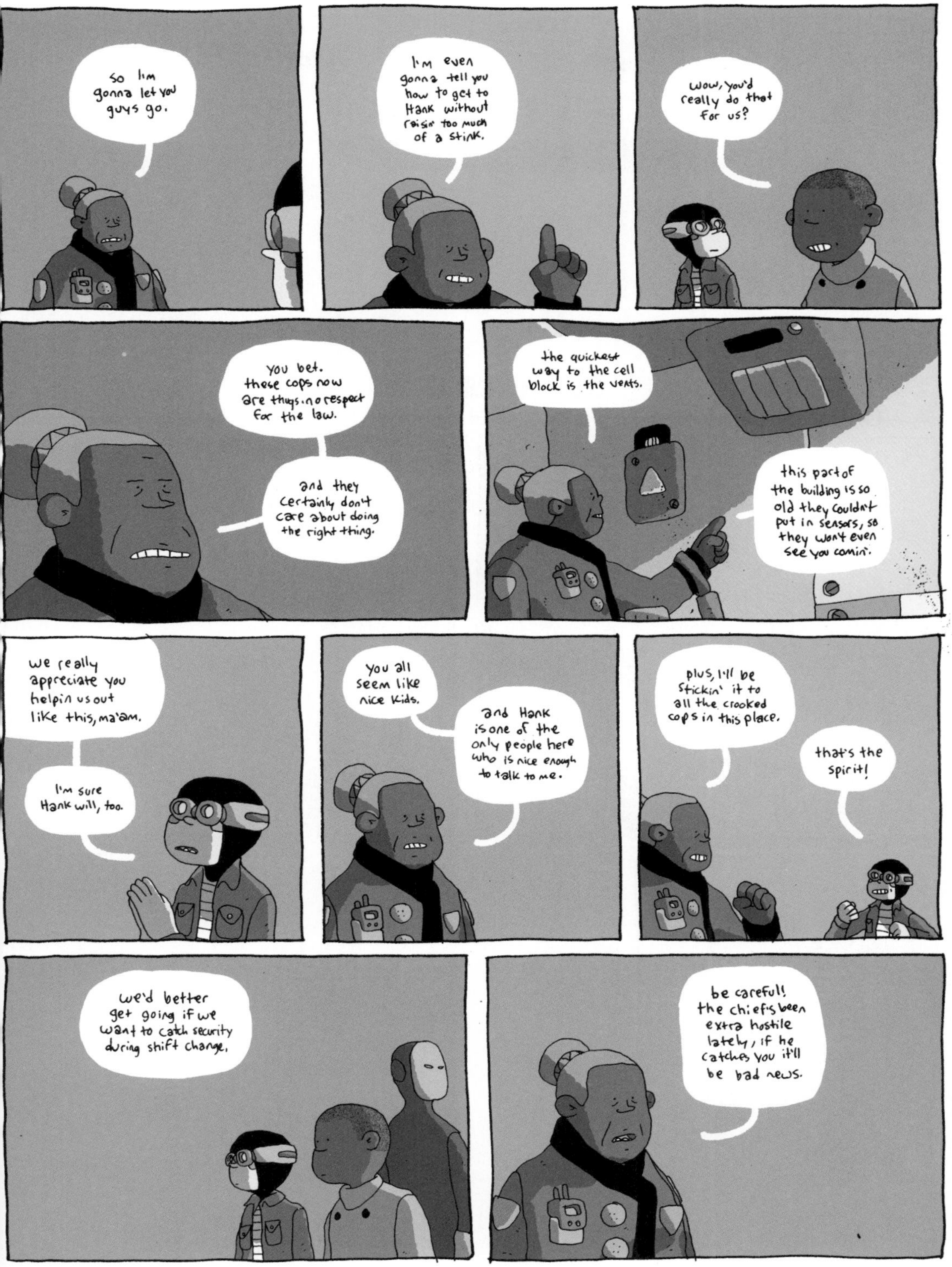
so I'm gonna let you guys go.
I'm even gonna tell you how to get to Hank without raisin' too much of a stink.
wow, you'd really do that for us?
you bet. these cops now are thugs. no respect for the law.
and they certainly don't care about doing the right thing.
the quickest way to the cell block is the vents.
this part of the building is so old they couldn't put in sensors, so they won't even see you comin'.
we really appreciate you helpin us out like this, ma'am.
I'm sure Hank will, too.
you all seem like nice kids.
and Hank is one of the only people here who is nice enough to talk to me.
plus, I'll be stickin' it to all the crooked cops in this place.
that's the spirit!
we'd better get going if we want to catch security during shift change.
be careful! the chief's been extra hostile lately, if he catches you it'll be bad news.

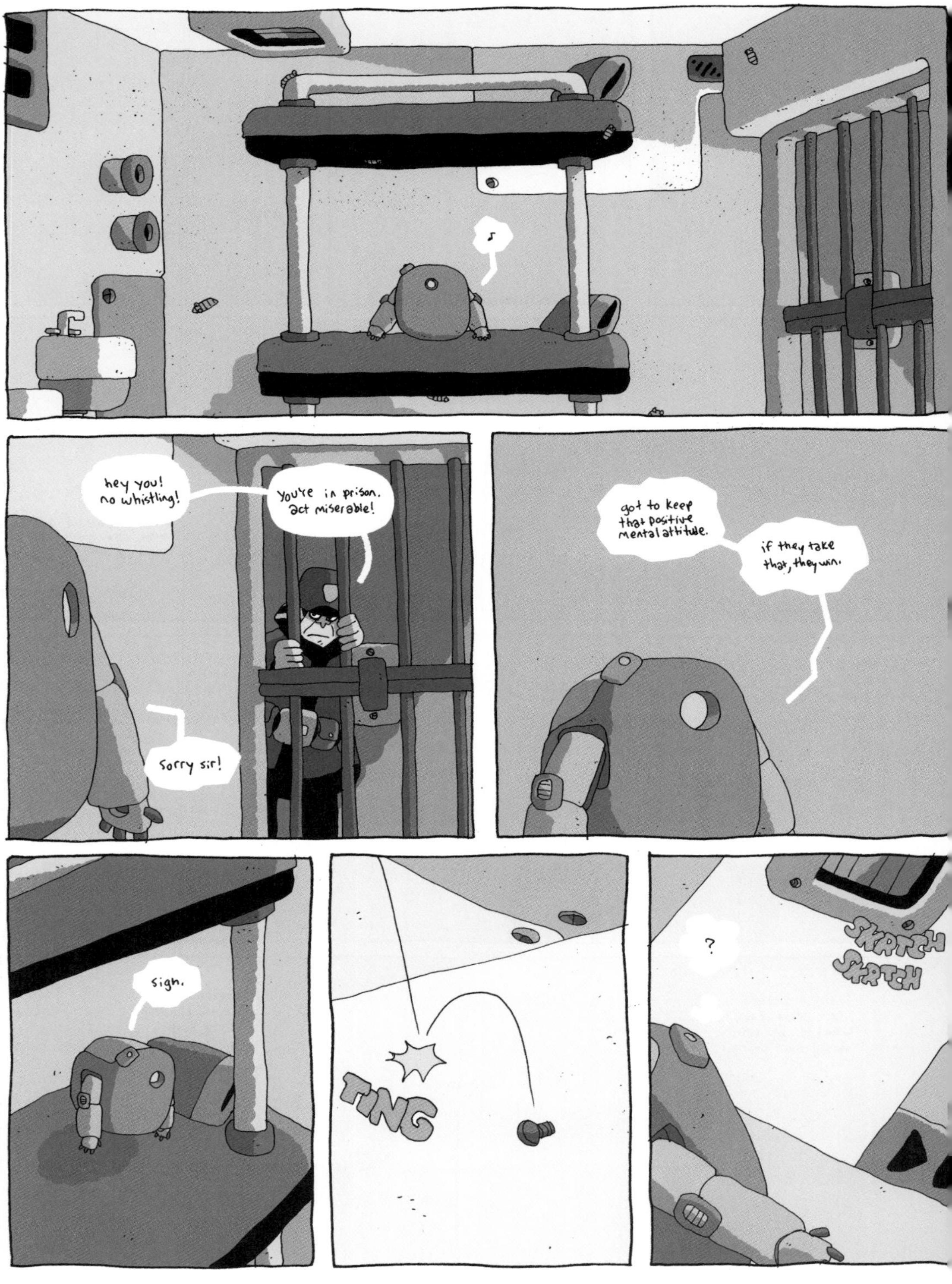

hey you! no whistling!
You're in prison. act miserable!
sorry sir!
got to keep that positive mental attitude.
if they take that, they win.
sigh.
TING
?
SKRTCH
SKRTCH

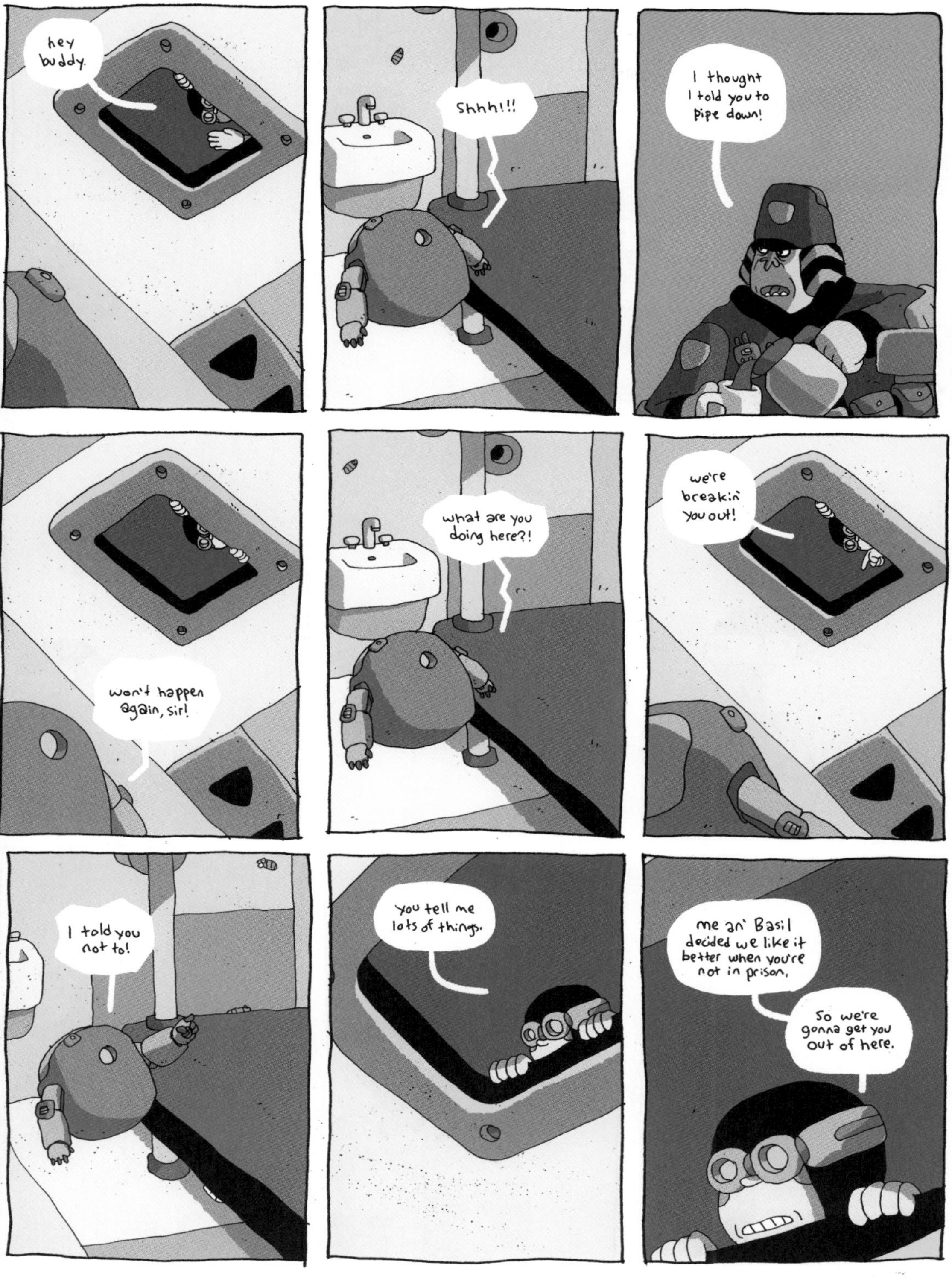
hey buddy.
Shhh!!!
I thought I told you to pipe down!
won't happen again, sir!
what are you doing here?!
we're breakin' you out!
I told you not to!
you tell me lots of things.
me an' Basil decided we like it better when you're not in prison.
So we're gonna get you out of here.

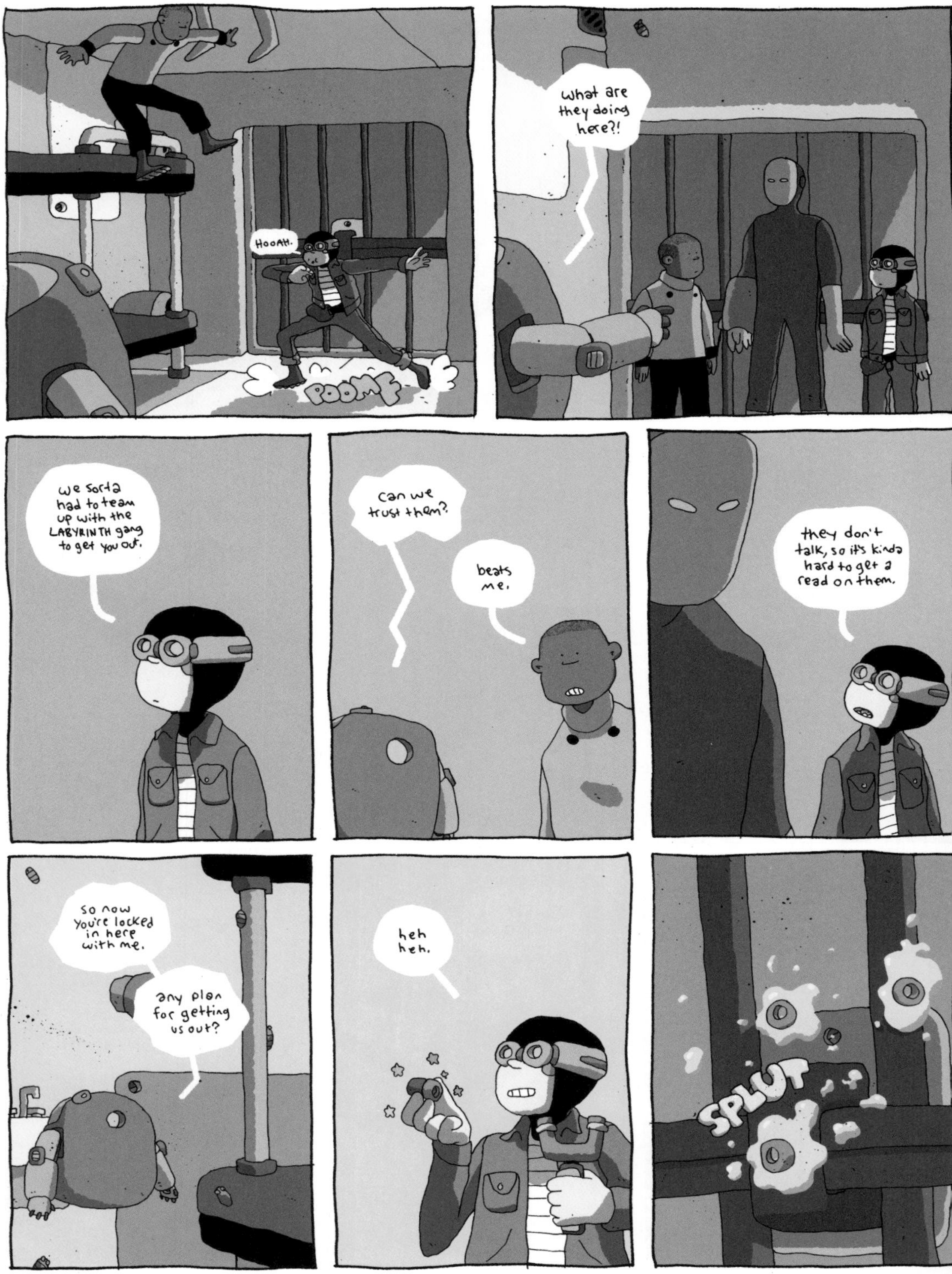
HOOAH.
POOMF
what are they doing here?!
we sorta had to team up with the LABYRINTH gang to get you out.
can we trust them?
beats me.
they don't talk, so it's kinda hard to get a read on them.
so now you're locked in here with me.
any plan for getting us out?
heh heh.
SPLUT

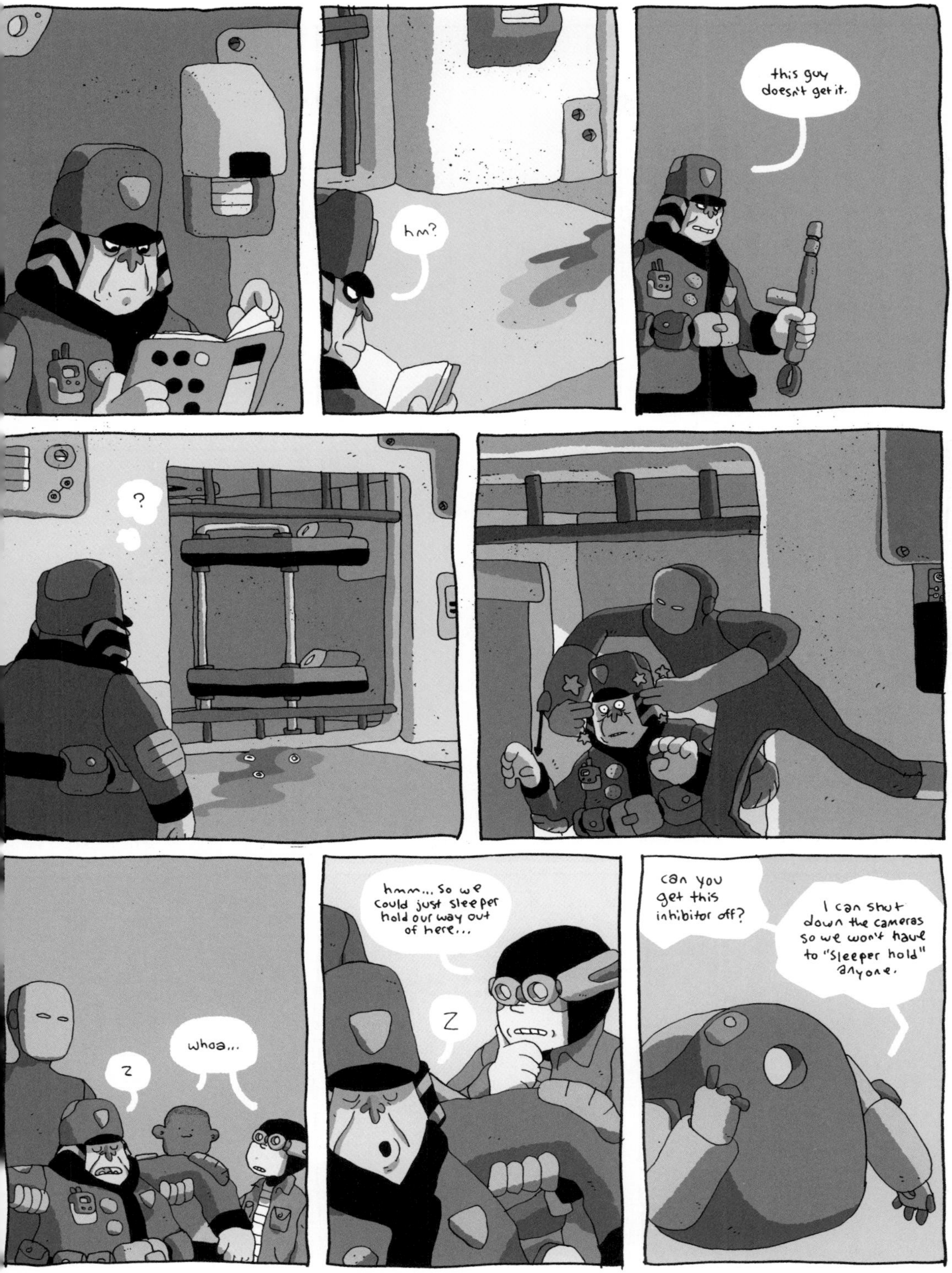
hm?
this guy doesn't get it.
?
whoa...
z
hmm... so we could just sleeper hold our way out of here...
Z
can you get this inhibitor off?
I can shut down the cameras so we won't have to "sleeper hold" anyone.

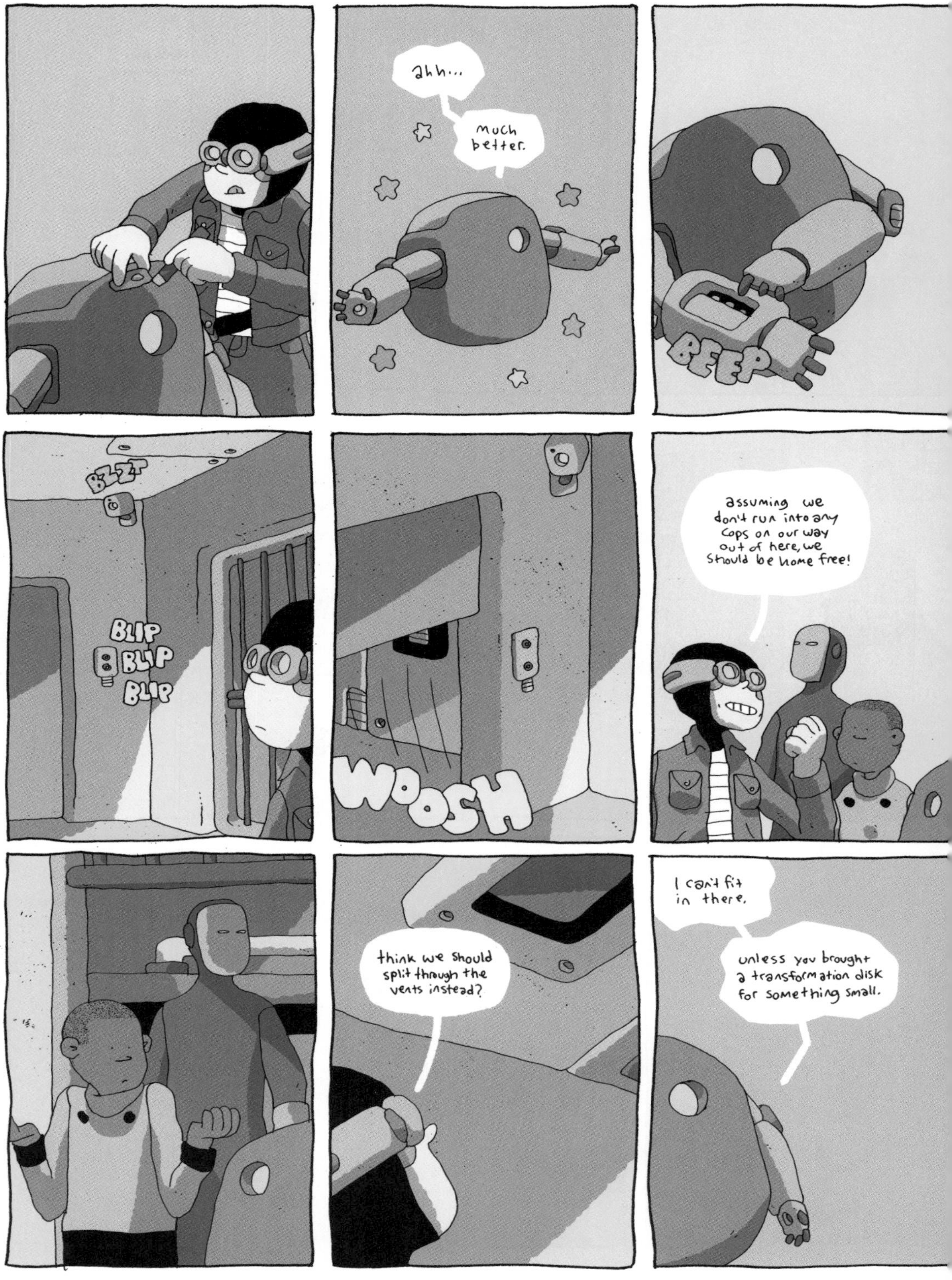
ahh...
much better.
BEEP
BZZT
BLIP
BLIP
BLIP
WOOSH
assuming we don't run into any cops on our way out of here, we should be home free!
think we should split through the vents instead?
I can't fit in there.
unless you brought a transformation disk for something small.

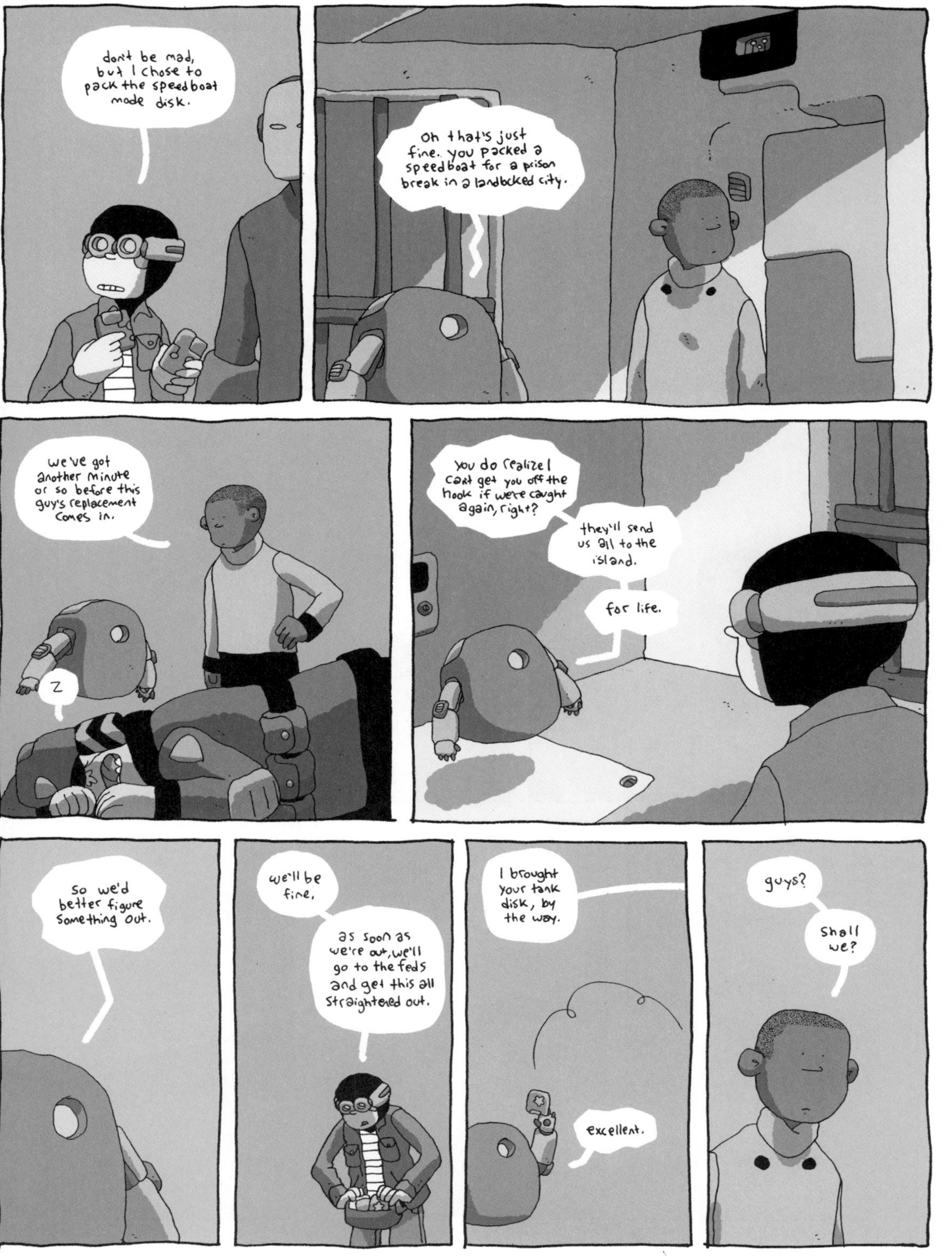
don't be mad, but I chose to pack the speedboat mode disk.
Oh that's just fine. you packed a speedboat for a prison break in a landlocked city.
we've got another minute or so before this guy's replacement comes in.
Z
you do realize I can't get you off the hook if we're caught again, right?
they'll send us all to the island.
for life.
so we'd better figure something out.
we'll be fine.
as soon as we're out, we'll go to the feds and get this all straightened out.
I brought your tank disk, by the way.
excellent.
guys?
shall we?

several minutes later...

get this door open, Hank!

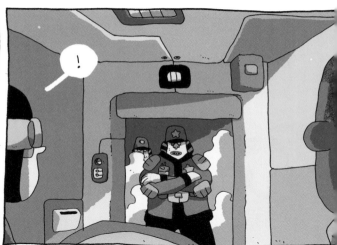

!

Well, well, well.

look what we got here.

a couple of punk kids,

a robot,

and some weirdo wearing tights.

hey man, these are the only pants that fit.

everything else looks like clown pants on me.

oh, he meant you.

heh heh.

kid, you better shut your mouth.

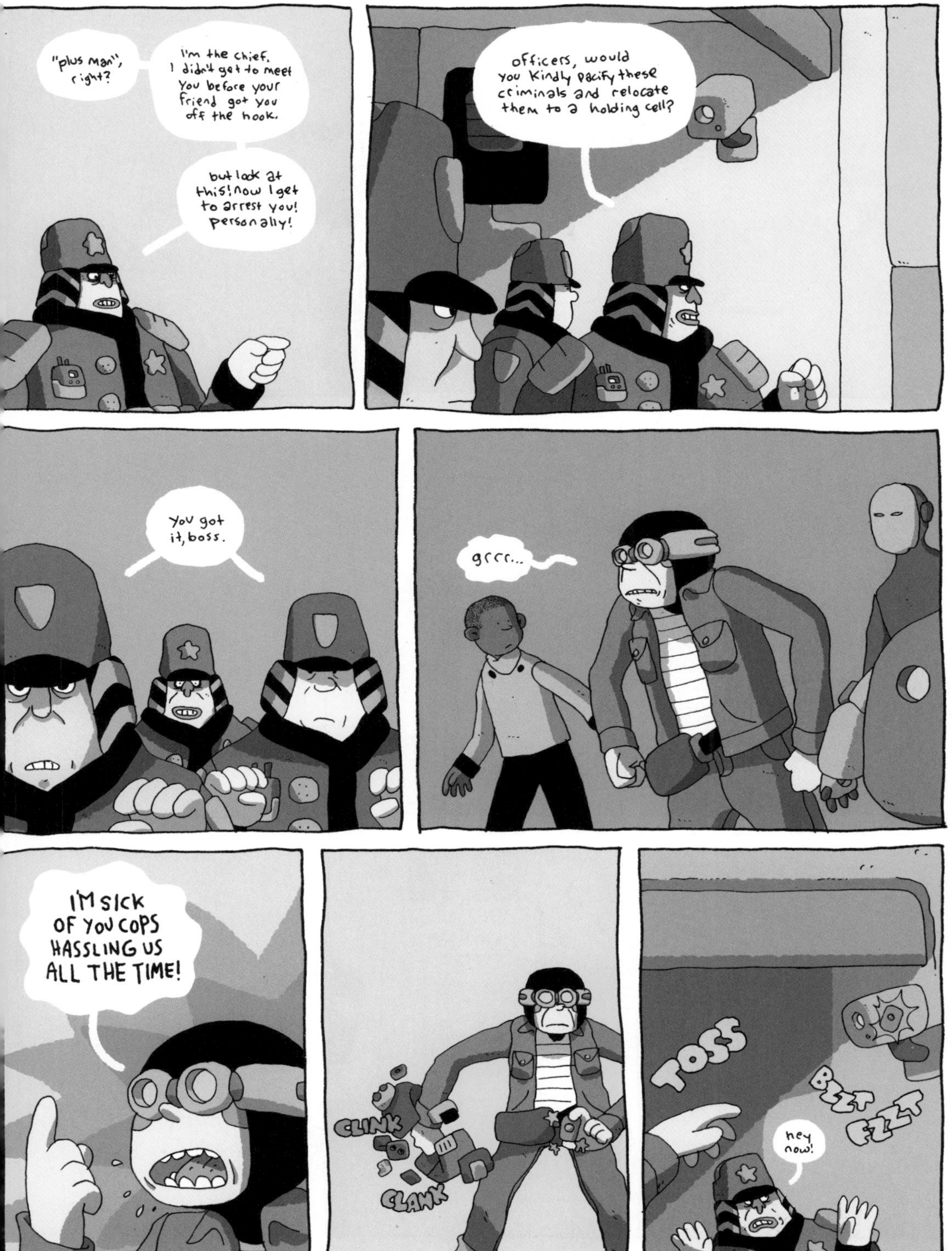
"plus man", right?
i'm the chief. I didn't get to meet you before your friend got you off the hook.
but look at this! now I get to arrest you! personally!
officers, would you kindly pacify these criminals and relocate them to a holding cell?
you got it, boss.
grrr...
I'M SICK OF YOU COPS HASSLING US ALL THE TIME!
CLINK
CLANK
TOSS
BZZT
FZZT
hey now!

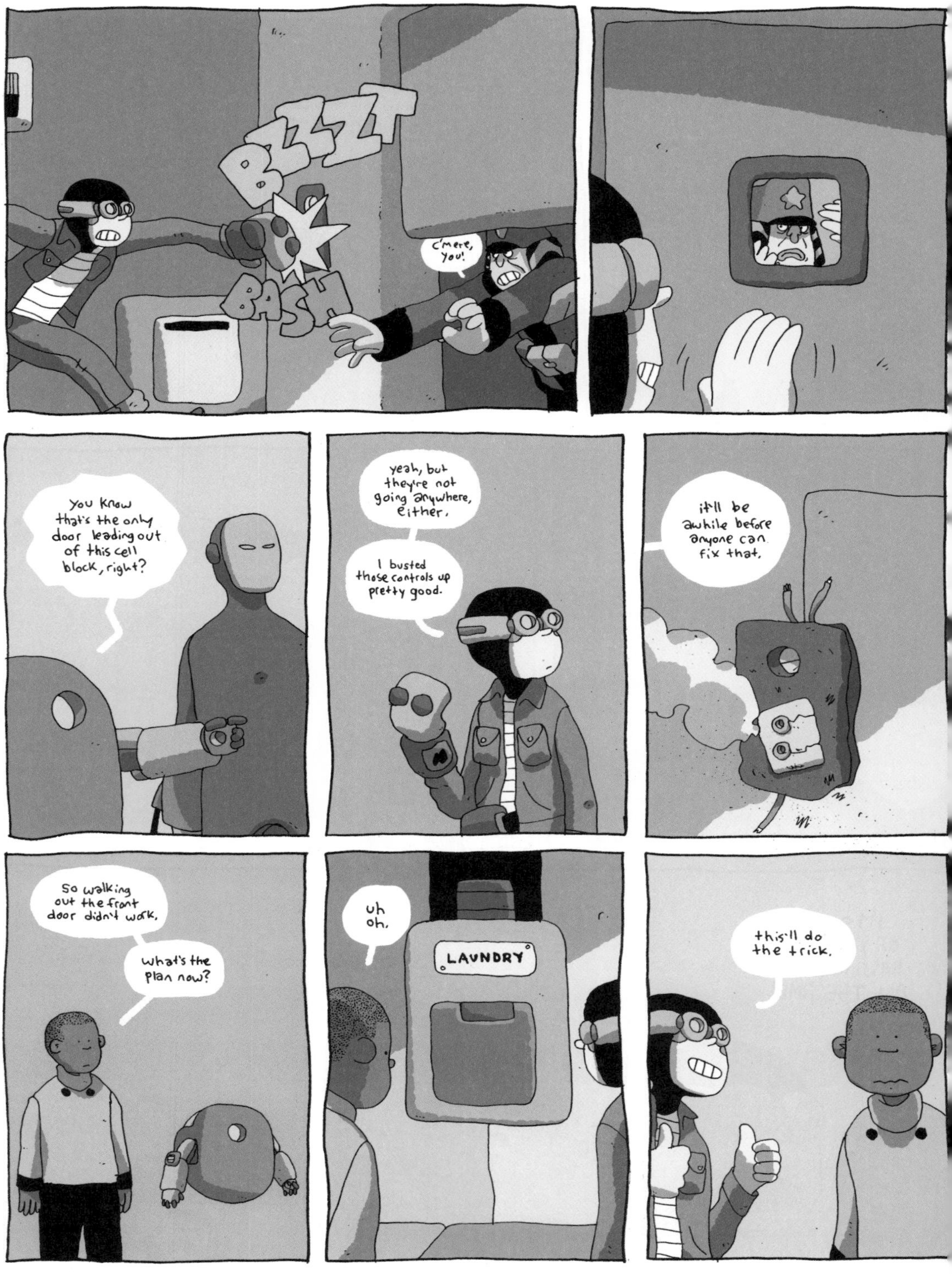

BZZZT
BASH
c'mere, you!
you know that's the only door leading out of this cell block, right?
yeah, but they're not going anywhere, either.
I busted those controls up pretty good.
it'll be awhile before anyone can fix that.
so walking out the front door didn't work.
what's the plan now?
uh oh.
LAUNDRY
this'll do the trick.

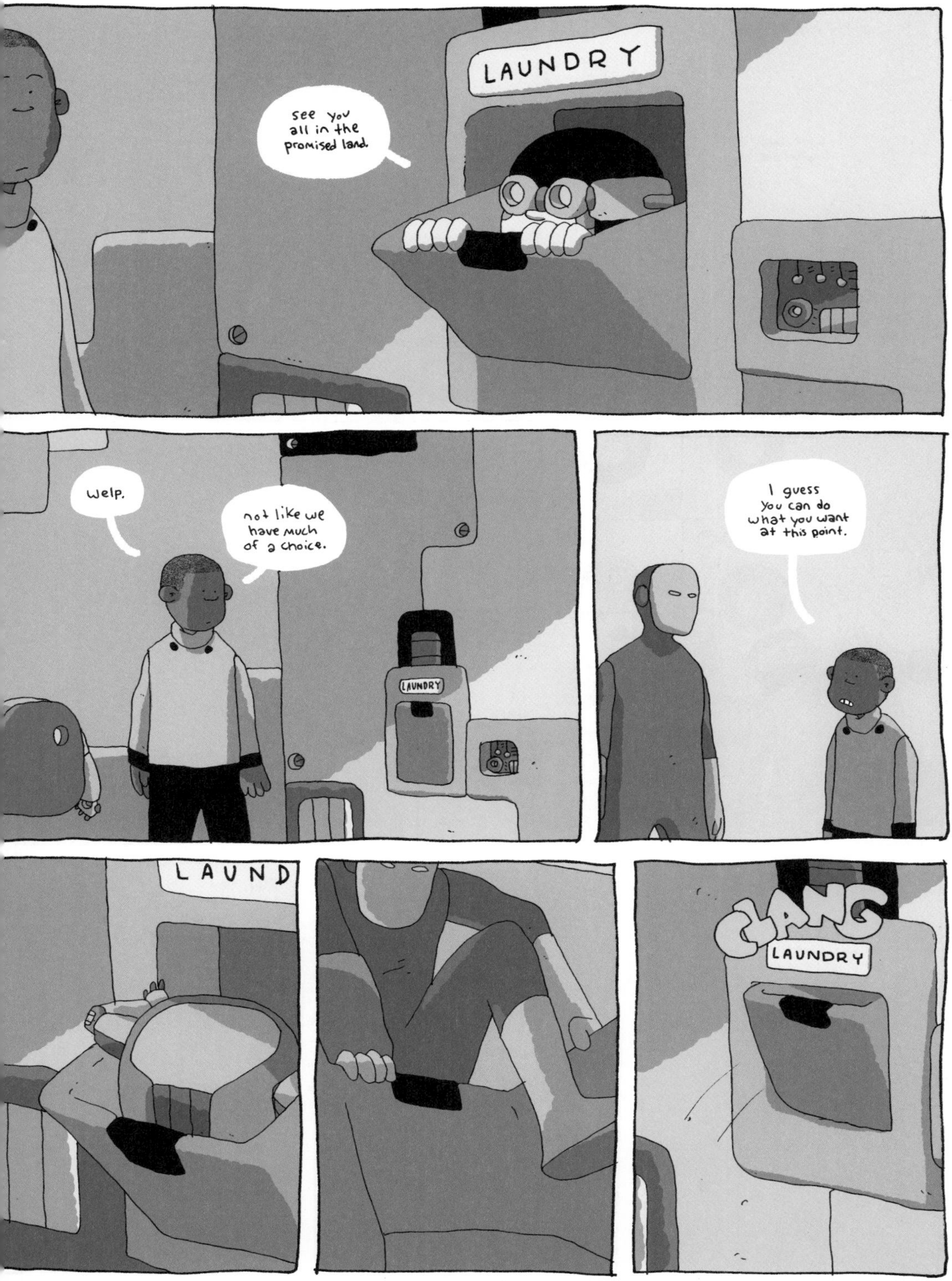
LAUNDRY
see you all in the promised land.
welp.
not like we have much of a choice.
LAUNDRY
I guess you can do what you want at this point.
LAUND
CLANG
LAUNDRY

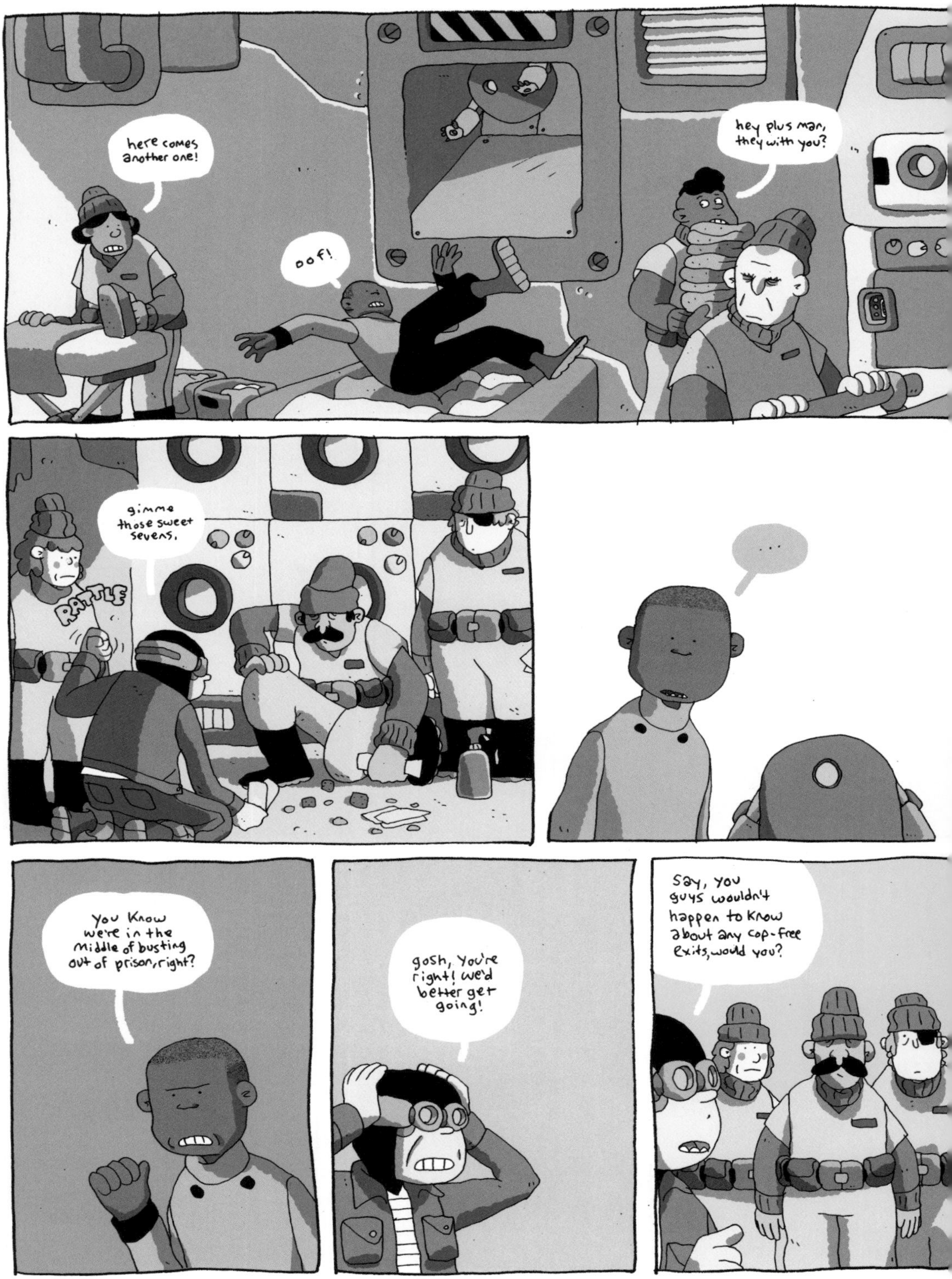
here comes another one!
oof!
hey plus man, they with you?
gimme those sweet sevens,
RATTLE
...
You Know we're in the middle of busting out of prison, right?
gosh, You're right! we'd better get going!
Say, you guys wouldn't happen to Know about any cop-free exits, would you?

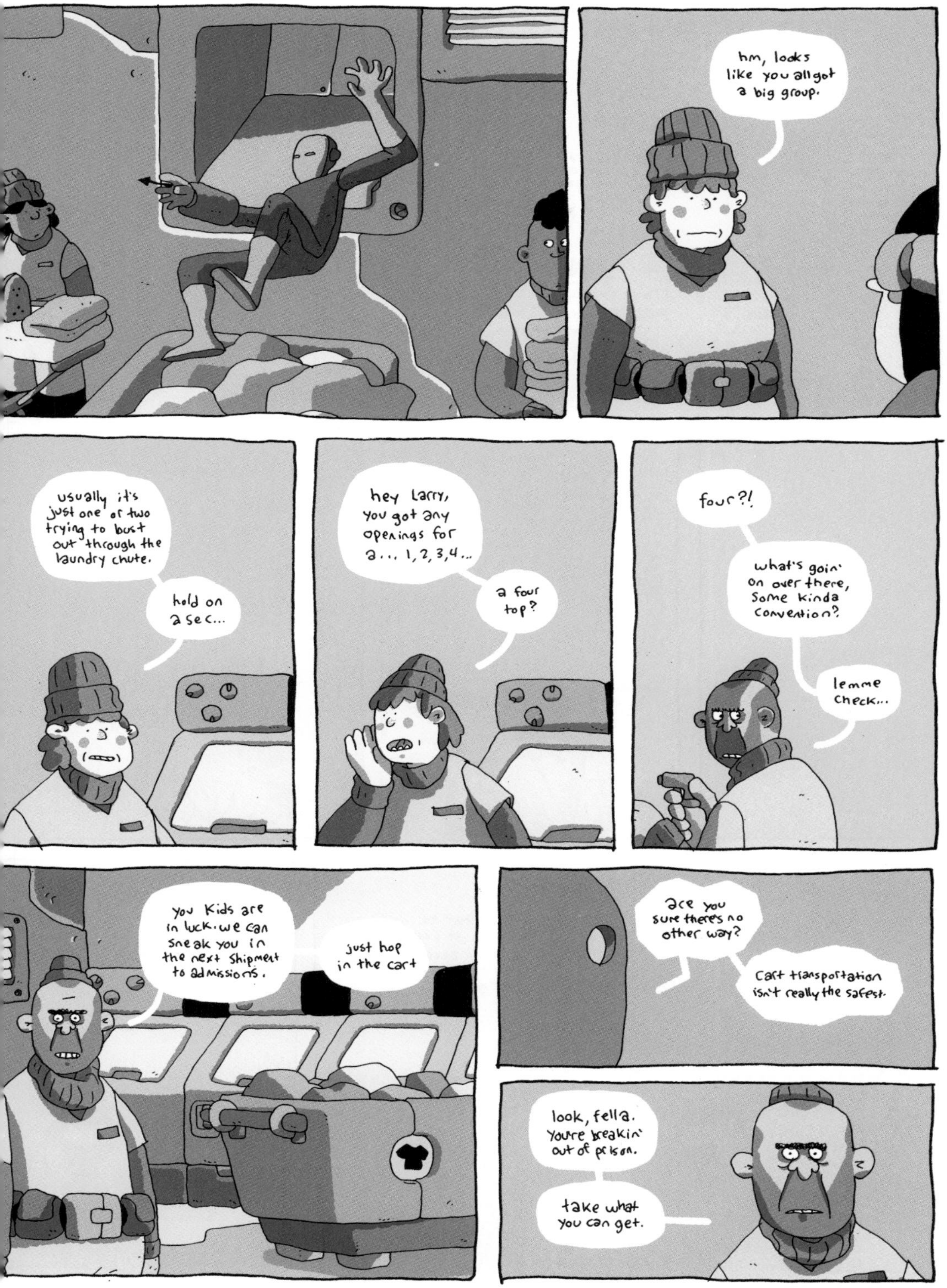
hm, looks like you all got a big group.
usually it's just one or two trying to bust out through the laundry chute.
hold on a sec...
hey Larry, you got any openings for a... 1, 2, 3, 4...
a four top?
four?!
what's goin' on over there, some kinda convention?
lemme check...
you kids are in luck. we can sneak you in the next shipment to admissions.
just hop in the cart
are you sure there's no other way?
cart transportation isn't really the safest.
look, fella. You're breakin' out of prison.
take what you can get.

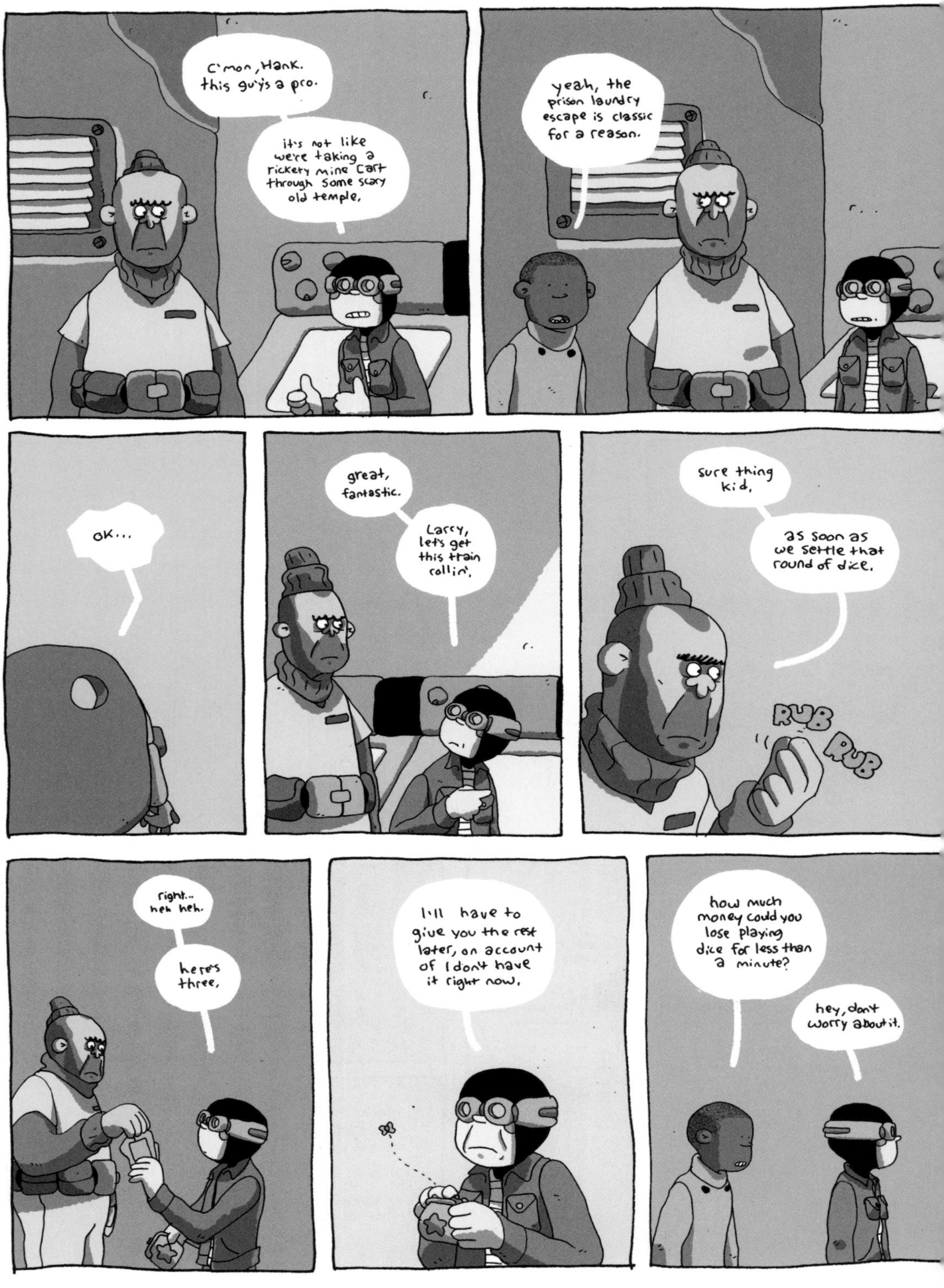
C'mon, Hank. this guy's a pro.
it's not like we're taking a rickety mine cart through some scary old temple.
yeah, the prison laundry escape is classic for a reason.
ok...
great, fantastic.
Larry, let's get this train rollin'.
sure thing kid,
as soon as we settle that round of dice.
RUB RUB
right... heh heh.
here's three,
I'll have to give you the rest later, on account of I don't have it right now.
how much money could you lose playing dice for less than a minute?
hey, don't worry about it.

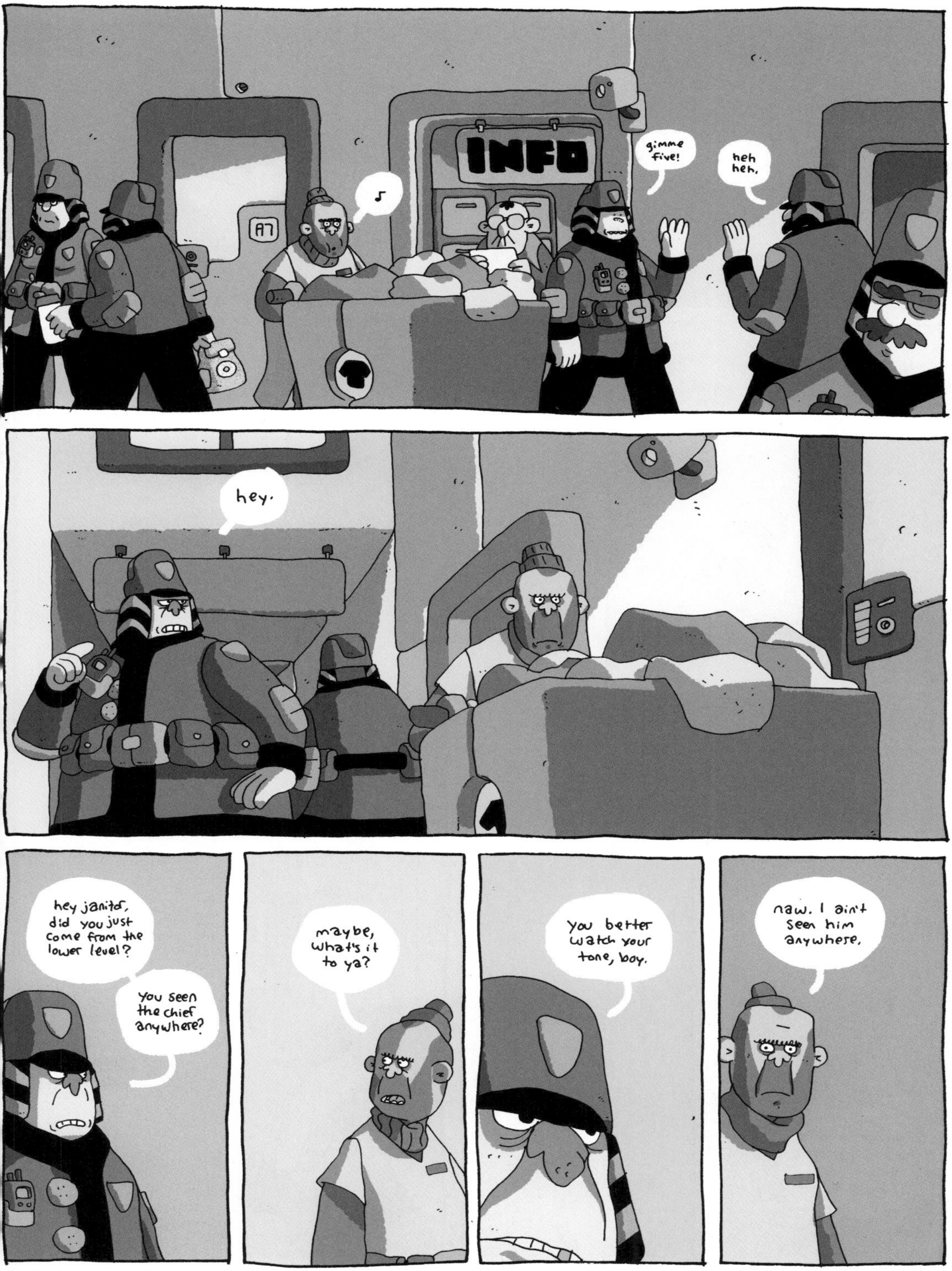
♪
INFO
A7
gimme five!
heh heh.
hey.
hey janitor, did you just come from the lower level?
you seen the chief anywhere?
maybe, what's it to ya?
you better watch your tone, boy.
naw. I ain't seen him anywhere.

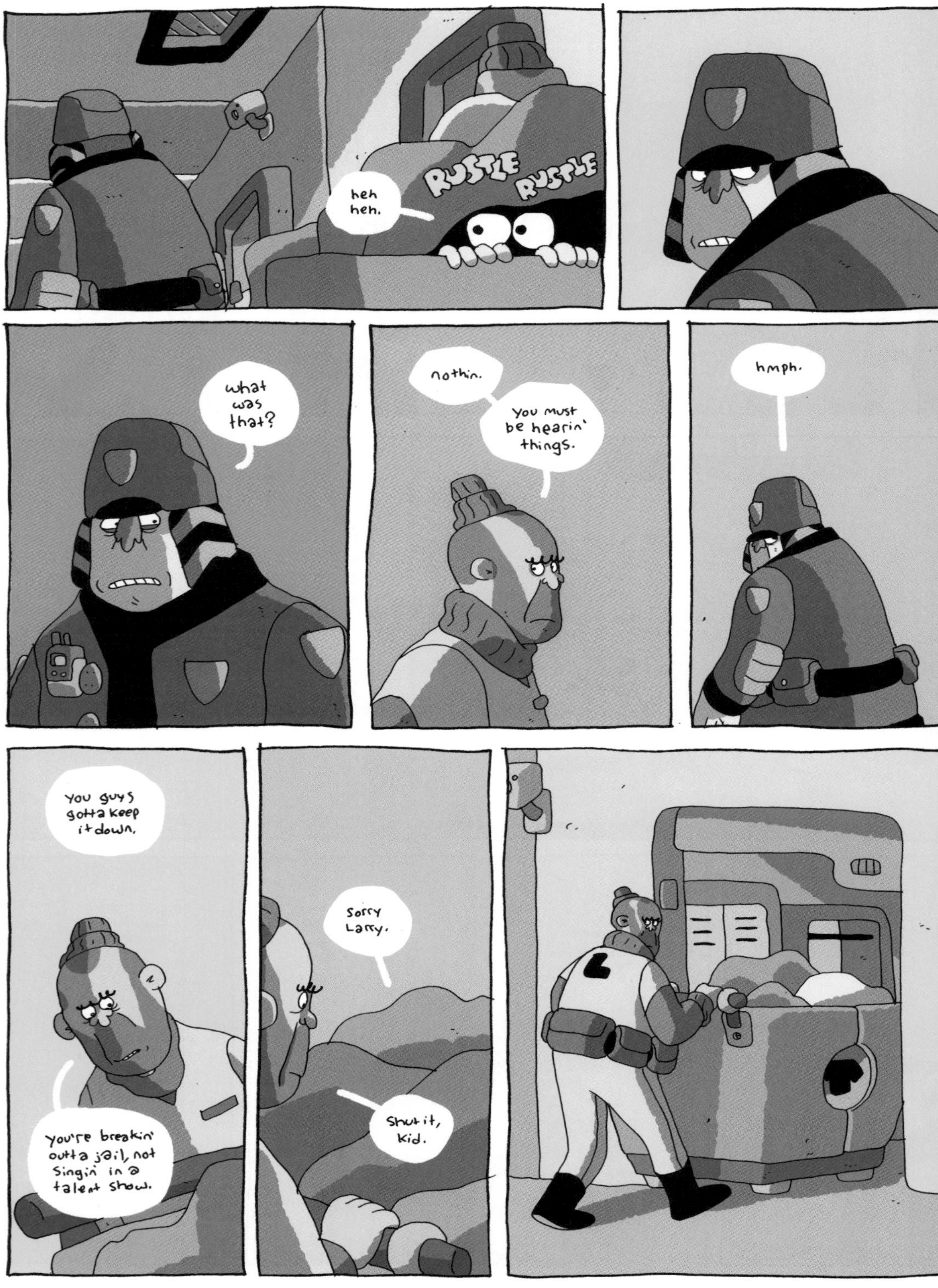

heh heh.
RUSTLE RUSTLE
what was that?
nothin.
You must be hearin' things.
hmph.
You guys gotta keep it down.
You're breakin' outta jail, not singin' in a talent show.
Sorry Larry.
Shut it, kid.

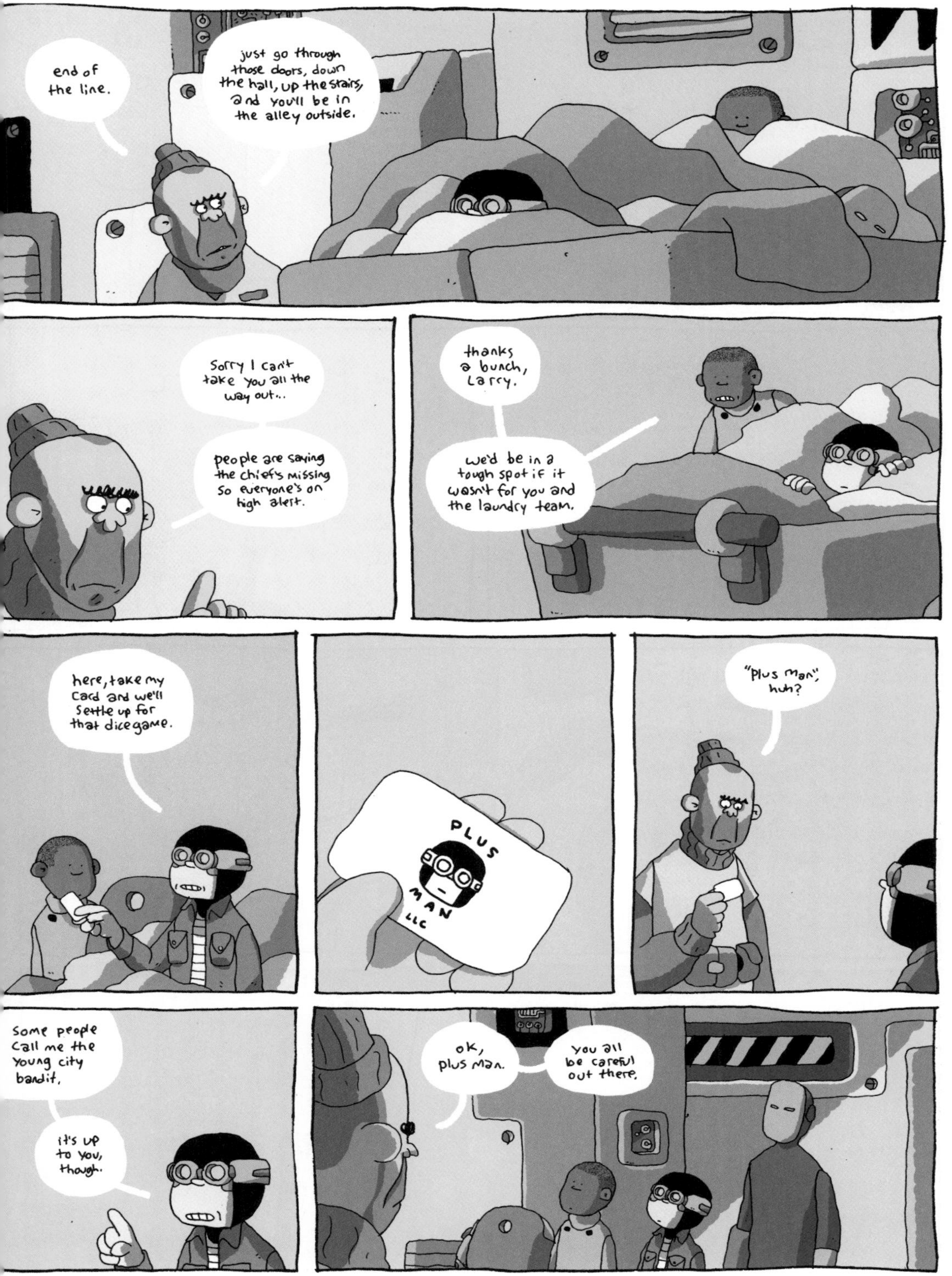
end of the line.
just go through those doors, down the hall, up the stairs, and you'll be in the alley outside.
Sorry I can't take you all the way out..
people are saying the chief's missing so everyone's on high alert.
thanks a bunch, Larry.
we'd be in a tough spot if it wasn't for you and the laundry team.
here, take my card and we'll settle up for that dicegame.
PLUS MAN LLC
"plus man", huh?
Some people call me the young city bandit,
it's up to you, though.
ok, plus man.
you all be careful out there.

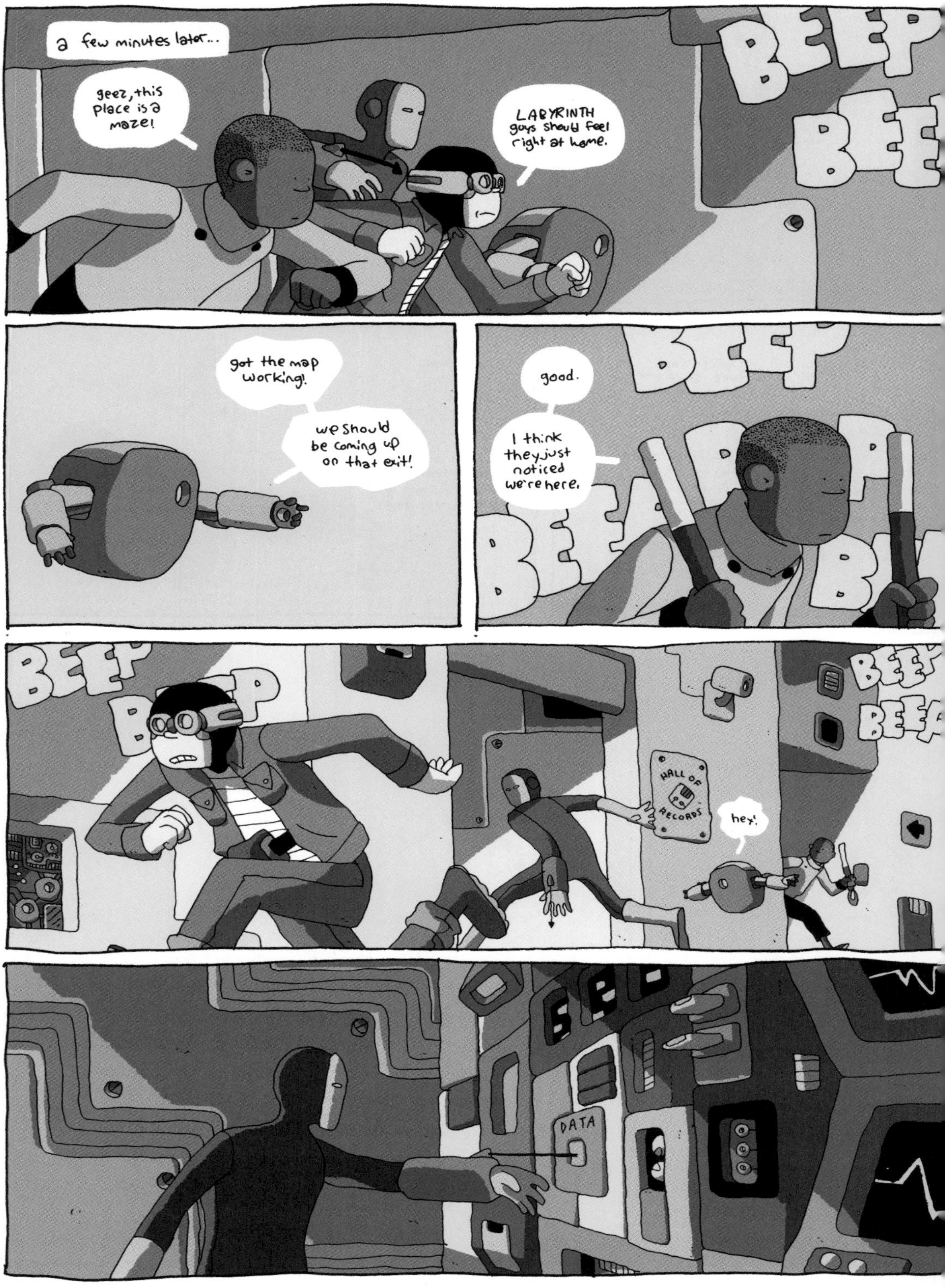
a few minutes later...
BEEP
BEEP
geez, this place is a maze!
LABYRINTH guys should feel right at home.
got the map working!
we should be coming up on that exit!
BEEP
good.
I think they just noticed we're here.
BEEP
BEEP
BEEP
BEEP
HALL OF RECORDS
hey!
DATA

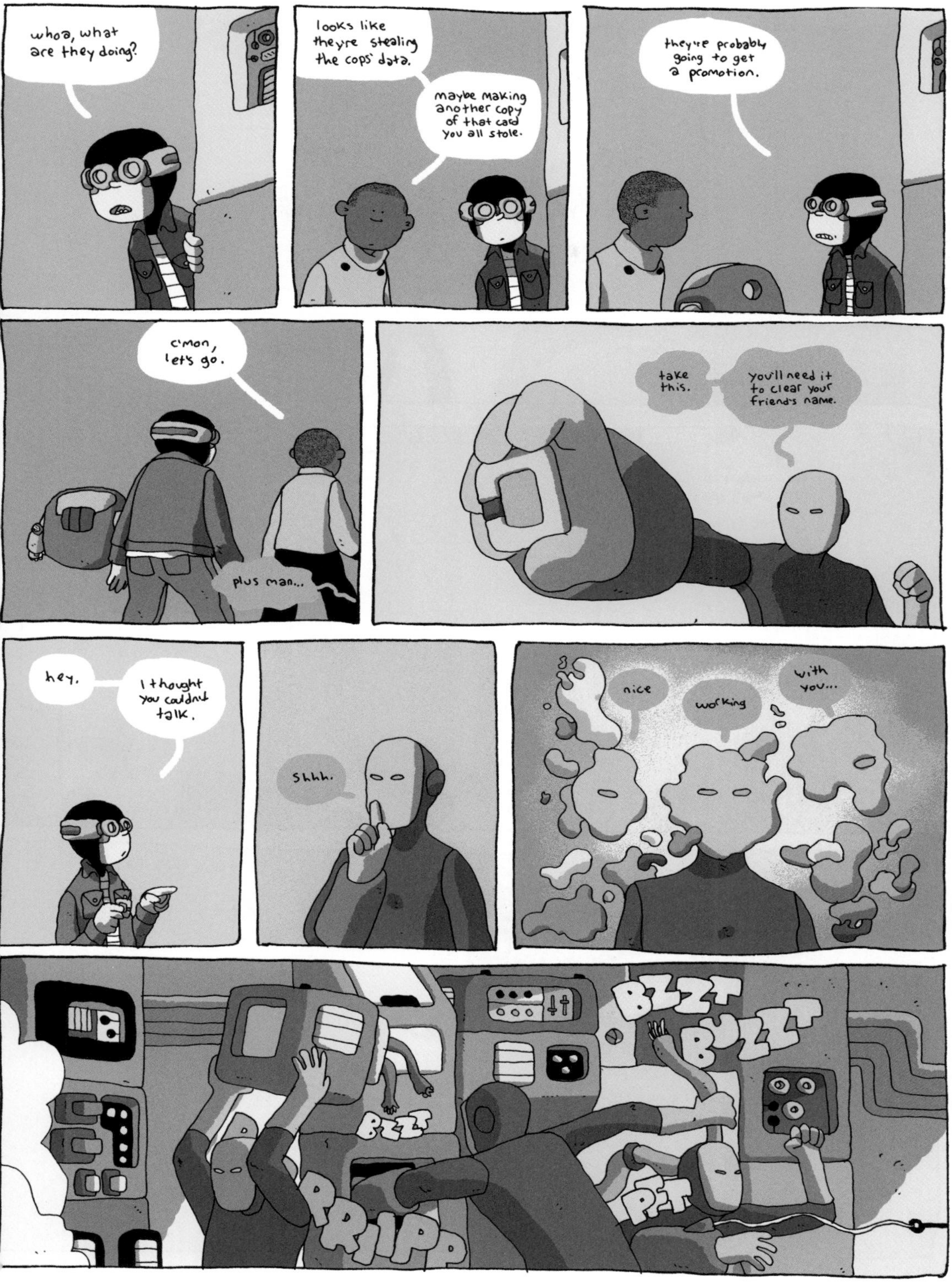
whoa, what are they doing?
looks like they're stealing the cops' data.
maybe making another copy of that card you all stole.
they're probably going to get a promotion.
c'mon, let's go.
plus man...
take this.
you'll need it to clear your friend's name.
hey.
I thought you couldn't talk.
shhh.
nice
working
with you...
BZZT
BUZZT
BZZT
PT
PRRIPP

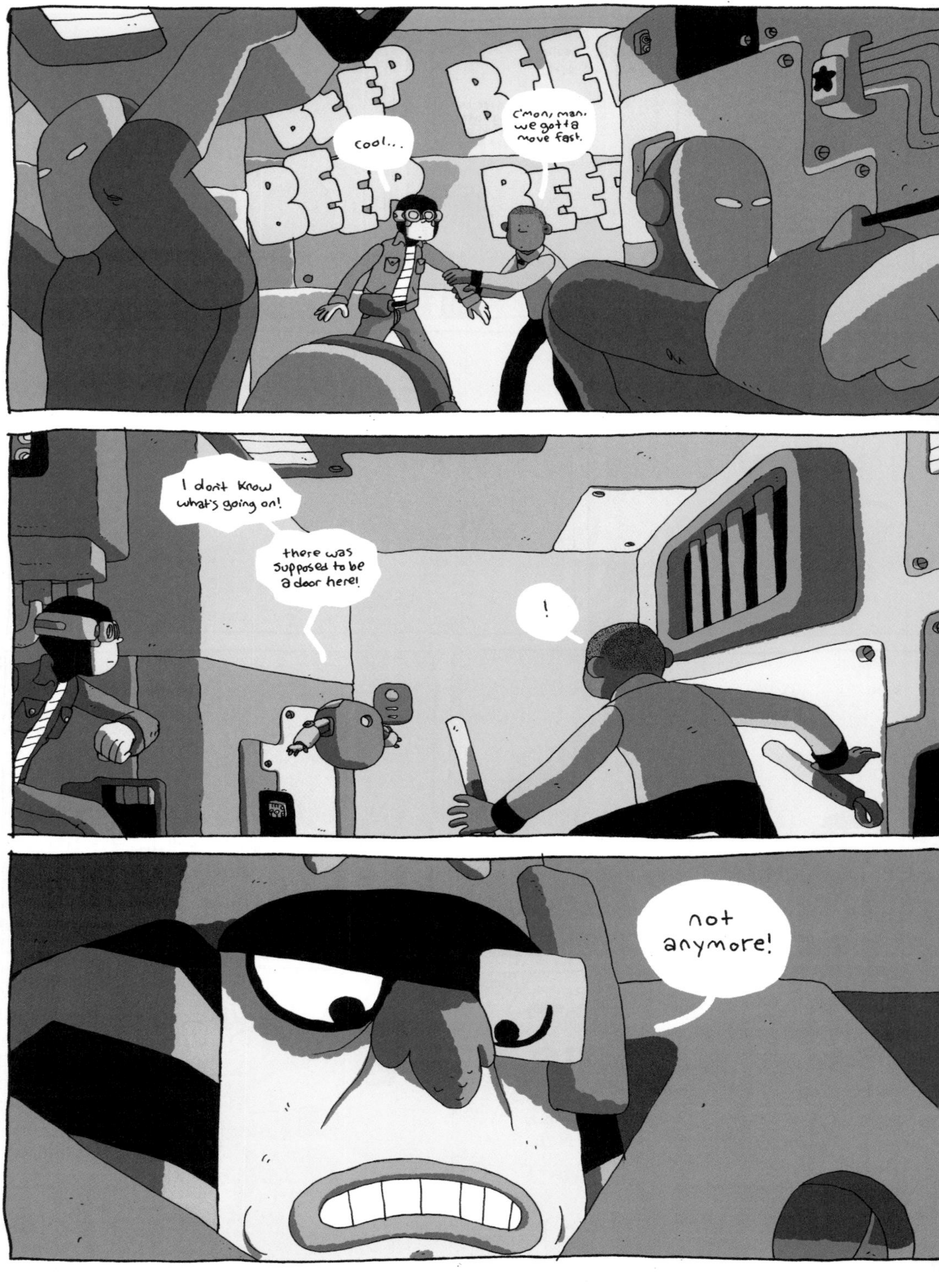
BEEP
cool...
c'mon, man, we gotta move fast.
I don't know what's going on!
there was supposed to be a door here!
!
not anymore!

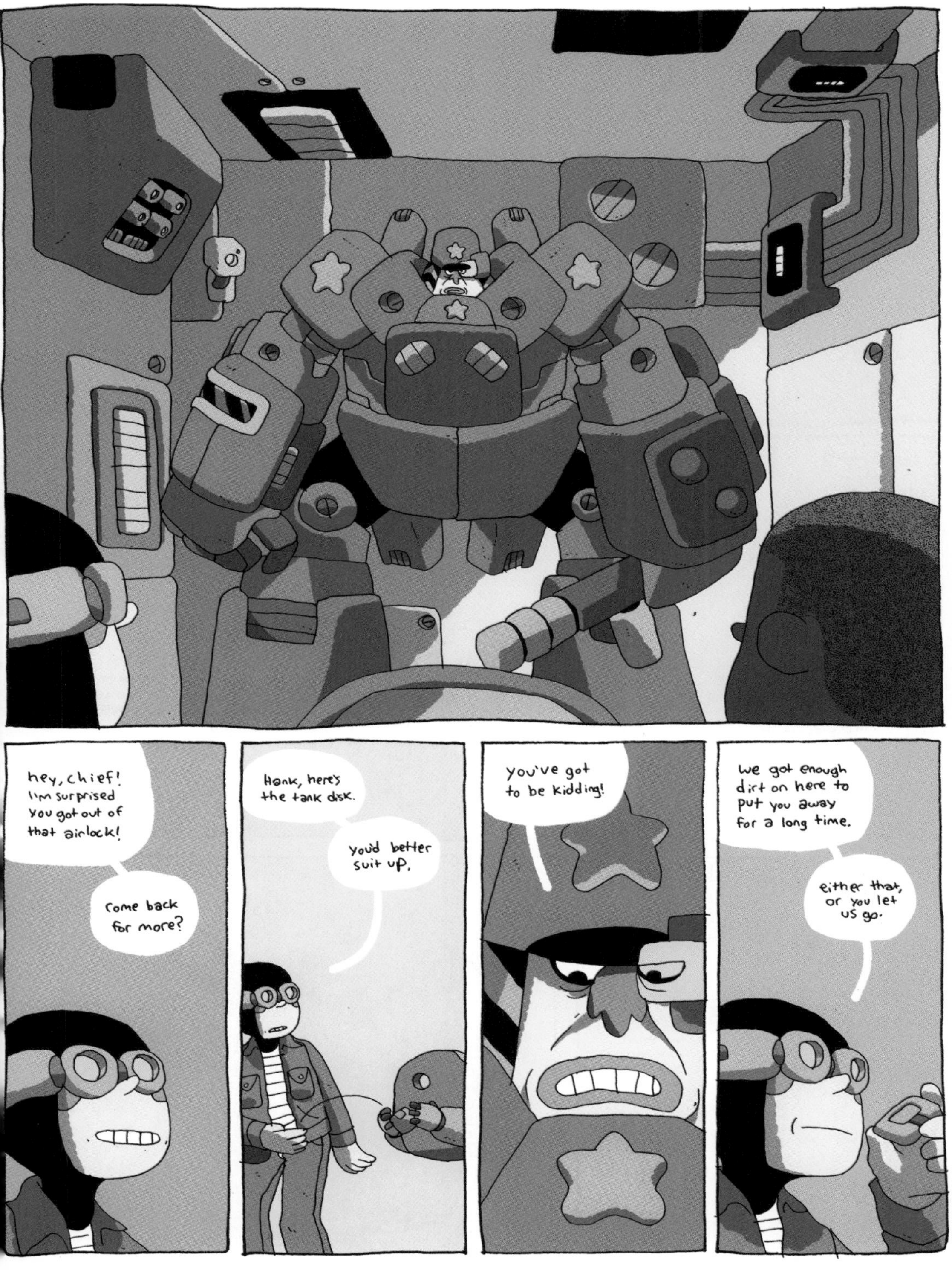
hey, chief! i'm surprised you got out of that airlock!
come back for more?
Hank, here's the tank disk.
you'd better suit up.
you've got to be kidding!
we got enough dirt on here to put you away for a long time.
either that, or you let us go.

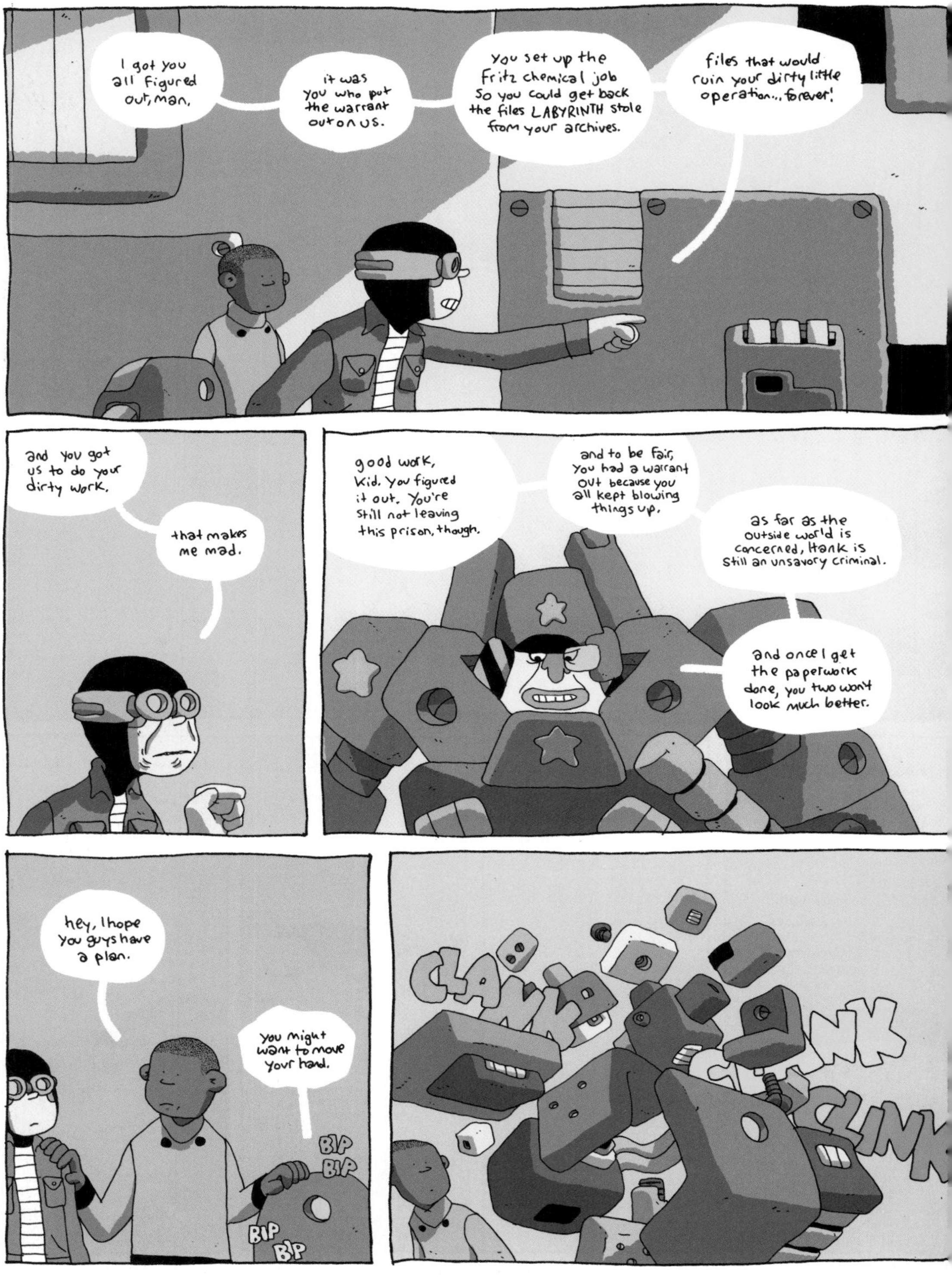
I got you all figured out, man.
it was you who put the warrant out on us.
you set up the Fritz chemical job so you could get back the files LABYRINTH stole from your archives.
files that would ruin your dirty little operation... forever!
and you got us to do your dirty work.
that makes me mad.
good work, kid. You figured it out. You're still not leaving this prison, though.
and to be fair, you had a warrant out because you all kept blowing things up.
as far as the outside world is concerned, Hank is still an unsavory criminal.
and once I get the paperwork done, you two won't look much better.
hey, I hope you guys have a plan.
you might want to move your hand.
BIP
BIP
BIP
BIP
CLANK
CLANK
CLINK

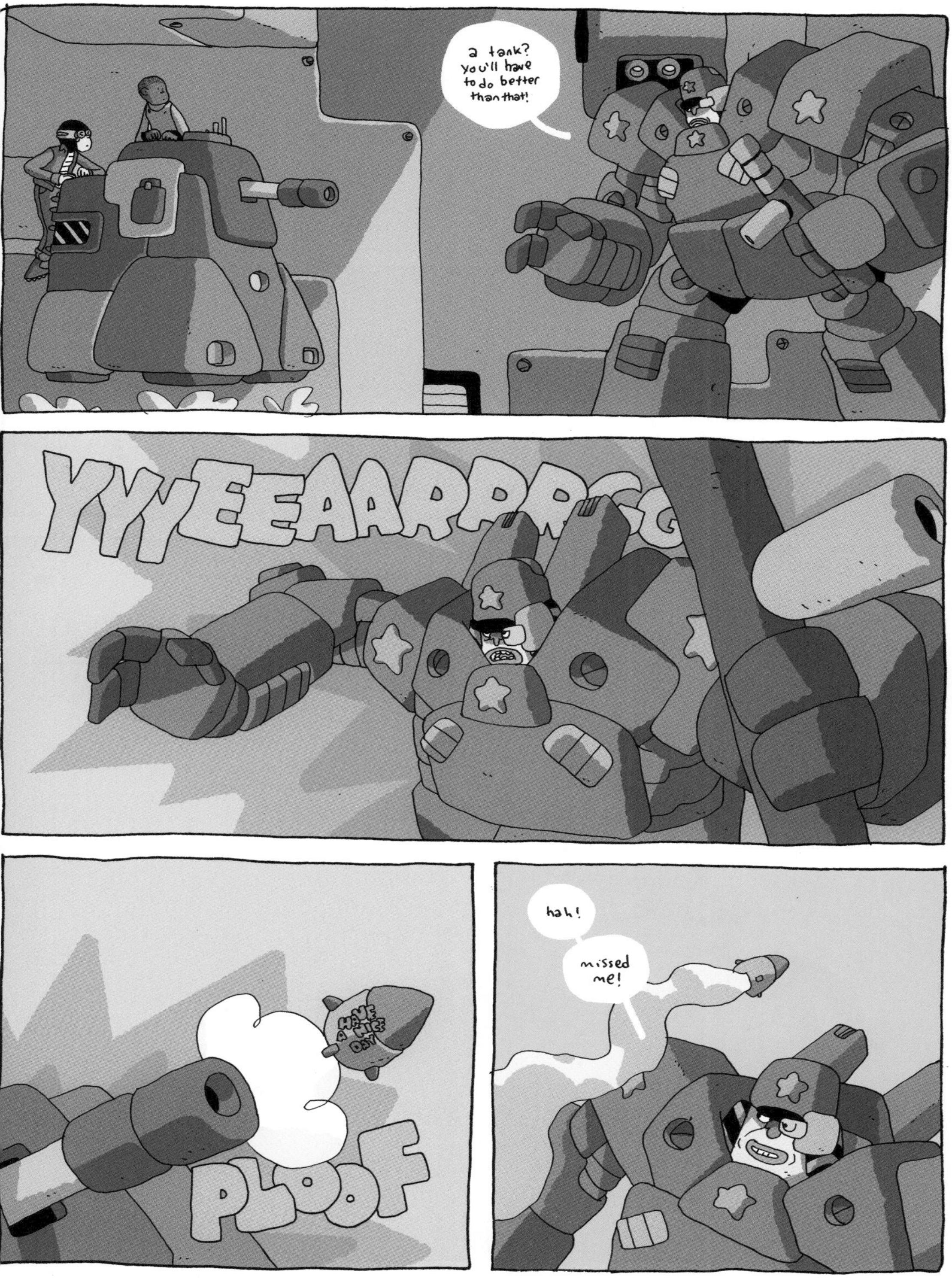
a tank? you'll have to do better than that!
YYYEEAARRRG
HAVE A NICE DAY
PLOOF
hah!
missed me!

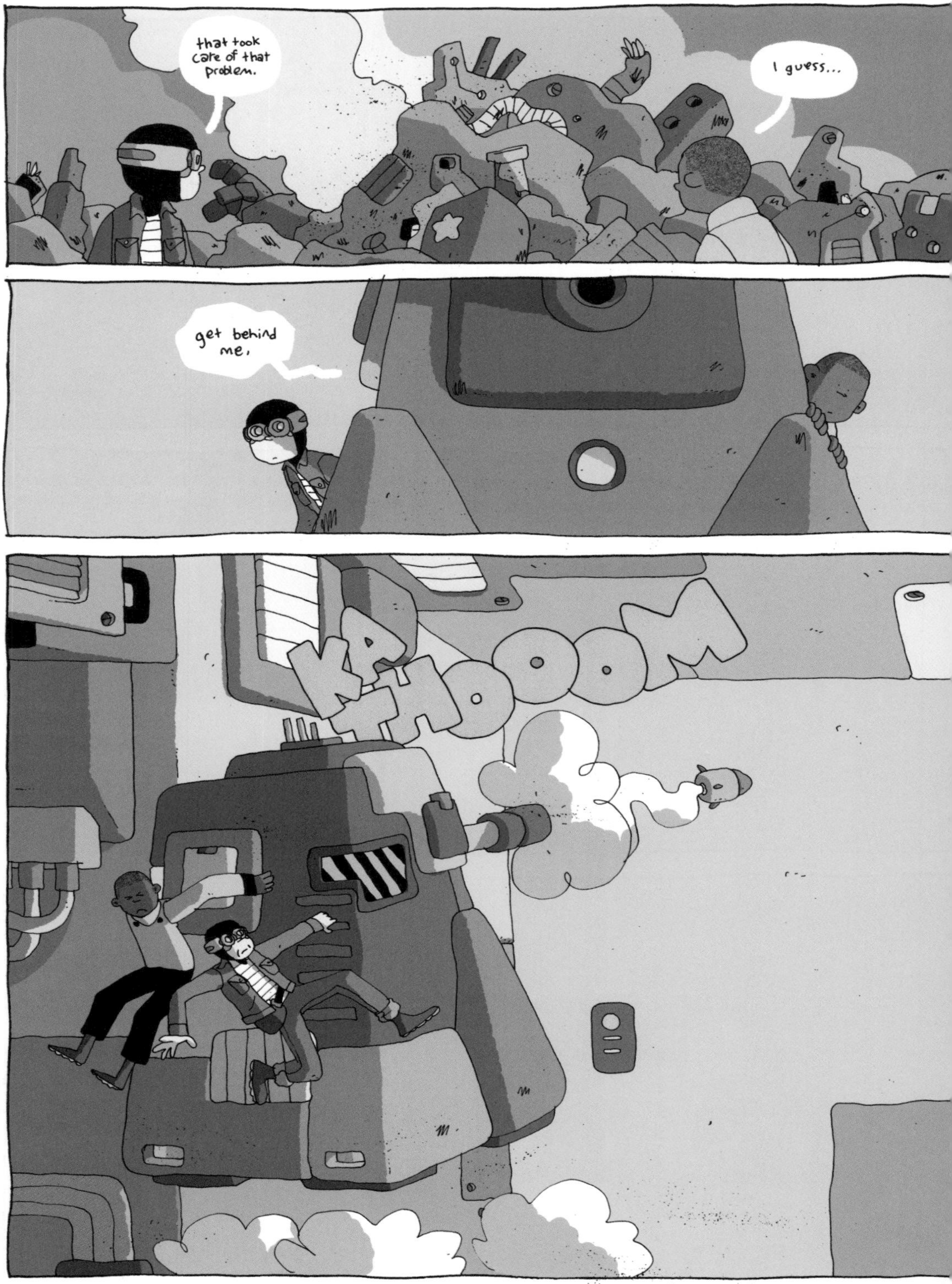
that took care of that problem.
I guess...
get behind me,
KA THOOOM

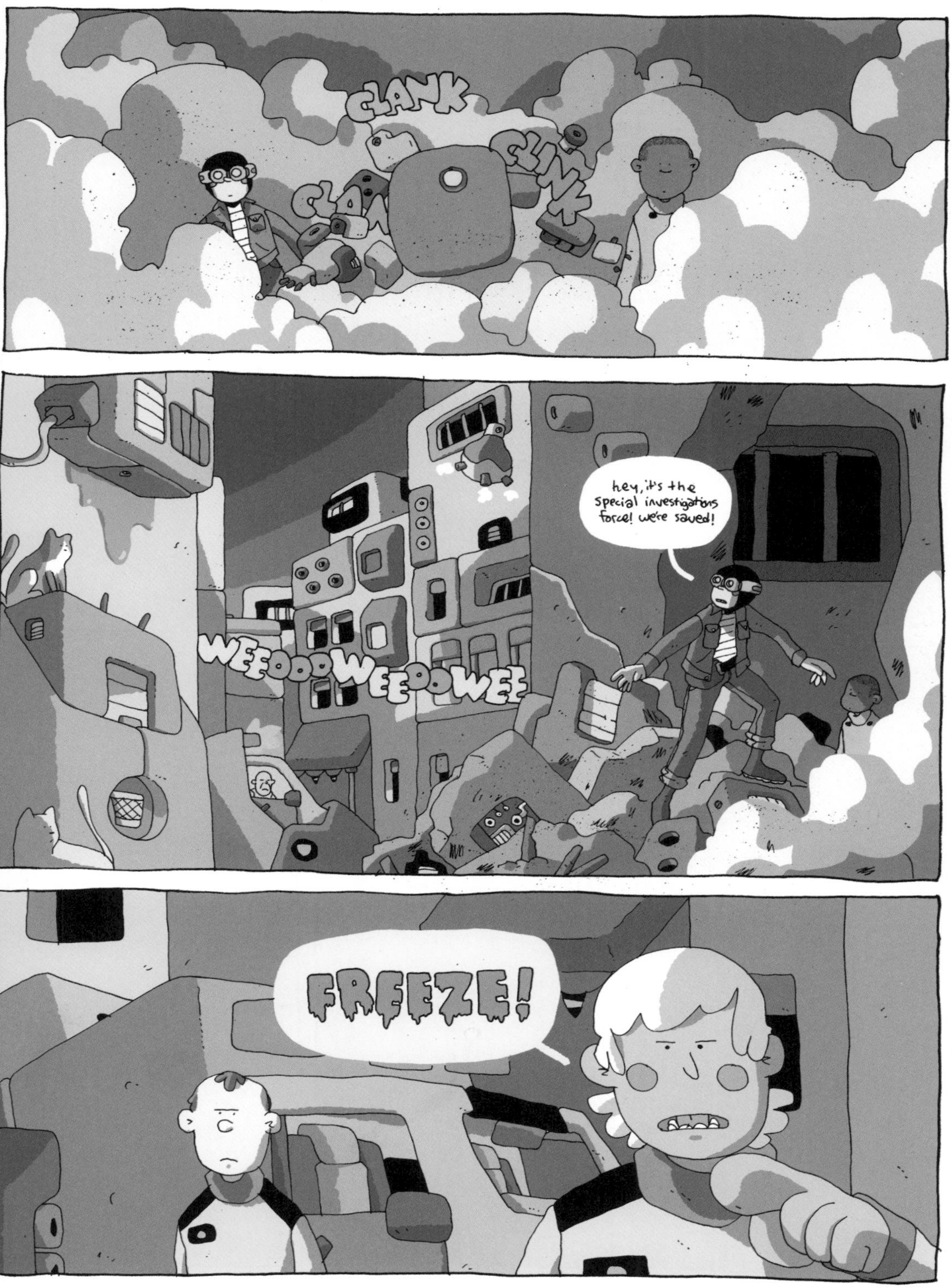
CLANK
CLINK
CLA
hey, it's the special investigations force! we're saved!
WEEOOOWEEOOWEE
FREEZE!

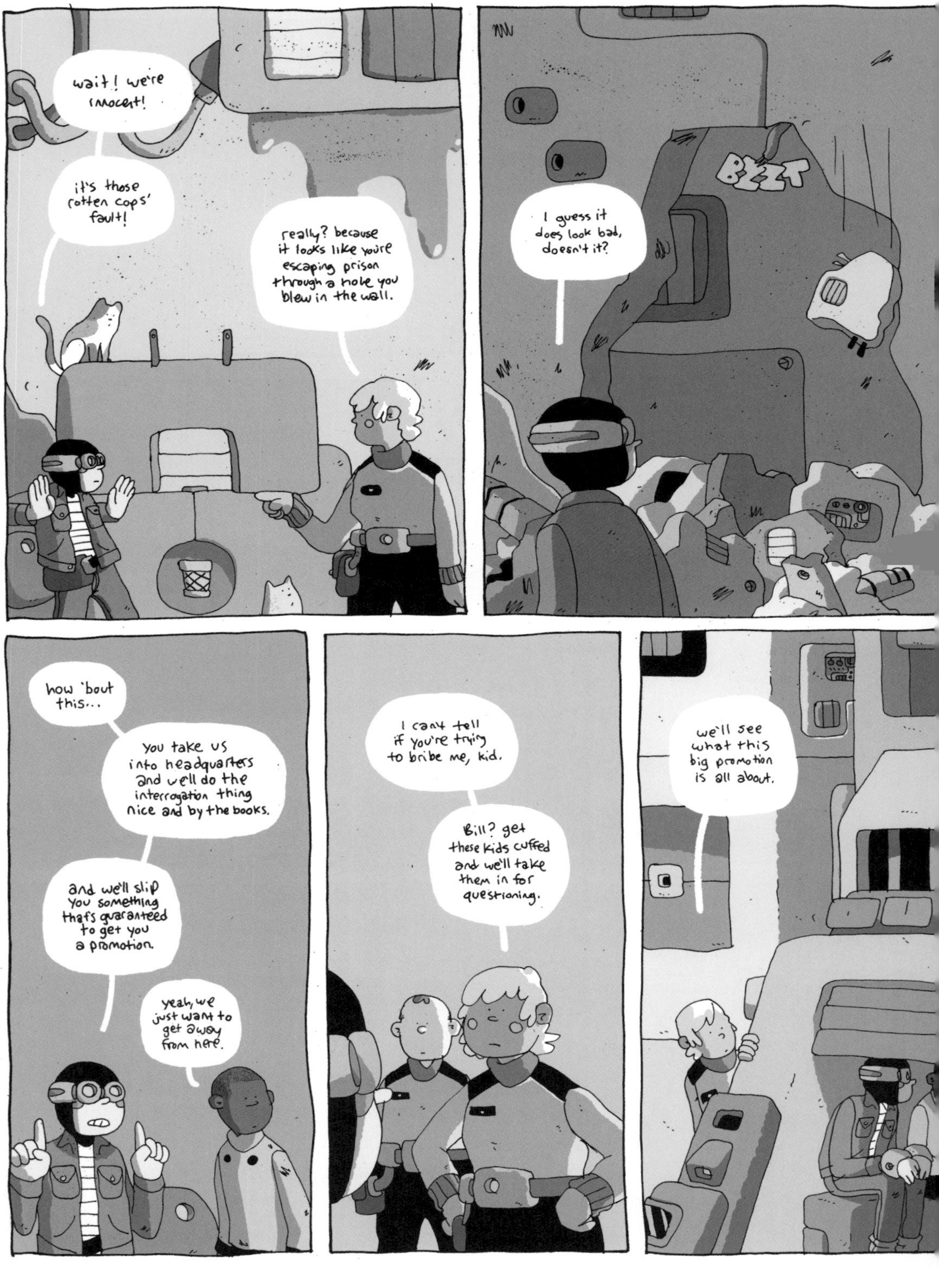
wait! we're innocent!
it's those rotten cops' fault!
really? because it looks like you're escaping prison through a hole you blew in the wall.
BZZT
I guess it does look bad, doesn't it?
how 'bout this...
you take us into headquarters and we'll do the interrogation thing nice and by the books.
and we'll slip you something that's guaranteed to get you a promotion.
yeah, we just want to get away from here.
I can't tell if you're trying to bribe me, kid.
Bill? get these kids cuffed and we'll take them in for questioning.
we'll see what this big promotion is all about.

EPILOGUE

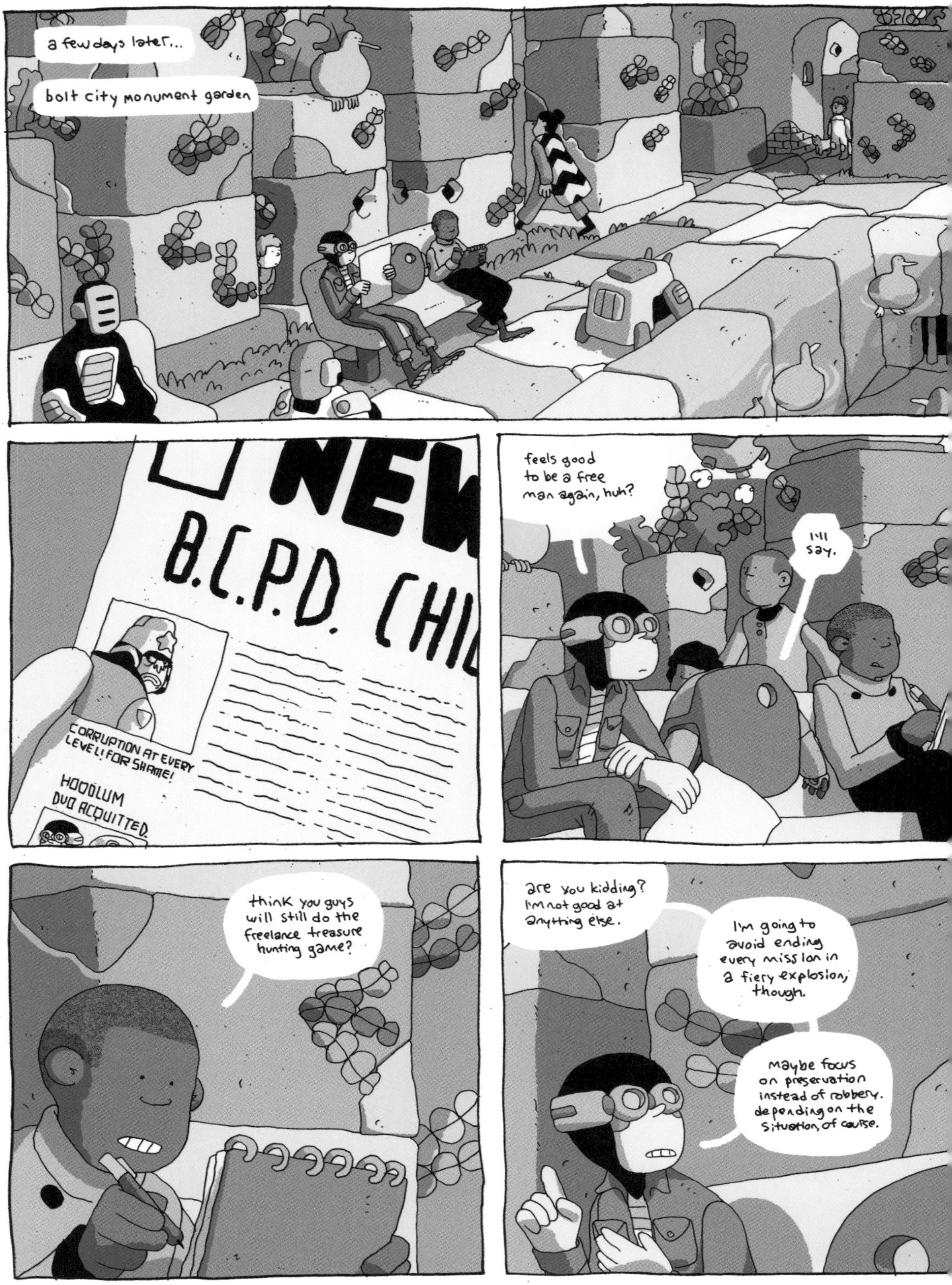
a few days later...
bolt city monument garden
NEW
B.C.P.D. CHI
CORRUPTION AT EVERY LEVEL! FOR SHAME!
HOODLUM DUO ACQUITTED
feels good to be a free man again, huh?
I'll say.
think you guys will still do the freelance treasure hunting game?
are you kidding? I'm not good at anything else.
I'm going to avoid ending every mission in a fiery explosion, though.
maybe focus on preservation instead of robbery. depending on the situation, of course.

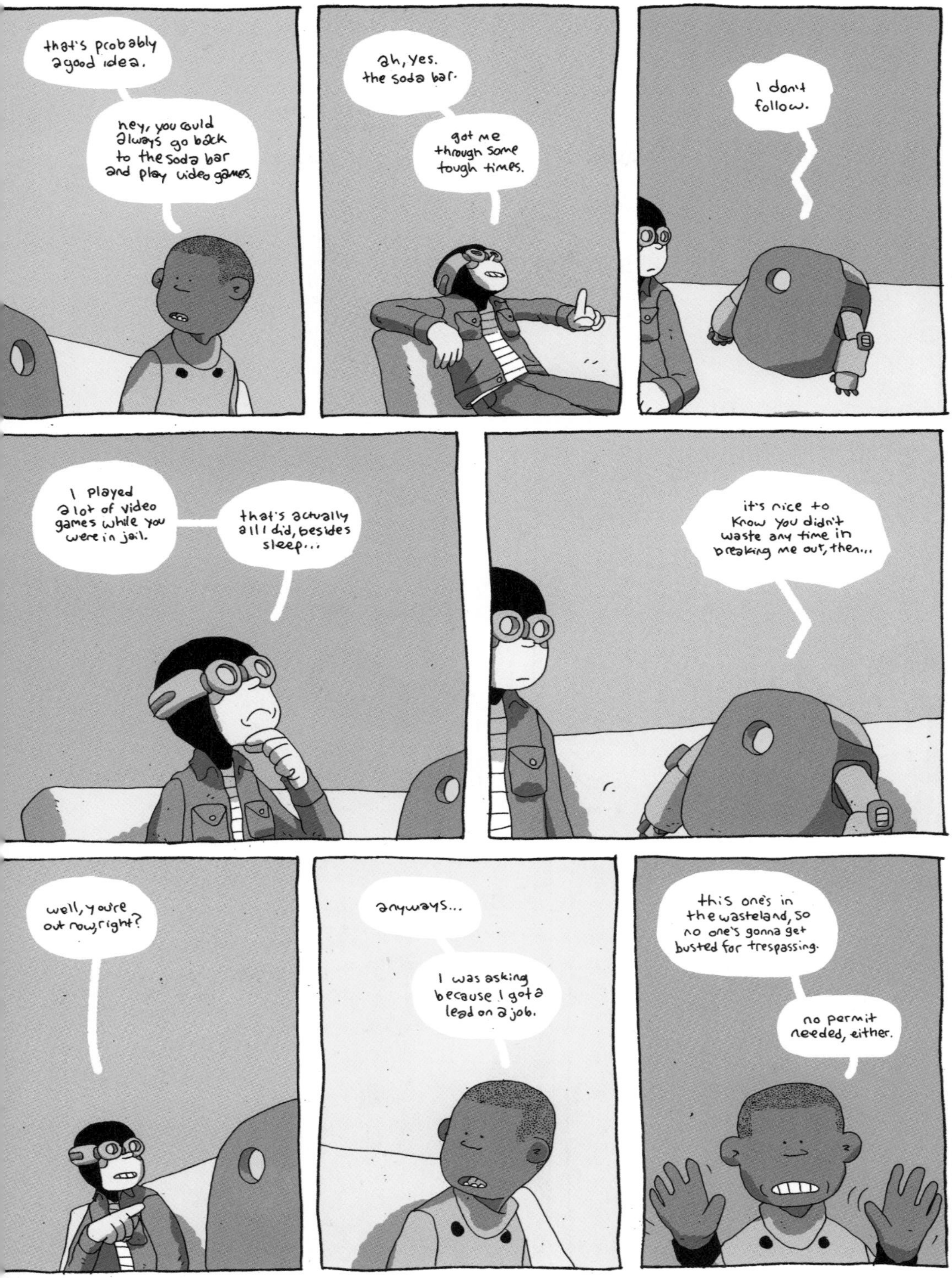
that's probably a good idea.
hey, you could always go back to the soda bar and play video games.
ah, yes. the soda bar.
got me through some tough times.
I don't follow.
I played a lot of video games while you were in jail.
that's actually all I did, besides sleep...
it's nice to know you didn't waste any time in breaking me out, then...
well, you're out now, right?
anyways...
I was asking because I got a lead on a job.
this one's in the wasteland, so no one's gonna get busted for trespassing.
no permit needed, either.

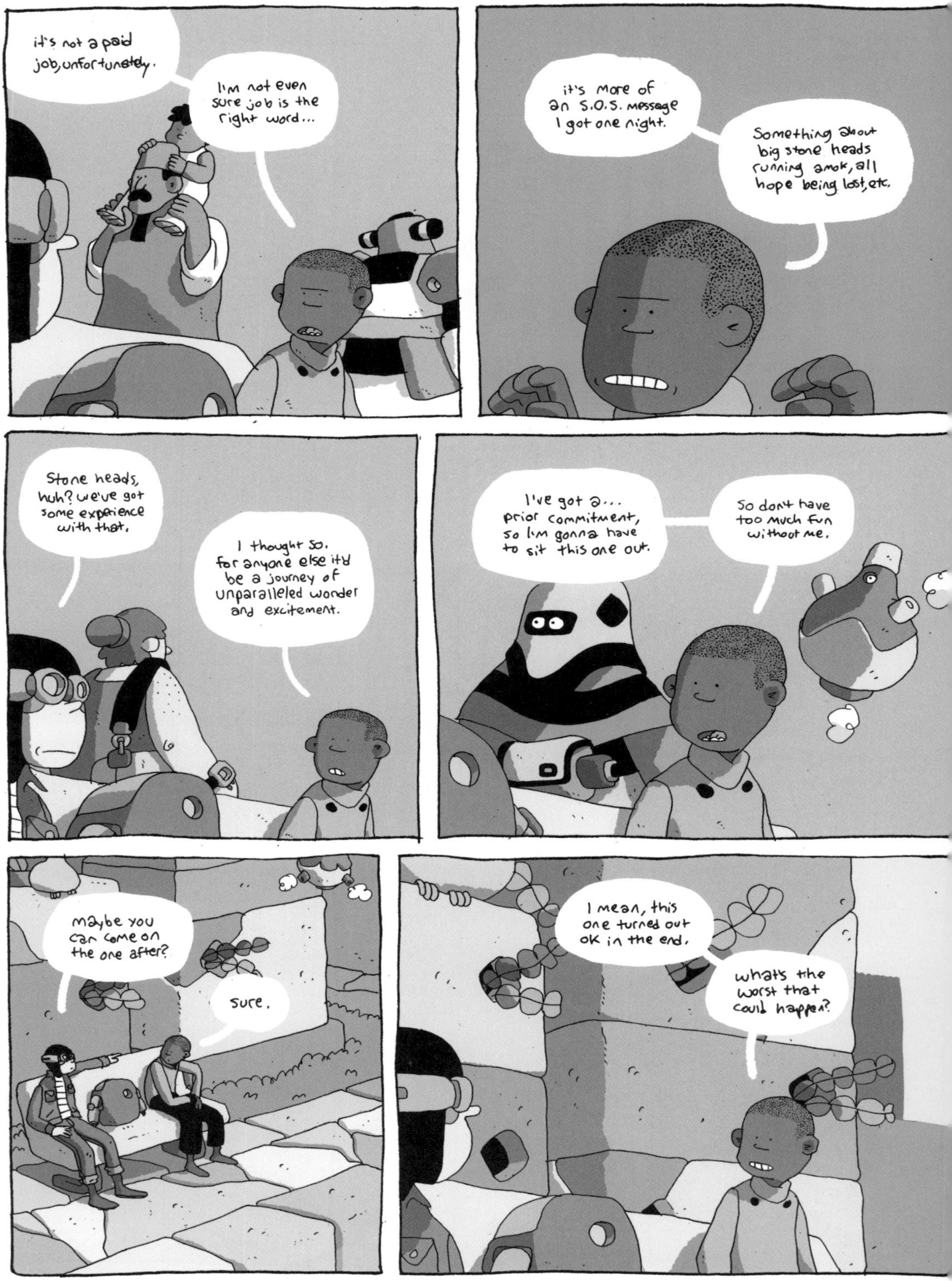
it's not a paid job, unfortunately.
I'm not even sure job is the right word...
it's more of an S.O.S. message I got one night.
Something about big stone heads running amok, all hope being lost, etc.
Stone heads, huh? we've got some experience with that.
I thought so. for anyone else it'd be a journey of unparalleled wonder and excitement.
I've got a... prior commitment, so I'm gonna have to sit this one out.
So don't have too much fun without me.
maybe you can come on the one after?
sure.
I mean, this one turned out ok in the end.
what's the worst that could happen?

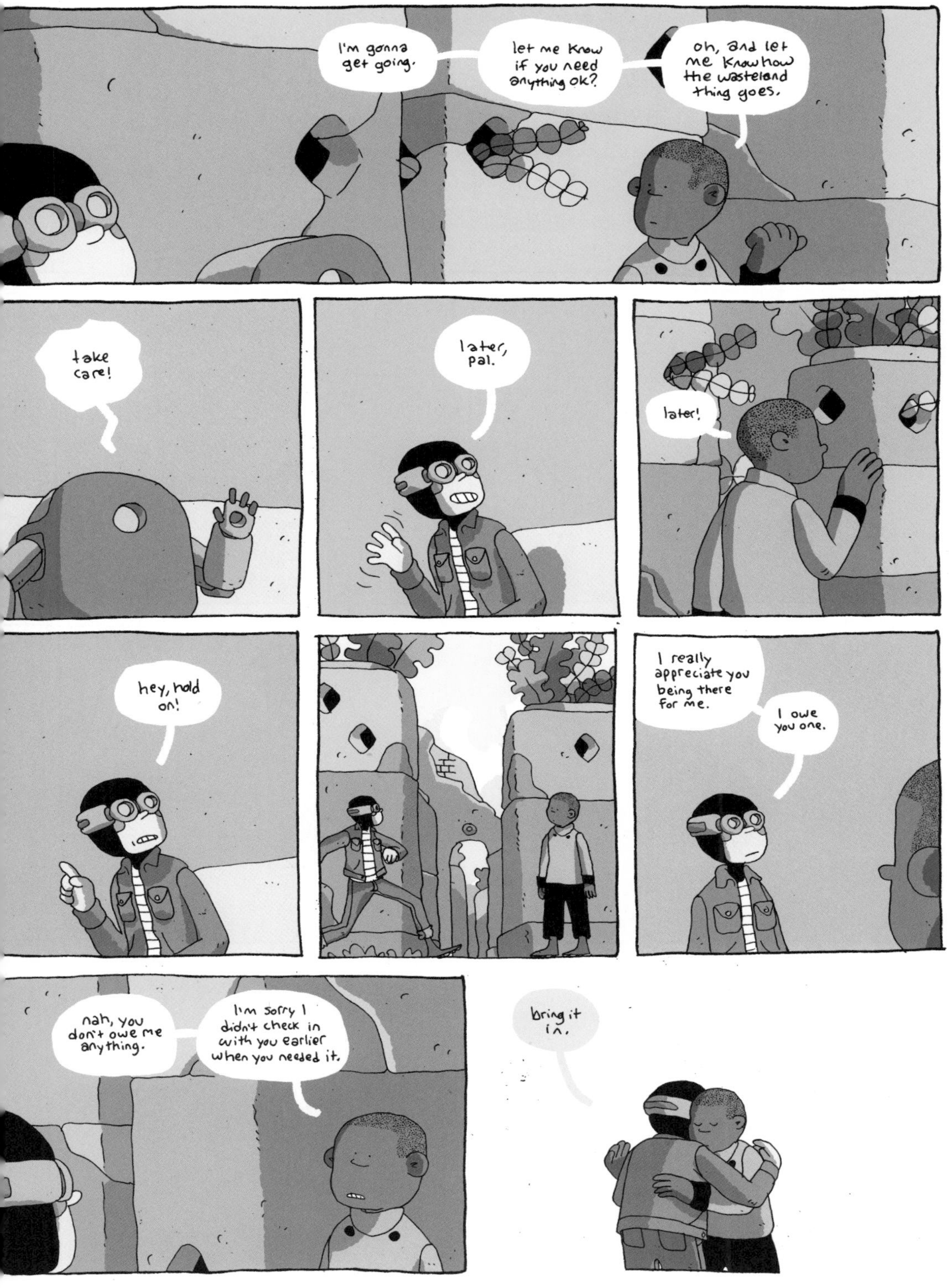
I'm gonna get going.
let me know if you need anything ok?
oh, and let me know how the wasteland thing goes.
take care!
later, pal.
later!
hey, hold on!
I really appreciate you being there for me.
I owe you one.
nah, you don't owe me anything.
I'm sorry I didn't check in with you earlier when you needed it.
bring it in.

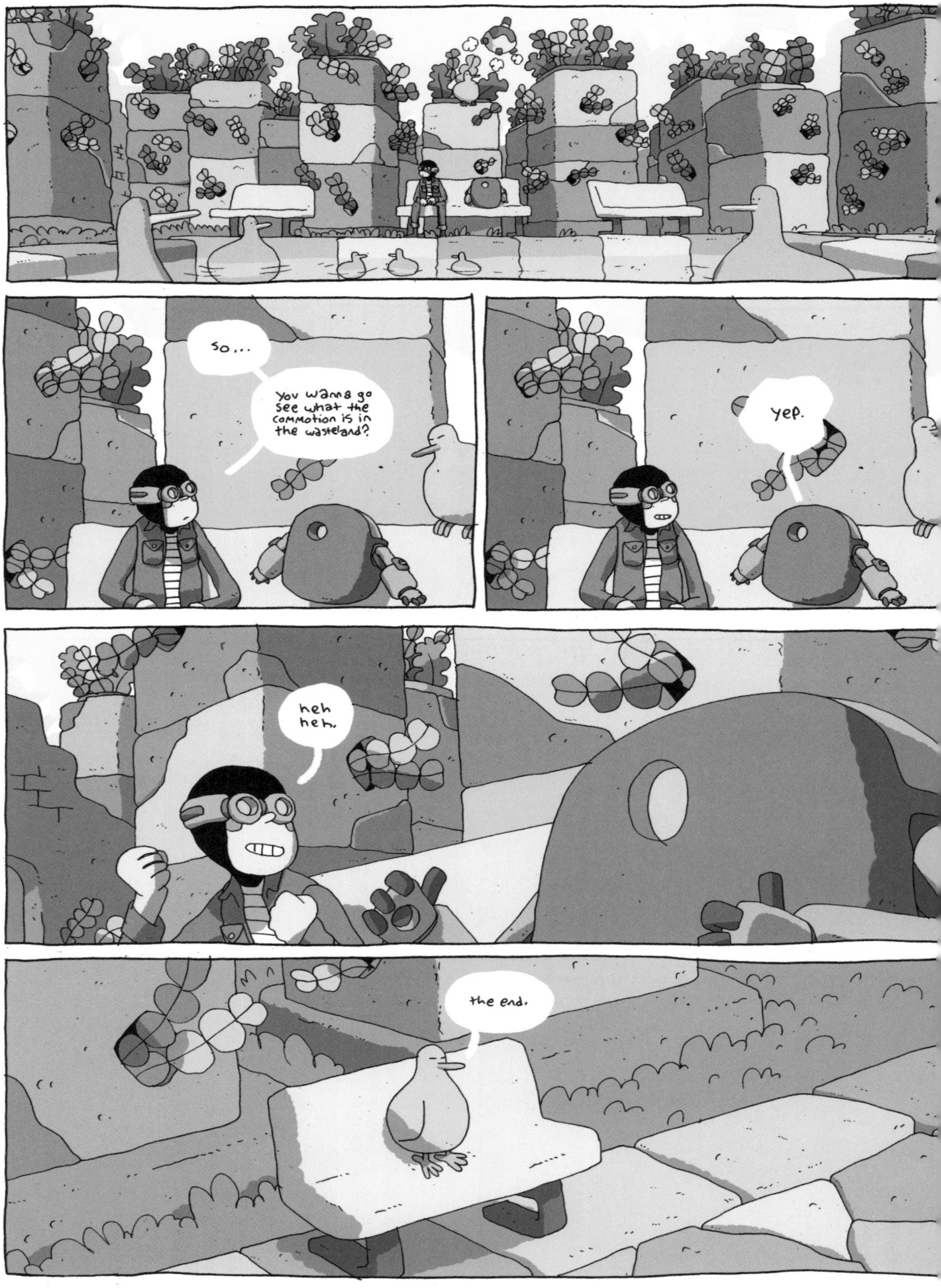
so...
you wanna go see what the commotion is in the wasteland?
yep.
heh heh.
the end.

PLUS MAN & HANK
WILL STRIKE AGAIN

DEDICATED TO TIM SEARS

SPECIAL THANKS TO ANNIE KOYAMA
& ELLEN SEARS, WITHOUT THEM THIS
BOOK WOULD NOT EXIST.